MW01677799

# The Scotty!

By Eric J. Hildeman

James,
"Beam me up," my good man!
E. Hildeman

Copyright May, 2024

# Table of Contents

## Introduction

You are about to read a novel which is actually a series of short stories linked together. Sometimes this is called a *mosaic.* Other times it is referred to as a *linked series* or *story cycle.* In bygone days, it might have been referred to as a "fix-up novel." But whatever term one uses, it is a conglomerate work.

Generally, this format is seldom used anymore, but back in the day, it was quite common. Some of the greatest science fiction novels from the Golden Age, such as Isaac Asimov's *Foundation* and *I, Robot,* Arthur C. Clarke's *Tales from the White Heart*, or Ray Bradbury's *The Martian Chronicles* used this writing technique. One animated science fiction movie, *Heavy Metal* (1981), used this same story structure. Of course, the entire genre was different back then. Quite often, stories which had been serialized in magazines or comic books would be collected and made into novels. In other words, the industry often necessitated the technique. This time, however, what links the stories together is a machine: *The Scotty*, named after the chief engineer on the original Star Trek television series, because it does just what that name suggests. It turns matter into energy, and then energy back into matter again, usually somewhere else.

Without spoiling things too much, the Scotty is so much more than merely a "transport." Every Trekkie knows that a transporter is also a replicator; the technology is essentially the same. But nobody has really thought through the other implications of such a device. For example, any user must also see where they're materializing something, or else that person/thing could end up below a floor, or inside a wall, or within some other obstruction. But that makes the Scotty a *spy* device – the *ultimate* surveillance tool! The Scotty is a *macroscope.* Or, consider that materializing an object at a distance basically means transmitting *information* instantaneously over that distance as well. That makes the Scotty a communications device. One could talk with someone instantaneously over a vast distance, even from one galaxy to another! The Scotty is an *ansible* (as well-versed sci-fi fans would refer to it). If you can do that, you've essentially exceeded the speed of light. And, because space and time are the same continuum, that means you could materialize something in the past, or the future. All it takes is adjusting the mathematics a little bit. The Scotty is also a *time machine!* Or how about this: If you can transport a dashing young captain from his starship down to a planet's surface, why not simply transport the entire starship to another star system, such as from Earth to Alpha Centaurii? The Scotty is an *FTL drive*. Or then there's *this* whopper: if you can turn matter into energy slowly and capture it, what would happen if you were to take a piece of matter and release all its energy at once and *not* capture it? The Scotty is even a *nuclear bomb!* Think it through, and there's very little one *cannot* do with such a device.

This book will explore each of these possibilities, plus a few more, chapter by chapter, story by story.

The earliest editions of this book lacked this introduction. As a direct result, some of my early readers, particularly contest judges who couldn't see my summary blurb on the back cover (because book covers are often judged separately or even excluded from consideration) were befuddled by the sudden shifts between one chapter-story and the next. It became clear that this introduction would greatly benefit my readers (especially contest judges), setting the stage, as it were, in a much deeper way than a back-cover blurb could do.

So, let me set the stage for you.

In this version of a future Earth, the Scotty is invented, developed and enhanced in the early 2070's. But humans have been very busy developing other things, too. For example, Mars has been slowly colonized from the 2050's through the 2060's, mostly by a motley combination of wealthy eccentrics, scientific expeditions, religious libertarians, and (of course) a few military outposts from Earth's more space-faring nations. This makes for an interesting political interplay on the red planet. "Musk City" is the only colony of any appreciable size. All the others are tiny, far-flung communities. Meanwhile, *N.B.I.'s* have emerged (that's *non-biological intelligences* – one does not refer to them as "A.I.'s" because calling their intelligence "artificial" is considered racist). Many of these N.B.I.'s still exist as immobile computers, but by the 2070's, some have built humanoid bodies and walk among humans. A few have even become politicians, which has ignited global controversy. And humans themselves have begun merging with machines. Many humans have computer-enhanced brains, colloquially referred to as "Ex-drives" (external hard-drives), giving them perfect memory and instantaneous learning, like a smart-phone plugged directly into the brain. Most humans are becoming part cyborg.

Who knows about the Scotty? Well, that's left somewhat ambiguous. A private industry initially invented it, and boasted of that momentous event to the press, so the general public is already aware of its existence. But then the U.S. government acquired it, and facts about the device were kept hush-hush as much as possible. So in this future, the Scotty sits somewhere on the fence between general knowledge and state secret. Naturally, the more years go by, the more things go from "classified" to "declassified." Where exactly certain facts cross that line isn't all that important. The important thing is that, slowly, more and more facts about what the Scotty can do become well-known.

Even time is measured differently in this future. Although the common Gregorian calendar (which we use today) is still used, a slightly modified calendar, known as the "Tranquility calendar" has become popular. It counts the years beginning from the date mankind first stepped on the moon. In other words, July 20th, 1969 is New Year's Day, Year One. You will sometimes see the Gregorian date juxtaposed with another date written as "A.T." (after Tranquility).

I should mention one additional thing about my future universe, which is touched upon briefly, but which might confuse readers if they don't know about it beforehand. In the late 2060's, a 10-year-old boy genius named Iosef Irfan sues his parents for the right *not* to be indoctrinated into Islam. The World Court, recently empowered by the New United Nations, hears his case in the year 2073, the same year the Scotty is invented. By this point, the boy is 16. Yet he pleads his case as eloquently as any seasoned lawyer. The court sides with the boy, and just like that, religious indoctrination of those 13 years or under is rendered illegal. This sets the stage for political retribution, as depicted in two of my chapter-stories, as well as the beginnings of a mass exodus from Earth to the outer planets. (After all, if the religious cannot indoctrinate their young on Earth, they must do so elsewhere.) If you wish to know more details about this watershed event in my future history, you can read all about it in my novelette, *Sariah's Run* (to be published in 2025).

You will meet various characters throughout this book, but most of them do not return in subsequent chapter-stories. So be prepared to love my characters, only to see them disappear. But a few do reappear. Sarita Shantay is the most frequent recurring character. Randall Gosling also makes a few encore appearances. Still, you will most often not meet a main character a second time. The beginning of each chapter-story spans years, sometimes even decades. And the final chapter, well, that one takes place in far-flung future millennia. The only consistent recurring "character" in this book is the Scotty device.

Chapter 1 is a story about the Scotty's invention, and its unfortunate inventor. Chapter 2 tells the story about how the U.S. government began using the Scotty as a surveillance device, and its time-travel capabilities are hinted at. In Chapter 3, the Scotty is used as a communications device on

Mars, and its capabilities as a time-travel device are exercised in a limited way. But by Chapter 4, the Scotty's time-travel capabilities have spawned a *Temporal Bureau* to "police" the timeline, and like with most bureaucracies, things go haywire. Naturally, there are also historians who "work with" the Temporal Bureau to research historical events, often by sending "agents" back in time. That too, goes awry. The fifth chapter sees the Scotty beginning to be used for space exploration. And so on, and so forth. Naturally, I saved the best story for last.

So sit back and enjoy. You will consume in a few hours what took me well over a decade to write. Each of these chapter-stories has been reviewed multiple times and honed by many eyes and critiques. Those reviewers all liked the stories as stand-alone works. I hope you will agree, they are even better when linked together as part of a greater story.

# Chapter 1: Omphalos Psychosis

**Private Journal, April 8, 104, A.T. [*the year 2073, Gregorian*]:**

My latest government assignment ordered me to the Peace Frog, which was a Mary Jane establishment in Pasadena, California. The air inside was filled with a thin haze caused by constantly smoking patrons and, because nearly all the ganj was flavored, the indoor fog smelled of berries, peppermint, chocolate, vanilla, as well as cannabis. It was a candy-chronic conglomeration; a reefer redolence; a *pot*-pourri. Like most marijuana bars, this one was a nostalgic dive into the 20th Century, when pot was actually illegal, and only rebels smoked it, as opposed to the young and well-heeled conformists who generally frequented here. So, naturally, someone like a middle-aged scientist, my target, stood out like a whole handful of sore thumbs.

I wish I could say my feminine wiles lured him in, but really all I needed to do was show up. He hit on me almost instantly and, when I didn't actually run away like all the other women did, he opened up like a cave full of treasure to Ali Baba. In theory, my job was to get him talking, and *keep* him talking, until he accidentally gave us what we needed. In practice, it was damned near impossible to shut the motherfucker up.

"That's right," the scientist slurred. "I *invented* the thing. I invented the Scotty. I get to say that because I was head of the department, you know. Pretty cool shit, right? But believe me, it wasn't easy."

I tried to appear absent-minded as I listened to the condescending babble of this old fool who was high enough to paint stars. What a lame pick-up line, telling strange women that he was the one who actually invented the Scotty! He might as well claim to have invented Velcro. Okay, sure, he *was* telling the truth as it turned out (about inventing the Scotty, not about the Velcro), but I was the only one besides him who actually knew that. I'm also certain I was the only woman that line had ever worked on, and *that* only because I had to pretend it did.

"You see," he paused, taking a drag from some absurd miniaturized hookah, "the main problem was resolution. We were easily able to transport matter from point A to point B in an instant, but if we dematerialized, say, a block of stone, all we'd get when it re-materialized at its destination was a pile of sand. If we used a block of wood, all the receiving end got was something resembling sawdust."

"But then you realized that the process had to be fine-tuned to below the Planck-length level," I completed the thought for him, trying to speed things along.

His bloodshot eyes gave me a look of surprise. "How the hell did you know that?"

"I was an engineering major. Besides, it isn't like this stuff isn't common knowledge, or anything." That was certainly true, at least to a certain extent. Name a matter-transport device 'The Scotty,' after the Chief Engineer on the Starship Enterprise, and every science fiction geek will want to learn all about it, which they did, sort of. Truth be told, all the general public *really* knew was that the Scotty existed. Only the nerdiest nerds knew any details.

He finally looked at my face instead of my tits for one damned second.

"Oh," he finally said. "That's impressive, uh – sorry, sweetheart, what was your name again? I forgot."

"Sarita," I answered, trying not to look annoyed as I offered him my hand. "Sarita Johansson."

"Roger Avon," he said, accepting my hand, and then planting a disgustingly wet kiss upon the back of it.

"Yes, I remember." I snatched my generously moistened hand back. Jeez, this guy was as baked as a Hostess cupcake, and just as healthy. For the record, I *hate* hash bars. If Uncle Sam hadn't ordered me to be there, I wouldn't be.

"Um, okay. Well, uh, where was I?"

"Resolution."

"Ah, yes. Well, we did eventually get the resolution issue solved, but it took five whole years of trying to refine the goddamned process. Brownian motion wreaks havoc with the whole thing, you know. Stray atoms got nudged into the wrong places. Wood blocks came out intact, but without any visible grain pattern. A G.I. Joe action figure would come out looking alright, until you tried to pose it, and found that the movable pieces were welded together. But *then*, you see," he brought his face uncomfortably close to mine, "we finally realized that *speed* was the key. Transport an object fast enough and it doesn't have any time for the random jostling motion of atoms to have any effect."

"And that's when you decided to attempt transporting living animals?" I said, trying to skip to the end of the story.

He gave a startled laugh which sounded like the snorting of a pig. "Of course not! First, we had to *fine-tune* the process. We eventually did this, of course. You know, we got so good at it, that we could pour out a pitcher of water on one side and watch the stream never even hit the ground, but on the other side see it materialize into a perfectly positioned glass! So, we started fooling around with it. We put a Mr. Potato Head toy into the Scotty, and had it re-materialize with eyes, mouth and nose in the wrong places. We put a mixed-up Rubik's cube in, and had it re-materialize solved. Then and *only* then did we feel that we were ready for living test subjects."

"But they didn't materialize quite right," I said. It was a flat statement rather than a question. I felt I already knew what he was about to say. But he surprised me.

"Oh, no! They materialized just fine. We used bacteria at first, and they survived perfectly. Then yeast cells and then plants, and they all came through with no problems. But then we tried our first mouse. It also came through in perfect condition – except that it was dead. We did an autopsy but couldn't find any cause as to why it died. The same thing happened with the second mouse, and the third. It took us a long time to figure out what was killing the poor, little devils."

"You know," I said, trying to coax more out of him, "anybody could learn all this stuff by watching Science News on the Wideweb. It's a popular Netstream show."

"Yeah," he said, "but *I* know stuff that was never documented."

I narrowed my eyes on him and lured him in further. "Like what?"

"Like how the nanotech people got involved."

This didn't strike me as anything like an important detail, but I decided to go off on this tangent with him anyway. "Yeah, well, I understand that matter-energy and nanotechnology were neighboring departments in the same R&D division of Gormann Industries. Naturally, they ended up collaborating. So what?"

He softly chuckled at me. "Oh, no, no, no. We may have been divisions in the same company, but that didn't mean we got along. We hated each other! The animosity originated with minor stuff like budget disputes and squabbles over resources, and the nanotech people usually won because they were the corporation's biggest cash-cow. But over the years it got personal. One division manipulated extra work onto the other one just before the CEO's inspection tour, or one scientist undermined another's promotion, sometimes minor sabotage of experiments – you know, stupid, petty shit. Still, we needed some insight into why only animals died when put through the Scotty, and we determined that experimenting with a batch of nanobots just might give us a clue. So, we swallowed our pride and asked the nanotech division for two tiny batches of 100 general-purpose nanobots –

enough for only a few experiments. You know what? They refused even that! Can you believe that shit? They had *billions* of nanobots at their disposal, and they couldn't spare a mere two C's. And all because somebody made a pass at somebody else's wife at last year's Christmas party, or some other such nonsense. So, there we were, totally stuck! We didn't know what to do. So, we decided, maybe because we were a little bit desperate, to do the only thing we really *could* do after that."

He paused for an agonizing length of time as he sucked on his stem. That was some *very* coherent talk for someone who was supposedly wasted! I certainly wasn't so eloquent the few times I'd gotten stoned, and indeed, I was struggling to stay focused just from the second-hand smoke in this place. Then again, certain people become *more* coherent and philosophical the higher they get. High-functioning stoners. Perhaps this was that sort of guy. Just my luck. A little more curious about the story now, I asked, "You simply *bought* some nanobots?"

He gave me a look as though I'd just suggested he ought to wear a tutu. "You mean spend *our own* money?! Don't be silly. No scientist worth their salt ever does that." He drew a long drag off of his hookah, and while exhaling the smoke, softly breathed, "We *stole* them."

I raised my eyebrows. He was right, that little detail never got onto the Net. "You stole them?"

"Sure. Some fool left them on a counter right near the door. All a body had to do was walk in and palm the vial."

Okay, this was getting interesting. But how long did I have to keep him talking before he would finally stick his head into the noose?

He was gawking at my chest again as he spoke. "We had swiped about 500 nanites, so we decided to put them through in batches of fifty. That would give us ten trials. But the first five all had the same results."

"What results?"

"They died."

I crinkled up my brows at him. "That doesn't make any sense. Nanobots can't die. They're microscopic *machines*."

"Well, stopped working is what I mean."

Odd mistake for a scientist to make, even a baked one. "How come?" I pressed.

He annoyingly took another hit before answering. "That's just it, we didn't know. The only people who could tell us were in the nanotech department. So, we were forced to confess to our crime and ask them for a post-mortem." He snorted. "You can imagine their reaction! They complained loudly about how that particular kind of nanobot had taken months to develop and then went on at excessive length about how much work and money our little stunt had cost them. Not only did they refuse to tell us what had killed their little bots, but they went and infested *our* lab with a new variety of nanite which coated everything with an ultra-slick substance that wouldn't wash off. We were slipping and sliding all over the place for *days* before we were finally able to replace all the affected surfaces!

"But we got back at them. You see, we struck a deal with the quantum-linking development team. They'd perfected a technique which allowed them to link to a specific point anywhere in space using gamma radiation inter-dimensionally."

"They did what?" I asked, playing dumb.

"Uh, they figured out how to operate a nanobot by remote-control," he clarified. "Pretty useful, since nanobots are too small to be controlled with radio waves. They even developed a way to move distant atoms around using this same trick."

"You mean, like a long-distance laser-tweezers?" I asked him.

"Yes, exactly!" he answered, beaming. "Just imagine, a doctor in Sri Lanka could do molecular-level gene therapy on a patient in Los Angeles!"

"Yes, yes, but how does all this relate to the Scotty?" This guy was turning out to be a lot of work.

"Oh, right. Sorry, I got a little distracted. Anyway, the quantum-link people also had an axe to grind with the nanotech people. I won't bore you with the details as to why…"

*Too late*, I thought.

"… but when we offered them a few of the nanobots we'd swiped earlier – oh, you didn't think we returned *all* the ones we'd stolen, did you? – they were quite ready to help us in return. Using the bots we gave them, they quickly perfected the ability to remote-link with them, and even worked out a method on how they could *build* one remotely by joining the necessary atoms together out of ordinary dust particles.

"And here's where we *really* lucked out." He started getting wild-eyed, even for a pothead. "Those type of bots were so valuable because they could not only replicate themselves, but any *other* type of nanobot as well! Build one of *these* babies at a distance, they can replicate and then then *specialize* into specific task-oriented bots. Before you know it, you can build anything, anywhere!"

A lightbulb was beginning to brighten over my head at this point. "So, let me guess: You decided to build a Scotty receiver in a hidden spot right inside the nanotech department?"

He laughed. "You bet we did! And then we materialized an unwrapped wheel of *limburger cheese* beneath one of their workbenches. Have you ever seen what a typical laboratory workbench looks like? It's completely enclosed and bolted to the floor! It took those nanotech morons over a *week* to figure out where the smell was coming from!" He cackled like a banshee, taking over a minute to recover.

When he finally did, he went on. "Well, after that, they begrudgingly agreed to help us. After all, if we could transport anything into or out of their laboratory at will, there was no telling *what* we might do! They diagnosed the reason the nanobots had ceased functioning, and it was so simple, I'm ashamed to admit that *we* didn't figure it out."

I had to wait as he paused to smoke again, the infuriating bastard. "What *was* it?"

"Well, anything that re-materialized did so in a nearly stationary state, you see? That's why the nanobots stopped. Give the bots a little electro-chemical jolt and they would start right back up again. No big deal for plants or eukaryotic cells, Brownian motion will make them start up again on their own. But an animal materializes without any heartbeat or neural activity. Those had to be *re-started* after materialization. So, we sent through another mouse, and immediately defibrillated it as soon as it appeared at the receiving end. Wouldn't you know it, the little critter revived splendidly! The quantum guys then figured out a way to do a remote jump-start without having to use a defibrillator, and the next mouse barely even realized it had been transported at all. Before long, we were transporting dogs, cats, monkeys, and then we all volunteered to go through the machine at least once, and we all made it! I went through a few times, myself. We now had the makings of a true matter-transport system."

"Wow!" I answered, enthusiastically. I *was* genuinely impressed, but was trying to appear more so than I actually was. "I can only imagine the sorts of things that you could do with this new device. Things which haven't been reported by the news feeds yet."

He smiled broadly. "You don't need to imagine it anymore," he said. "Now it's *reality*. You know, if you can re-materialize the original thing, all it takes is a little more energy, plus the computer-memory of the molecular pattern, and you can materialize it again to make a copy. A working replicator! With a Scotty attached to a solar array in every desert, you could turn acres of harvested energy directly into good, nutritious food!

"And if you can make things you need, you can also get rid of things you don't need. You can remove all the salt from seawater at a rate of mega-gallons per minute. Landfills for garbage become unnecessary. Plastic in the oceans becomes a thing of the past. Or perhaps you want to lose a little weight? You can step onto a Scotty pad and have your fatty tissues transported *right off* your body. Women could eat up, have all their belly fat removed and none of the fat removed from, uh, well, *other* parts of their body, if that's what they want."

I knew perfectly well what he meant. He was staring at my "other parts" as he said it.

"Or men could make themselves, um, *taller*. Or maybe the bodily patterns of someone aged 21 could be stored and then applied to someone who is older, thus making him or her young again. An endless fountain of youth! Or how about space travel? If you can build a Scotty to another laboratory, nothing keeps you from building one to a nearby star-system, except maybe the additional math. You could remote-build an entire *ship* in Alpha Centauri, then Scotty on board a crew, and *voila!* An instant Starship Enterprise. We were so right to name it the Scotty! And if you can travel through space in an instant, there's nothing to prevent you from traveling through time as well, because space and time are the same continuum. You could build a Scotty receiver in the past. Or the future! You could visit your grandparents, shake hands with Einstein, maybe even meet Jesus! Or maybe you could see how your favorite stock is going to do years from now…"

That last comment in his tirade caused him to trail off, so I tried to prompt him into going on. "Sounds wonderful."

"Wonderful? *And* terrible!" he said, turning somber. "Do you realize how truly evil this invention could be if it were ever weaponized? A few elites having knowledge of future markets could easily undermine the global economy overnight! Soldiers could materialize inside of any compound, no matter how secure. Or prisoners could escape from any jail. A bomb could appear suddenly, anywhere, anytime! One tank could become a thousand. The Scotty could be used for super-surveillance, as any remote drone or camera could materialize or disappear at any hidden location. George Orwell's 1984 writ large. And if all this weren't bad enough, we have to realize that a person's *brain*-patterns are part of what is stored when the Scotty is applied for transport. No one has figured out how those Scotty-patterns translate into thought-patterns yet, but it would only be a matter of time before someone does. People could have their *minds* read. Or possibly even have their brains wiped and reprogrammed with *new* memories. Or maybe…" He stopped. It was as if he didn't want to think about it anymore. "No, it's simply too much. I *can't* let them have it. I *can't!*"

"Can't let *who* have it?" I asked.

"What? Oh." Apparently, I'd snapped him out of being lost in thought. "Sorry. The government, of course. The Pentagon has tried several times to buy our patents. To be honest, I'm surprised we haven't sold them yet. I can only assume that Mr. Gormann is holding out for more money. But this has made the Feds desperate for an excuse to simply declare eminent domain and seize the technology outright. You can imagine why."

That's when I decided to go for the kill. If I let him dwell on *that* thought too long, he might cast it my way. "Well, then," I said, cheerily, "we might not have much time to lose. When do *I* get to try it?"

He looked startled. "Huh?"

"Oh, come on, when do I get to travel somewhere with a Scotty? I'd love to see the Great Wall of China. Or how about the Coliseum in Rome? No, wait, I've got it." I took his hand and gave him one of my sexiest looks. "How about a romantic weekend in Paris? Wouldn't that be grand? We could tour the Louvre tonight."

He pulled his hand away, looking very worried. "Um, look, I really can't…"

That's when I pounced. "Yeah, I thought so! You're just some huckster who sells that story to every woman who catches your eye in here. Jesus Christ, I should have known!" And with that, I started to storm off.

"No! Wait! It's not that. It's just…"

He trailed off as I stopped on my heel to turn around and give him one last annoyed look, doing my best to feign total exasperation.

"There are *side-effects*," he confessed.

I sneered, putting on my best jilted-woman look. "Side-effects to *what?*" I was trying to sound pissed, but I was excited. I almost had him.

"Side-effects to using the Scotty," he said. "Only a few of us know about it. We're calling it omphalos psychosis."

"Ompala-*what?*" *Gotcha*, I thought.

"*Omphalos*," he tried to explain. "It's the Greek word for *navel*, you know. Not naval as in maritime, navel as in belly-button. You see, it was once thought that Adam and Eve had no belly-buttons because they were instantly created in the Garden of Eden, and so would never have needed an umbilical cord, much less a belly button, because they were brand new people…"

"What *are* you babbling about?" Of course, I knew damn well what he was babbling about, but I was *so close*.

"Don't you see?" He held his hands out, palms up, imploringly. "I went through the Scotty transporter three weeks ago. That means I'm only *three weeks old!*"

I stared at him, knowing what he meant, but needing more. "*What?*"

"When the original Roger Avon stepped onto the transporter pad of the Scotty, he was instantly converted from matter to energy. Don't you see what that *means?*" He really looked worried, now. "He *died!* The *real* Roger Avon died at that moment. *I*, that is, the *new* Roger Avon, was created at the receiving pad, with all Roger's memories *implanted* within me!"

All I could do was stand there and shake my head from side to side with a puzzled look on my face. "That's crazy talk," I said, baiting him.

"Is it? It wasn't a slip of the tongue when I said that the nanobots died when put through the Scotty. In a real way, they did. So did I. Maybe I have all the same memories, the same fingerprints, even the same allergies, but some part of me knows that I'm not *really* Roger. I'm his facsimile. Little more than a copy. Maybe I'm a strange kind of clone, even, but definitely *not* the original. Do you realize how that knowledge can *fuck* with your mind? Do you?"

I gave him a look as though he'd just told me that he was Elvis returned from the dead. After all that yakking he'd done, did he really just go and make it *this* easy for me?

"No," he finally said, shaking his head. "I can't put you through that. There's probably even *dementia* caused by slight copying errors from getting copied over and over again. No big deal for the body, that heals itself. But the mind? That's permanently fucked. I mean, look at me! The original Roger never smoked weed a day in his life. But *I'm* smoking like a chimney, drinking like a fish, and being totally reckless with women I don't even know. I'm not doing it because that's a healthy state of mind, I'm doing it because I *know*, fundamentally, that I'm a copy of a dead man, and I can't stand it. And on top of that, at any given moment, I'll probably have to demonstrate my little invention to others by getting onto that damned transporter pad and dying *again!* So, I just figure, what the hell? What could it matter, you know?" He paused in his sermonizing, and then accidentally tripped over the reality of his situation with what he said next. "You'd just end up being one more liability walking around. All your friends would notice your changed behavior. And if the *government* ever learned about this particular side-effect, they'd have just the excuse they've been looking for."

"Truer words were never spoken," I said, and then showed him my badge.

"Wha-? *Department of Homeland Security?!*"

"I lied to you, Doctor Avon," I confessed. "I didn't study engineering, I studied psychology. And my name isn't Sarita Johansson. It's Sarita Shantay."

His eyes grew wide. "*The* Sarita Shantay?" he whispered.

Yeah. You might already know this, especially if you've read my other journal entries, but I'm kind of famous. I don't like to brag, but I'm the most publicized undercover Fed agent since Donnie Brasco. I've taken down more domestic terror cells than any field agent in history. They even made a movie about me once. Of course, that means many people recognize my face, but it's amazing how well a bit of red hair coloring masks my identity.

"As a licensed mental-health professional employed by the Federal Government, I'm forced to officially diagnose you as mentally ill. And because the nature of your work constitutes a significant potential threat to public safety, to say nothing of the United States and her allies, we'll have no choice but to seize the work you've done at Gormann Industries in the interest of national security. I'm personally placing you under arrest for recklessly endangering the safety and well-being of the general public."

"No!" he shouted. "You can't do this! It's *my* project! *Mine!*"

"It was the *original* Roger Avon's project," I corrected him. "But you're not the original Roger Avon, remember?"

"*No!*" His hands flew up to his temples as if his head were about to explode.

"We had a fair case against you before," I said, removing the surveillance device from my cleavage, "but your recorded admission as to your imbalanced state of mind makes things so much easier."

"You can't do this! You *can't!*" he wailed.

"Oh, come now," I scolded. "Blabbing information that could undermine your research to any Jane Doe who happens to catch your eye in here? That's not very rational behavior, doctor. You even said so, yourself. You were practically *begging* Uncle Sam to intervene on this."

"No! I won't let you do it! I *won't!*" And with that, he bolted out the front door – right into the arms of the two fellow agents whom I'd had waiting outside.

Such a shame, really. He was such a brilliant man, and he and his team made a truly remarkable breakthrough. Funny how some scientists are destroyed by the unforeseen side-effects of their own discoveries. Marie Curie died of radium poisoning, Wilhelm Röntgen died of exposure to X-rays, Elon Musk got killed while on board one of his own tourist space shuttles, and now Roger Avon has succumbed to omphalos psychosis, induced by his own matter-transport device. How very tragic. Still, that meant that he was out…

And *I* was now in.

# Chapter 2: Macroscope

Inside a converted aircraft hangar, Doctor Gregory Lampert, the diminutive and bespectacled director of DARPA, the Defense Advanced Research Projects Agency, worked quickly to begin the demonstration of his agency's newly acquired device, like John Hammond preparing to show off his dinosaur-maker at Jurassic Park. But this device did not make dinosaurs or sequence DNA. It did something much more terrible. It was dubbed the "Scotty," and in its present form, it looked very much like a treadmill, with a simple platform instead of a moving tread. Lampert was standing on the non-treadmill, operating the control pad at the top of the machine and, suspended right above him, a large flat-screen display allowed several other people to see what he was seeing.

Two of those others were none other than the President and Vice President of the United States.

The flat-screen showed images of the control icons, but those soon faded away to reveal another image – that of a brightly-lit room containing four metallic colonnades. Lampert turned to address the group.

"As you can see on the screen," he announced, "the Scotty is currently showing us another location. When we procured this device, we envisioned it merely as a matter-energy transport. But we soon realized that we needed to see the destination area clearly in order to prevent objects from materializing within walls, below floors, or inside other obstacles. In so doing, we have perfected not only a way for the Scotty to avoid such pitfalls, we've created the ultimate surveillance device. There are no hidden cameras at the site you are currently viewing. No bugs have been planted. We can see *everything* that is happening. With the mere touch of a control pad, we can look anywhere. And, Madam President, this image is of the 14$^{th}$ Administrative Corpus Building at the Kremlin in Moscow!"

There was a moment of silence as the weight of Dr. Lampert's words were felt. President Lauren Cullen in particular, a tall and stern woman in her 50's, looked simultaneously both intrigued and puzzled. Eventually, Carla Jeffries, the president's short yet powerful Secretary of State, broke the silence.

"Um, actually, Dr. Lampert, that is *not* the reserve residence of the Kremlin. In fact, it strongly resembles the women's locker-room showers inside the Congressional Fitness Center."

"What!?" exclaimed Lampert, who took a good look at the image on the screen for the first time. "Why you're right! That's not where I left the calibration!"

"Getting an advance look on what the Scotty is capable of showing, doctor?" asked Vice President Martin Guevara. The twinkle in his eye seemed to show that he found the situation amusing, but he didn't really find the situation especially humorous. Guevara was simply an old-fashioned, affable sort of politician who was constantly smiling and found a bright side to everything. His personality counterbalanced the tough-as-nails attitude Cullen presented.

"Wipe that silly grin off your face, Martin," scolded the president. "I have yet to see this new technology in action and *already* somebody's apparently been using it to get his rocks off!"

"It wasn't me!" Lampert protested.

"Actually, I'm quite sure it was just an accident, and that Madam Secretary is quite mistaken regarding the remarkably coincidental current image," interjected Randall Gosling, the Scotty Research Team Leader. The skeletal and dark-haired man wasn't a nervous figure, and his voice seemed steady enough, but the president noticed the color in his cheeks had gone rather red.

"Okay, got it, now," said Dr. Lampert. "*Now* we are seeing the Kremlin."

The president's eyes grew wide. "Why, it *is* the Kremlin! There's Premier Molodinov. And President Kolojnivka! Are we able to hear them as well?"

"Sound presents an additional obstacle at this time," Lampert explained. "Photons pass through the P.O.V. easily, but sound waves involve air molecules which are simply too large. We're confident that we can eventually develop a workaround."

"Is this in real-time?" the president continued.

"In this case, yes," Lampert answered. "But bear in mind, information being transferred instantly through space also means that it could be transferred across time as well, since space and time are the same continuum. With some specific adjustments we are currently working on, we could see the Kremlin in the future, *or* the past."

"You mean, we could see what the Russians are planning for us next year?" asked the vice president. "Or in five years? The FBI could investigate a cold-case murder? Or learn the future intentions of Beijing?"

"Not just now, sir," Lampert answered. "Our range is limited to only several minutes. But with time and experimentation, yes. We will be able to see that far into the future."

"My God!" Guevara exclaimed, suddenly losing his cheerful demeanor. "This is too much power for any one nation to possess, even us! What if this technology were to be used *against* us?"

"Ah," interjected Gosling, as if this were his cue. "We have a solution for this concern, and I'm proud to say I was instrumental in developing it. Allow me to show you." He tapped an icon on his own computer pad, and then grinned at everyone with an air of self-satisfaction. "We are now surrounded by a field which allows us to see if anyone is utilizing a Scotty-type device against us. Because a Scotty's macroscope works by feeding gamma radiation through space-time at the quantum level, we can generate an EM field which makes the surrounding air molecules at the point of view give off light. Dr. Lampert? Could you please tune the macroscope to this location so that we might see the effect?"

"Of course," Lampert replied, trying not to sound annoyed at being given an order by his subordinate. He changed the image on his pad, and the view screen now revealed the seven people who were currently in the hangar at DARPA.

"There we all are," said the president. "Which means the point of view of the macroscope must be about…" she experimented with pointing her finger while watching her own image on the screen, then turned to look as soon as she brought it to bear on the source. "*…there.*"

As she turned, they all saw it. A small patch of brilliantly blue light surrounding the macroscope's point of view, about ten feet in the air, like a halo suspended in mid-air inside the hangar. It was about three inches in diameter and pulsated slightly.

"Well, hello there!" said Defense Secretary Pollock. Such a term of endearment sounded strange coming from a man whose chest medals were so numerous he looked almost lopsided.

"Indeed," said Vice President Guevara. "Eerie little blue light, isn't it?"

"And *this* will allow us to know if someone else is using a Scotty device to spy on us?" asked the president.

"Yes," answered Gosling. "If anyone tries to spy on us, that tell-tale blue light will let us know."

"But what if someone chooses their point of view carefully, and the blue light ends up being concealed in a clever hiding place?" asked Pollock.

"Yes, that is a concern," Gosling admitted. "The P.O.V. could be situated in a chandelier, or a Christmas tree, or within a bauble, and it would be very hard to tell it was there. But if one is vigilant about such things, one should make certain that such hiding places are not present in a secure meeting room."

"We should go light on the decorations in the oval office is what you're saying," said the president.

Everyone besides her exchanged looks.

"Was that a joke, ma'am?" asked Carla Jeffries.

"I don't joke," she answered.

"Pardon me for asking," said a red-haired woman, "but what good is it to know we're being spied on if we can't tell who or where the spy is?"

The president turned and looked at her, truly noticing her for the first time. "Carla, who is this woman?" she asked.

Carla stepped forward to answer, but was interrupted by Marlin Kettrell, the Director of the Department of Homeland Security. "Madam President, this is Special Agent Sarita Shantay. She's part of my detail. And she's also the person who procured the Scotty technology for us."

"Ah, yes," the president nodded towards Sarita. "I saw that movie based on you. So, *you're* the one who tricked Roger Avon into letting us militarize this new gadget. Very deft of you." Coming from her, it wasn't clear if she was giving a compliment.

"Like taking candy from a baby, Madam President, I assure you," Sarita answered. "But my question for Dr. Gosling still stands. Is it possible to do more than simply locate the P.O.V. the spies are using? After all, it's one thing to see a blue light and know that *someone* is spying on us, but that does us no good whatsoever if we cannot tell whether that light belongs to the Chinese, the Russians, the Saudis, or even the Republicans."

"Quite right, quite right," replied Gosling. "Which is why we've developed the ability to ping any P.O.V. which should happen to appear. Allow me to demonstrate." He picked up what looked for all the world to be a child's ray gun from the 1950's and aimed it at the blue light. He then pulled the trigger, and the device emitted a comical buzzing sound which oscillated in pitch. It was an utterly juvenile-looking display, and more than one person in the hanger hung their heads and covered their eyes at the embarrassing spectacle.

"And that little ray gun is supposed to help us get the *bad guys*, Buck Rodgers?" joked Secretary Pollock.

"Scoff if you must," Gosling answered back, "but the silly-looking design is rather pragmatic. What I've done is 'ping' the P.O.V.. I've sent a targeted burst of gamma rays back through the macroscope's quantum aperture. The particular Scotty doing the viewing, *our* Scotty, in this case, will now emit a coded gamma ray transmission at its source, which we can monitor by satellite. Anyone who might be spying on us will have their location instantly known to us, because we can detect the signal."

"That's quite impressive, but I see a problem with that," said Vice President Guevara. "What if someone decides to spy on us from the future? Or the past? If the spy is in the future, the satellites won't detect the 'ping' until that future date. And if the spy is in the past, the satellites won't be able to detect it at all."

Gosling beamed. He had a ready answer for this objection. "In that case, we can know exactly *when* the spying is taking place as well. You see, the 'ping' sends back a small return echo, and that echo has the quantum spin of the source, which we can use to determine the exact date and time the spying is taking place. You see, it was once assumed that the universe's expansion was taking place at an accelerating rate. Then, we discovered that the increasing rate of expansion was actually an optical illusion caused by the dimension of time growing *smaller*. In other words, time is actually *slowing down* as the universe gets bigger. So, any return echo from the ping will be faster or slower in its quantum spin depending on when…"

"Jesus, Gosling," interrupted Lampert. "You don't have to give them the *whole* encyclopedia."

Gosling recovered. "Yes, of course. Suffice it to say, the 'ping' tells us *when* as well as where."

"Very good so far, Doctor," said the president. "But just one thing. Are you prepared to install these detection fields throughout the White House yet? And please for the love of *God* say yes."

"Of course," replied Lampert. "We only await your order."

"Good. The order is given," she told him.

"How could you have someone spying on you from the past?" asked Secretary Jeffries. "I mean, if the Scotty wasn't invented back then, how could anybody use it?"

"The Scotty could eventually be used to set up another Scotty device in the past which could be used by similarly Scottied spy agents," replied Lampert. "It's tricky to do today, but with a few advancements it really wouldn't be all that difficult to do a few years from now."

"Good God!" Jeffries cried. "I hadn't thought of that. The Scotty is a *time machine* too! Martin, I'm starting to agree with you. This is too much power for any one nation to possess."

"Indeed," agreed the vice president. "And 'good God' is an appropriate expletive, because we are *literally* playing the role of God, here, and I don't mind telling you, I don't like it."

"You don't have to like it," said the president. "But we simply have no choice but to work with it. Because if we scuttled all of this due to our moral scruples, this technology would almost certainly leak out to some other nation, and we'll be left defenseless. No, the genie is out of the bottle, and if we don't make it work for *us*, it will work for someone else."

"It's still not right," said Guevara. "I..." But he was unable to continue.

"Here's a question," began Defense Secretary Pollock. "Suppose someone in the future were to spy on us for legitimate historical purposes. Would we be able to tell the difference?"

"We thought of that," said Gosling. "We've drawn up a list of protocols for historians to witness historical events in the White House and elsewhere. All such activity must be within prescribed parameters. And I'm pleased to say, Madam President, that all such activity has *already* been so ordered."

"*What?!*" yelped the president. "You mean, historians are *already* viewing us?"

"Oh, yes," said Gosling. "All viewers have originated from Ivy League schools, except one from Oxford."

"That's *unacceptable*, Randall." scolded the vice-president. "You show us your supposedly initial demonstration of this device, and *already* it's gotten into the hands of every trust-fund baby college kid?!"

"No, no, you don't understand!" Gosling pleaded. "The technology is simply more available in the *future*, that's all. It's top secret today, sure, but 50, 100, even a thousand years into the future, more and more people will progressively have access to the Scotty."

"And you've spoken with these Futurians already?" asked the Vice President.

"I don't like this at all!" the president nearly yelled. "For some as-yet-unborn college voyeur to spy on me in the bathroom on the pretext of some history lesson is..."

"No, no, ma'am!" Gosling rushed to correct. "Nothing like that. State rooms and meeting rooms only. That's one of our *key* parameters."

"I would have appreciated it if you let me in on your parameters *beforehand!*" she huffed, oblivious to the logical paradox behind what she'd just said. "Well, fine then. Just how many future historian-voyeurs do we have peeking in on us?"

"Leading up to this moment," Gosling said, "forty-three viewings have been made."

*"Forty-three!?"*

Gosling gulped. "Yes, ma'am."

She shook her head. "To be fair, that's actually less than I *thought* you were going to say. All right, fine. But when this is all over, Randall, I promise you I'm going to have a serious talk with my staff about whether to promote you or *fire* you."

"Um," Gosling started, unsure of where to go with his thoughts. Finally, he simply said, "Yes, ma'am."

"Forty-three, you say?" asked Sarita Shantay.

"Um," began Gosling. He had forgotten Sarita was even there. "Yes. That's right. Forty-three. Why?"

"You mean forty-*four*," she replied, and pointed to a far corner of the hangar.

There, as all turned to see, was *another* blue light!

"Randall, is *this* within one of your protocols?" asked the president.

"No, ma'am! This demonstration was strictly forbidden to all press, present *or* future!"

"Then *ping* that P.O.V. *Now!*"

Gosling didn't hesitate. Grabbing his comical gamma-ray gun, he aimed at the blue light and squeezed the trigger. The archaic-sounding buzz indicated that he'd gotten off a good shot, and hit the blue light squarely.

"Now," said the president, "*where* is he? Where's that spy?"

Gosling and Lampert both examined the equipment on the Scotty with perplexed expressions. Finally, Lampert said, "*Nowhere*, Madam President. We get no return on our signal."

"You missed!" accused Pollock.

"No, I got a return echo." said Gosling. "The signal went through."

"Then he must be in either the future or the past," said the vice president. "What time period is this spy operating in?"

Gosling examined his gun, but his furrowed brow furrowed even more in puzzlement. "I don't understand," he said. "According to this, the quantum spin on the echo is the same as ours. Whoever this guy is, he's spying on us from another location *at this very moment*."

"Could the spy have developed some way of thwarting your signal?" asked Carla Jeffries.

"I don't see how," said Gosling. "If you block the gamma-ray signal, you also prevent the Scotty from working."

"I disagree," said Pollock. "Somehow, someone's probably *improved* on your technology. DARPA has a mole."

"Impossible!" Gosling shot back. "Too few people. No communications go in or out of the facility."

"Bullshit!" said Pollock. "Gormann industries was probably *crawling* with corporate spies before the technology came to us."

"Not true," said Lampert. "We vetted everyone."

Everyone was moving towards the mysterious intruding blue light now, and it was only a matter of time before someone voiced what they were all thinking.

"Whoever is watching us," said Secretary Jeffries, "they obviously don't give a damn that we're all looking right at the point where he's spying from."

"Either that," added the vice president, "or he-she-it isn't paying attention."

"This is unbelievable!" shouted Pollock. "The most powerful surveillance device ever invented, and it utterly fails on its maiden voyage. I can't believe your incompetence, Randall!"

"It isn't *me!*" Gosling protested. "Nothing I'm seeing makes any sense. Unless…" he trailed off.

"Unless *what*, Gosling?" The impatient voice of the president made it clear she would brook nothing less than a good explanation.

"No, you'll think it's crazy…"

"Wrong. I *already* think it's crazy. Now *spill* it!"

Randall Gosling looked as though he were fending off several imaginary birds that were flying at his head. Then, he seemed to recover enough to try to speak. "Well… Okay, look, if this particular Scotty's macroscope were… *extraterrestrial…*"

Nearly everyone guffawed at once. "Oh, *come o*n, Gosling!" bellowed Marlin Kettrell. "Are you seriously arguing that *aliens* are spying on us?"

"No, wait!" said Lampert, trying to yell above the din. "That actually makes *sense.* If the Scotty spying on us were several light years away, the gamma-ray signal from the ping wouldn't reach us until several years later as it traveled the speed of light back to Earth. And *that's* assuming the signal would even be strong enough."

"I've never heard anything so ridiculous," chided the vice president. "You're telling us that *E.T.* ate your homework!"

"Couldn't the spy's signal be bounced off of a satellite?" asked Secretary Jeffries. Confuse your location tracking?"

"No, we would detect the gamma signal, even if it bounced off a satellite," said Lampert. "Our satellites monitor *other* satellites, you know."

"Wait a minute," said Sarita Shantay. "We can probably *test* Gosling's alien origin hypothesis."

"We can?" Pollock frowned at her. "How?"

"Well, Gosling, didn't you tell us that you could always determine *where* and when a P.O.V. was coming from?"

Gosling looked momentarily frozen. Then simply said, "Yes."

"How does that work?" Sarita asked.

"Um, well the ping signal never reaches you if it comes from the past, and you have to catch up to it if it comes from the future. But the *echo* gives us the quantum spin, and from that you can determine the time and direction the other Scotty originated from. Compare that against the Earth's spin and orbital revolution and you can determine a probable point of origin. But we *can't* use that technique this time, because the quantum spin is the same as ours! They're spying on us in real time, so the Earth's position is the same."

"Wrong," said Sarita. "We have 180 degrees of arc above us, and 180 degrees of arc below. The time is the same as ours, so only the direction matters. If the other scotty originates in the 180-degree arc *below* our horizon line, then the origin could be either Earth or outer space. But if it comes from the 180 degrees *above* us…"

"It could *only* originate from outer space!" Gosling completed her thought for her. "Why, that's brilliant!"

"Brilliant?" said Lampert. "It's a 50-50 shot."

"Which is 100% better than what we had before," pointed out Marlin Kettrell. "I hope you can see, Madam President, why I insisted that Ms. Shantay be part of our team."

"Indeed," the president agreed. "Okay, Dr. Gosling, do it. Find the direction this other Scotty is operating at."

It took several moments, but he did so. He had to ping the P.O.V. once again, but once he did, he got a clear direction. 15 degrees *above* the horizon. Right ascension 17, declination +30. The constellation Hercules.

"Well, I'll be damned," said Pollock.

"You and me both," said Kettrell. "Who would have thought that aliens would actually be *watching* us?"

"Maybe they've been watching us from the beginning," suggested Carla Jeffries.

"It makes sense, in a way," said the vice president. "The aliens must have developed the Scotty and its macroscope centuries before we did. What better and cheaper way to explore the cosmos than to simply peer through a spyglass?"

"It really *is* a macroscope!" exclaimed Lampert. "Just like Piers Anthony wrote about more than a century ago. How could we have been so blind? We saw this as a tool for spying on our own species, but why shouldn't we have first considered it as a tool to explore the cosmos?"

"Or affect it?" asked Gosling. "I mean, if aliens possessed technology like this millennia ago, as the vice president said, then who's to say they didn't use that technology to do more than merely watch? Who's to say they didn't help guide humanity's development?"

"How?" asked Marlin Kettrell. "By using a Scotty to appear to humans as Zoroaster? As Moses? As Jesus Christ maybe? Or a vision at Muhammed's mountain?"

"Maybe," admitted Gosling. "Maybe Erich Von Däniken was right. The gods really might be aliens."

"You're nuts," said Lampert.

"You're suggesting," said the president with deliberate slowness, "that we are currently staring into the eye of *God?*"

Almost as if in response, the blue light suddenly vanished.

For a long time, no one said anything. Instead, they all began looking everywhere else in the warehouse, trying to see if there was another blue light somewhere.

"Where is it?" asked the president.

"There!" said Jeffries.

"No, that's the original one," said Lampert.

"Shut it off, just to be sure," ordered Guevara.

Lampert did so, and the search for another blue light continued. When it became clear that there wasn't one, it was he who broke the silence. "What could it mean? Are they done watching us?"

"Who knows?" said Agent Shantay. "Maybe, now that they know we're aware of them, they've granted us autonomy. Maybe we've just graduated to a new level of technological development that they respect."

"Maybe they're waiting for us to make contact with them, now," said Gosling.

"Or maybe they're just waiting for us to turn the detection field *off*," said Pollock.

"In any case, this is the discovery of the millennia," said the vice president. "It will require a new agency. One whose sole purpose is human-alien relations. And a Bureau of Space Exploration, akin to the old NASA, that's undoubtedly warranted. Why, when the world learns of the proven existence of space aliens whom we can actually *contact…*"

"It will also learn about the Scotty's spying capabilities," the president interrupted.

The hangar went silent. That thought had not yet occurred to anyone else.

"Are you willing to let that happen, Madam President?" asked Secretary Pollock.

"Not just yet," she replied. "No, the Scotty's macroscope must remain a secret for now. I think that in the meantime, Dr. Lampert, you should simply record this as a successful test of your Scotty device and leave it at that. This entire project will remain classified at the highest level. We will discuss the formation of new agencies to deal with the aftermath of this – *event* at a later time. That is all."

Everyone began to reluctantly disperse, and President Cullen and Vice President Guevara began walking towards the exit where their motorcade was waiting. But before she reached the door, the president motioned Sarita Shantay over to her.

"Kettrell has you working with Lampert and Gosling on this project?" she asked her.

"Constantly," Sarita replied.

"Well, if you catch Gosling trying to get a peek at the women's showers again, I want you to use the Scotty to dematerialize him, and *never* rematerialize him again."

"Yes, ma'am," she replied, thinking she was joking.

Then she remembered the president's earlier comment, *'I don't joke.'*

## Chapter 3: The Red Race

Carly Mancuso had a feeling of dread, almost as if a dust storm were rising. But there was no dust storm, not where she stood. Not anywhere else on Mars, either. And none was impending, according to the meteorological feed on her forearm pad. From where she was standing, which was the tip of the "nose" on what was popularly known as the "face" on Mars, it was so quiet it seemed even death itself was taking a nap.

Still, she felt certain something bad was about to happen.

"See? I told you there was nothing here," said Bobby Mancuso, Carly's younger brother.

Jack Ng stood there, a kid who looked as though he'd arrived at an empty candy store. He was so down in the mouth his lower lip could have taken a core sample. Bobby, his best friend, was right. There was nothing. Just a few knolls on an ordinary mountain. By Martian standards, it was almost a collection of hills. "Aw, man," he said. "I thought maybe we'd find *something*, at least."

"Oooh, you mean like a message in a bottle from a long-lost alien princess who hopes that same brave boy would rescue her millions of years later?"

"Shut up!" said Jack. Bobby was rubbing it in.

"Come on, you two," said Carly. She was fifteen, and the oldest of the three. "We've got to get headed back if we don't want to miss dinnertime."

It was Carly's presence that made the excursion possible. She was a top student, a mathlete, and her parents, along with all the other adults of the settlement, completely trusted her. There was already talk of giving her a permanent duty assignment. With her chaperoning, they approved Jack Ng's request to go out and see Camelback Mountain, a.k.a. the "Face on Mars." Of course, he then insisted on taking Bobby with him. Her younger brother Bobby was equally bright, but more physical, and loved picking on Jack, even though Jack followed Bobby everywhere.

"I mean, what did you even think would be out here?" asked Bobby as they headed back to the rover.

"I dunno," said Jack. "That guy Hoagland said there was a flash in one of the satellite pictures, like the glint of something metal."

"You mean *Richard* Hoagland?" asked Carly, climbing into the dune-buggy-like rover. "That guy was a crackpot. Died decades ago. He never even set foot on Mars. Where did you find that kooky guy's crap?"

"Um… On an old Netstream show?" Jack admitted.

Bobby laughed. "Yeah, *that's* a reliable source of information."

"Well, it sounded really interesting," Jack said, seating himself and clasping his seat belt. "I thought maybe it was worth a look."

"You're such a sucker. People have been searching that place for years and they all found the same thing. You know what they found?"

Jack's eyes got wide. "*What* did they find?"

"How not to be so *gullible!*" Bobby said, punching Jack in the shoulder.

"Hey!"

"Come on, Bobby," said Carly as she put the rover in drive and engaged the motor. "Learning how to be a skeptic sometimes means going over things that were debunked years ago. It's healthy to re-explore, especially when still young. Jack's only eleven, you know."

"He's ten. *I'm* eleven," Bobby replied.

"I thought you and he were in the same class," said Carly.

"Next month," Jack said, sulkily. "I turn eleven next month."

"Oh. Well, happy early birthday, Jack."

"Yeah, thanks," he moped.

"Hey, cheer up!" said Bobby. "You got us out of the Habitrail for a while. That's always good."

Jack smiled, weakly. It *was* always good to get out of the "Habitrail." The underground Habitation unit, or "Hab," and the tunnels that branched out from it, had been nicknamed the "Habitrail" right from the beginning, because it was almost impossible to think of the tunnels and rooms as anything other than a giant hamster cage. Getting outside once in a while was mentally healthy, even when the excuse was to chase a long-dead conspiracy theory.

It was a roughly 45-minute drive from Cydonia back to Bequerel Crater, and the underground tunnels which they called home. It was a boring ride home, and the boys took to playing games on their forearm-tablets almost immediately, leaving Carly to quietly mind the driving. All three kids were born there, at the crater, right after the Bequerel Hab was constructed in the year 86 A.T. (2055 Gregorian) by Musk City and its ruling government. The kids had never known anything like blue skies or green grass in their entire lives.

The "road" they followed wasn't really a road at all, merely a path where boulders had been shoved out of the way, thus making transit a bit easier. All Martian roads were like that. Dust was only a minor concern and there was never an issue with mud on Mars. The ride was a reasonably smooth one.

It was Martian dusk when their home crater came into sight. The sky was going from its usual light pink to a dark red, where soon it would fade into an almost impenetrable black. But as Carly brought the rover closer, her sense of unease reasserted itself. Something wasn't right. She brought the rover to a stop and looked over the entrance to the Hab carefully.

"Why'd you stop?" asked Bobby.

"Something's wrong," Carly answered.

"What could be wrong?" asked Jack.

"The docking light," she said. "It's out."

"Maybe they just forgot," said Bobby.

"Mom wouldn't forget," she told him.

She was right. Not only would their parents not forget that they were out there, but they would also have called in a few times to check by now. If the radio somehow wasn't working, someone would have met them on the way back. Nobody forgets about three kids out on their own, especially on Mars, and especially not when two of those kids happened to have the Base Commander as their father. Something really was wrong.

Carly turned off the headlamps on the rover. "I'm going to circle around," she said.

"Why?" asked Jack.

"Just to get a better look."

Carly took the rover off to the right of Bequerel Crater. The Hab was located on the crater's western ridge, so it appeared to be on the inner part of the right-hand side. Going around the crater to the right meant much of the crater's southern ridge was out of sight. But she hadn't gotten 30 degrees around the Hab before the southern ridge came into view and she saw that her instincts had proven correct. Behind the Hab's southern entrance, next to the southern ridge of the Bequerel crater, was an array of trikes.

"Whoa!" said Jack. "There must be dozens of them."

"Over *two* dozen, I'd say," said Carly.

"Who do they belong to?" asked Bobby.

"No idea," Carly replied. She turned off the remaining running lights on the rover. "You boys better turn off your helmet lights and radios. Once we're close to the Hab, our short-range communications might be overheard, or we might be seen."

"Aww," complained Bobby. "We won't be able to hear each other. And in a little while, we won't even be able to *see*."

"I'd rather not be able to see than have them see *us*."

Bobby and Jack complied, turning off their helmet lights and radios even as Carly did the same. Then, under the last remaining dregs of Martian twilight, she drove the rover up to the docking port. But instead of docking, she parked just outside of it.

Bobby unbuckled and touched his helmet to Carly's so she could hear him. "We're not going to dock?" he asked.

"No. Because as soon as we plug in, the charge indicator light will come on inside," she pointed out. "One of the strangers inside the Habitrail might see it and realize we're out here."

Bobby grinned to himself. He sometimes hated his sister for being so smart, but he had to admit, in situations like this, it was handy to have her around.

All three of them disembarked and stood just outside the airlock. They didn't dare open it for fear of being discovered. It wasn't the only way in, but the other entrances were just as risky. Jack beckoned to Carly, and she obliged by touching her helmet to his so that they could hear each other. "What now?" he asked.

Carly kept her helmet on Jack's and beckoned Bobby to come over and join them. With the three of them helmet-to-helmet, she said, "I'm going to peek in the north porthole. Get a look inside."

The boys nodded and they all parted helmets. Carly went up to the porthole and strained to look in. She was tall for her age, even for someone growing up in Martian gravity, but she couldn't quite get up high enough to see through the ship-like porthole. She came back to Bobby and Jack and the three of them touched helmets again.

"I need someone to climb up on my shoulders so he can take a look."

Both boys answered simultaneously, with Jack saying, "*I'll* do it," and Bobby saying, "*He'll* do it."

"Okay, Jack. Hop on."

'Chicken fights' were never easy in the low gravity of Mars. Were this a swimming pool back on planet Earth, Carly would have had the weight of surrounding water to steady herself. But on Mars, there was only the thin air, and the slightest misstep would easily send both her and Jack tumbling out of control. Jack had an easy time climbing onto Carly's shoulders, but from that point on, it was an uneasy balancing act. At least the suits they were wearing didn't have external air-hoses that might snag on something or get pinched off with the weight of another person. Finally, Carly's feet steadied beneath her, and she did a careful zen-walk over to the North portal.

Jack took a careful look inside. Then, after less than a minute, he tapped against Carly's helmet, signaling her to let him down. She carefully backed away from the portal, and slowly crouched to let Jack climb off. When the three of them joined helmets again, he had a lot to say.

"They've got your dad!" he said. "I saw him. They have him tied up with one of those zip-tie handcuffs."

"*Who* has him?" asked Bobby.

"I dunno," said Jack. "They had beards, and their hair was done up in buns like Dr. Alpert's."

Carly almost laughed, in spite of the situation. Dr. Alpert had his long, grey hair done up in a silly man-bun which all the kids made fun of relentlessly.

"Their skin was dark," continued Jack. "Not as dark as yours and Bobby's, but definitely brown."

"How *many* were there?" asked Carly.

"I saw three," Jack answered. "It looked like they were questioning your dad or something."

"*Questioning* him?" asked Carly. "Why would they question him up here? By the north airlock? Unless…"

All three of them realized it. *Unless they were threatening to throw him out of said airlock.*

"Oh, crap, oh crap!" said Jack.

"Damn! Who *are* they?" asked Bobby.

"I'm not sure," answered Jack. "But they had green symbols on their uniforms."

"Green symbols?" asked Carly. "What did they look like?"

Jack tried to find the words. "Um, I dunno, like an onion? Maybe? With a couple of curvy sticks on either side of it?"

Carly risked a little light and activated her forearm tablet. She selected an image and showed it to Jack. "Like this?"

"Yeah! That's it." said Jack.

Carly looked over at Bobby. She could barely make out the puzzled look on his face from the ambient light of her forearm tablet. "I don't get it," he said. "What is it?"

"The lantern and cross-sabers of a Sikh," she answered, shutting off her tablet. "They must be from Airy-Zero, the Indian Space Research Organization's encampment south of here."

It would fit Jack's description perfectly. Sikh males wore their hair in buns because the spatial constrictions of Martian vac-suit helmets didn't allow for the traditional turbans they wore on Earth.

"Sikhs?" asked Bobby. "I don't get it. I thought Sikhs were peaceful."

"They are," she answered. "This doesn't make any sense."

"I'm really scared," said Jack. "What are we going to do?"

Carly collected herself for a moment. Then she remembered one of her school lessons. "It's like what Mrs. Pautz says about people. If someone does something that doesn't make sense, you have to ask yourself why that person would act that way. So, what would the motive be? Why would a bunch of peaceful Sikhs suddenly decide to attack us?"

"Maybe they ran out of food?" suggested Jack.

"Maybe," agreed Carly. "But they wouldn't need to threaten us over that. Dad would just give them whatever they needed. Within reason."

"Maybe they're just disguised as Sikhs, and we're being attacked by someone else," said Bobby.

Carly thought about that. It was actually a pretty good theory. But something still didn't fit. "Could be. But I think we're missing something more basic. What could we possibly have that anybody else would want?"

"Water?" said Jack.

"Oxygen?" said Bobby.

"Medicines?" Jack continued.

"Maybe the asteroid busters," Bobby added.

"That's it!" cried Carly. "The asteroid busters!"

"Huh?" said Bobby.

"Don't you see? The asteroid busters are *missiles!*"

Bobby's face kept looking puzzled for a long moment. The asteroid busters were part of an anti-meteorite defense system. Musk City, on the opposite side of the planet, had a similar system, only bigger – more busters. But if the busters were hijacked, they could be reconfigured to fire at *anything*.

A grin slowly spread across Bobby's face as the realization dawned. Then it collapsed into a frown again. "Wait a minute, you're saying a bunch of peaceful Sikhs have suddenly attacked us because they want some *missiles?*" He shook his head, which only made the three of them sway back and forth a little with their helmets touching. "Not even the fundies back on Earth would do something that stupid. And *they've* been acting crazier than ever lately."

At that, Carly nearly started. "You're right!" She exclaimed. "They *have* been acting crazier on Earth lately. I think whatever's happening with the fundies on Earth is happening here on Mars, too!"

She couldn't see the faces of either Bobby or Jack, but from their initial silence, she presumed that they wore puzzled expressions. "Even if you're right, what craziness could possibly make even peaceful Sikhs want to attack us?" asked Bobby.

Carly shrugged, which was a useless gesture in the darkness. "I'm not sure. But I'm pretty sure the fundies want to take over Mars."

This time Jack answered, "Take over? Why?"

"Because of something mom and dad said," she replied. "I overheard them talking about four fundamentalist colony ships launched from Earth towards Mars several months ago."

"Really?" asked Bobby.

"Yep," said Carly. "The fundies are coming."

"That wouldn't explain why *Sikhs* are attacking us," Bobby pointed out.

"No," Carly agreed, "but we don't know they're *all* Sikhs, do we? We only know the patches of the men Jack saw. Jack, did they *all* have the same patch?"

"I couldn't tell," Jack admitted. "I only got a good look at one."

"Okay, then," said Carly. "It's reasonable to assume some of the others may be of a religion common to India but not necessarily Sikhs. Hindus and Muslims, probably."

"Are Hindus and Muslims less peaceful?" asked Jack.

"Pretty much," Carly answered. "They once killed each other for centuries. Sikhs alone might not be inclined to attack us, but a mixture of Sikhs, Muslims, and Hindus? Yeah, that just might work."

"And you believe they want to *conquer* Mars?" asked Jack.

"That's my theory, yeah." Carly stated.

"Yeah? Well, if they want to take over Mars, they're too late," said Bobby. "Mars is governed by Musk City. They'd never let a bunch of fundies take over."

"True," Carly answered. "But if Musk City were *destroyed…*"

The boys let that sink in. "That's crazy!" said Jack. "To do that, you'd need…"

"A bunch of missiles?" said Bobby.

Neither Carly nor Bobby needed to see Jack's face to know the expression he likely had. "Oh, *crap*."

Musk City ruled Mars, but the planet was still very lightly populated. With Musk City out of the way, the new religious settlers would probably have enough numbers to easily overrun the secular ones, especially with more fundamentalists on the way.

"I don't understand. What did *we* ever do to them?" asked Jack.

"Nothing," Carly answered. "We're simply in their way."

"Are you sure about this?" asked Bobby.

Carly huffed. "No! But we know enough to know that they're probably from Airy-Zero, and that they just threatened to throw dad out an airlock. That's enough to conclude that we need to do *something*."

There was a long silence before Jack spoke up. "So, what *do* we do?"

Jack was fortunate he couldn't see Carly's burning stare as she answered. "Well, *obviously*, we have to keep them from launching those asteroid busters!" she said.

"Don't be silly," said Bobby. "Our parents would never give them the codes to launch."

"If mom were drugged, and they threatened to throw dad out an airlock, *she* might cave."

Bobby was silent for a time at that. He knew she was right. "Okay," he eventually said, "Can we sneak inside? Disable the busters?"

"I don't see how," Carly answered him. "There's only three airlocks, and there's no realistic chance that we could use one of them without getting noticed."

"How about we jam the launch doors?" said Bobby. "We can do that from out here. The missiles can't launch if the doors are closed."

"Yeah, but if they don't know we've done that, and they launch anyway, that will blow up the entire Hab!" said Jack. "Along with our parents! *And* us!"

"And if they *do* know we've done that, that means they'll have realized someone is out here, come out to grab us, unjam the launch doors and then fire the missiles anyway," Bobby completed the thought for him. "So much for that idea."

"There *must* be a way," said Carly.

The three kids thought a moment before Jack spoke up. "If we can't jam the launch doors shut, maybe we can jam them open and get inside that way. Disable the busters inside the launch tubes."

"No way!" said Bobby. "Even *you* wouldn't fit down there."

"I wouldn't have to fit all the way," Jack countered. "Just enough to get the top of the warhead off and take the detonator out. The buster might launch, but it wouldn't blow up after it landed."

Carly smiled as she warmed up to the idea. "Hey, yeah! That just might work. But how long would it take?"

"A long time," Bobby answered for Jack. "There's *twelve* of those things. Jack's the only one small enough to get down those tubes, and we only have the tools from the repair kit in the rover."

"And here's *another* problem," said Jack. "We only have 35 minutes of air left."

Carly and Bobby both looked at their O2 gauges. Jack was right. They were running out of time.

Twelve warheads? In half an hour? Could a ten-year-old kid pull that off?

Just then, a huge roaring sound interrupted their train of thought. The three of them parted helmets, and they saw the launch doors open, and all twelve asteroid busters soared up from the center of the crater into the black Martian sky.

"Oh, *CRAAAAP!*" Jack shouted, even though the others couldn't hear. As they watched, the bright points of light turned eastward – towards Musk city. All except one, which seemed to veer off-course. But eventually it became obvious where that one, stray missile was headed – Communications Satellite Charlie.

Bobby came over to Carly and touched his helmet to hers. "What now?"

"I don't know!" Carly shouted back to him. "But I'm going to calculate how long Musk City has before the busters hit."

"Why?"

"Because we might have time to warn them."

Bobby was about to ask, 'Warn them *how?*,' but she'd already pulled her helmet back, so he couldn't argue.

Carly's mathlete skills really came in handy at this moment. She activated her forearm pad and began calculating using Newton's classic gravitation formula. She didn't know some of the variables – she had to guess how much the busters weighed, and she didn't know the exact distance to Musk City – but she figured each buster had a mass of no less than 2 tons with fuel, and since Musk city was nearly on the opposite side of the planet, the distance would have to be a bit less than half the planet's circumference, or roughly 10,000 kilometers. She calculated the missiles would have a maximum speed of 6 kilometers per second, because anything faster than that meant the missiles would break orbit and never land. At that speed, over that distance, that gave them…

"About 27 minutes," Carly said after turning off her tablet reconnecting her helmet to Bobby's.

"27 *minutes?*" asked Bobby.

"Well, more like 26 minutes, now."

"*26* minutes. And *34* minutes of air. How are we going to have time to warn anybody with *that?* I mean, that stray missile probably took out the communications satellite!"

He was right. Without the communications satellite, they were screwed. Carly's first thought was to use the rover's radio to send a warning to one of the other settlements. But they were too far away to radio directly, even if their attackers weren't jamming signals, which they undoubtedly were. With no communications satellite, that meant that any warning had to reach Musk City by relaying off something else. Someone could bounce a signal off of one of the bases on either of the Martian moons, Phobos or Deimos, but they were currently both behind the planet, so that couldn't work. The only other option was to send a message to Earth. When Mars and Earth were in conjunction, as they currently were, a radio message could go to Earth and back to Mars in about ten minutes. Except, damn it all, it was *nighttime* on Mars, meaning that Earth was behind the planet, too! They would have to wait *twelve hours* to relay a message via Earth, and by then it would be too late, even if their rover's radio were powerful enough, which it wasn't.

Those fundies had timed their attack perfectly.

There was only one other option, and it was a long shot.

Carly waved Jack to come over and join them, and he came back over and touched his helmet to theirs.

"I have a plan," she said. "We're going to Kasei Valles."

"Kasei Valles?" said Bobby. "That's a United States military outpost. Why are we going there?"

"Because we can warn Musk City from there. The Americans have something called a Scotty."

"A *what?*" asked Jack.

"A *Scotty*. It's a device that converts matter into energy and back into matter again. If they can use that device, they'll be able to warn Musk City before the missiles hit."

"Wow! Like, they can beam over a note?" asked Jack.

"Or a representative," Carly answered. "But it's also a basic communicator. It can transmit messages instantly without any time delay."

"You mean like an ansible?" asked Bobby.

"Yes, exactly," she said. "Besides, if anybody can rescue our parents, it's the Americans."

"How far away is Kasei Valles?" Bobby asked.

"I think it's a 20-minute drive," said Carly.

"Man, that's cutting it *close!*" said Jack.

"I know! So we have to make this count," Carly told them. "We're going to need a full charge for the rover, or else we'll never make it. So, I want to pull the old battery from the rover first."

"But as soon as we unplug the fresh battery from the docking bay, someone inside might see the indicator light!" Bobby protested.

"I know, so we're going to have to install the new battery *fast*," said Carly. "Then drive off right away."

"Why can't we just use the battery we have now and *sneak* off?" asked Jack.

"We could," said Carly. "But we wouldn't get there in 26 minutes. *Or* on 34 minutes of air."

Jack's disappointment was palpable. "Aww, man."

"I'll use night vision and keep the lights off," Carly said, trying to sound reassuring. "With luck, they won't even see the indicator light when the battery is pulled. But if they do, maybe we can get a big enough head start that they won't even be able to see us."

"What if they have night vision, too?" asked Jack. It was a good bet they probably did.

"Then we run like hell," said Carly. "One more thing, though. Turn your radios back on once we're underway. By then, it won't matter as much if they can hear us. Ready?"

Both boys tapped Carly's helmet to let her know that they were.

"Okay. *Go!*"

The boys scampered to the rover and wasted no time pulling the old battery. Carly watched them, and the instant the old battery was out, she pulled the new battery from the docking bay and brought it over. Then, they all tried to shove in the new battery, but in the darkness, that was a tricky thing to do. The battery jammed on something they couldn't see, and wouldn't go in.

"It's stuck!" said Jack, even though the others couldn't hear.

The light came on over the docking bay. They were discovered! But that same light allowed Carly to see what was keeping the battery from going in. It was a piece of rope, and she quickly got it out of the way. The battery slid into place.

"Go! Go! Go!" shouted Carly. She knew it was pointless with the radio still off, but she couldn't help herself. The boys got in just as quickly as she did, and she turned on the rover and drove off.

No sooner had the rover started to move than two people came out the north airlock and started chasing them. It was a short chase, however. Whoever they were, they were no match for the rover's speed on foot.

One by one, each of the kids turned his or her radio back on. From a distance, they saw the two people who came out the airlock go back in. Bobby was the first to say anything. "Did we lose them?"

Almost as if in response, they saw a row of lights come out from behind the southern ridge of the crater, and it wasn't difficult to discern that this meant that some of the trikes were coming their way.

"Ohcrapohcrapohcrapohcrap! They're coming *after* us!" cried Jack.

"Maybe they won't be able to see us," said Bobby.

Carly knew that was unlikely. Their lights were off, but their pursuers undoubtedly had night vision in their helmets, just like she did. And even if they didn't, those two men had seen her drive off to the West, and there weren't that many roads on Mars to choose from.

Sure enough, the trikes made straight for them, coming up the same road.

"Yeah, they see us!" said Jack.

Now, it was a race; a race across the red sands of Mars – and the winner of the race would win the whole planet.

The kids had a good head start. The rover was fast, but not quite as fast as the smaller, lighter trikes. Gradually, bit by bit, the pursuers gained on the rover.

"How many of them are there?" asked Carly.

"Eight," answered Bobby. "No, wait, *nine!*"

Nine trikes. And they were coming up the road two abreast to avoid the rocky areas off-road. All except for the lead trike, which was solo.

Bobby was pretty good at math himself. He did a quick estimate of the distance being gained, and did a calculation. "They'll probably catch up to us in about 15 minutes."

"Can't you be a bit more precise?" asked Carly.

"Hey, it's hard to gauge distance in night vision," he answered.

Carly didn't like that, but it gave her an idea. "Do you see the lights on the canopy bar?"

Bobby and Jack both looked up. The rover had a bar above the chassis like a dune buggy, and there were a pair of floodlights fixated on top of it. "I see them," said Bobby.

"Can you turn them around so they're facing backward?"

Bobby started working on one, and Jack the other. They could pivot the lights somewhat, but they didn't turn all the way around 180 degrees. Finally, Jack realized that if you slid the whole assembly forward, the lights could be made to hang down from the bar instead of being propped up above it, and that would allow the lights to shine backward. Jack showed this to Bobby, and soon both floodlights were pointing toward the rear.

"Okay, you're all set!" Bobby called out.

"All right. Turn off your night vision!" she ordered.

The boys did so, and she switched on the exterior lights.

Immediately, the lead trike threw an arm up over his helmet visor as the bright light blinded him, and he lost control. He wiped out, taking one of the trikes behind him out as well. But the other trikes got around this sudden obstacle with relative ease. They must have switched off their night vision right away. The chase was still on.

"We're down to seven," said Bobby. "That bought us some time, but they're still on us."

"Will we get there in time now?" asked Jack.

Carly thought for a moment. "Maybe not, but we might not have to. Once we're close enough, we should be able to radio them."

"They're probably jamming us!" said Bobby.

"I know," she replied. "But the closer we get, the easier it will be to get through the jamming signal." *I hope*, she added to herself.

They sped along like that for a while, and it soon became clear that the small amount of time the rover had gained by blinding the lead bike was long gone. Carly was beginning to make plans in her mind about how she might try running a trike off the road if it tried pulling alongside her, or maybe slamming on the brakes if the rider tried jumping aboard from behind. Those musings were interrupted by the sound of a ping that ricocheted somewhere off the rover's dashboard.

"They've got *guns!*" shouted Jack.

Guns were extremely rare on Mars. There was no wild game to hunt, and a stray bullet could easily crack the bulkhead of a Hab, killing everyone inside instantly. What's more, most guns needed oxygen to fire. If these fundies had somehow fashioned guns to work in the thin atmosphere of Mars, it meant they'd been planning this for a long while.

"Do we have anything we can *throw* at them?" asked Carly.

Bobby looked around. "I don't think so."

"Yes, there is!" shouted Jack. "The seats!"

Bobby was about to argue, and then realized what Jack meant. He reached over the back of the rear seat and grabbed the tool kit, just as another bullet whizzed past his head. He opened the kit and handed an adjustable wrench to Jack, took another one for himself, and the two of them got on their hands and knees and began unscrewing the rear seat from the deck of the chassis.

Another bullet grazed off the back of Carly's seat. "Whatever you're doing, you'd better hurry!" she shouted.

Bobby finished quickly. Then Jack finally managed to get the final bolt unscrewed on his side, and he and Bobby grabbed the underside, ready to throw.

"On three, ready?" said Bobby. "One… two… THREE!"

They heaved the seat over the back of the rover in a clean toss. The sudden appearance of this new obstacle in front of the trikes made them all swerve, and two more wiped out, but it didn't stop them all.

"We're down to five!" called Jack.

"Yeah, but they're gaining on us even *faster*, now!" said Bobby.

*What!? Why would that be?* Carly looked at the power indicator. The rover was at 85% charge. Normally, that was enough to get them anywhere, but in the freezing cold nighttime of Mars, batteries worked more sluggishly. The further the charge got from 100%, the less speed the rover would have, and the smaller, lighter trikes wouldn't have that problem so severely.

They were losing ground faster now, and still only halfway there.

It was then that she glanced at her O2 indicator, and got a *very* nasty shock. She saw that there was only *eleven minutes of air left!* But how could that be? Then she remembered. It was one of the first lessons they taught kids about vac suits: The number of minutes of air is only an estimate. It's based on the average amount of air consumed over a period of time. But she and the boys had racing heartbeats, and surging adrenaline. They were using up oxygen at a much faster rate than normal! She'd completely forgotten to take that into account.

Would they even *have* air when they arrived at Kasei Valles?

There was nothing she could do about it now, so she tried to put it out of her mind and focus on the things she *could* control.

Bobby was working on unscrewing the bolts to the passenger side seat in front – the only seat left with which they had to throw – but Carly knew they needed something more drastic.

"What about the spare tire?" she said.

"What?! You've *gotta* be kidding!" yelled Bobby.

Martian vehicles all had solid tires which never got a flat, but there were plenty of jagged rocks which could disable even one of those. That's why every rover had a light spare – just in case.

The problem was, it was attached at the *back* – and their pursuers were *shooting* at them. Getting the spare off meant becoming an easy target.

Another bullet pinged off of the back of Carly's seat. "These seats seem to deflect those bullets pretty well," she said. "If you got the other one off, could you use it as a shield?"

Bobby thought about that. It was a pretty good idea. "Yeah, I think so!"

"Good. *Do* that!"

The passenger side seat was already partially undone. Bobby just needed to unscrew two more bolts and it was free. He finished removing the bolts, pulled it up and over his helmet, and then turned to Jack.

"Hang onto the seat for me," Bobby told him. "I need my hands free to unscrew the spare."

Jack did as Bobby told him, and grabbed the edge of the seat so that the back stayed draped over Bobby's head. Bobby then crept towards the back where the temporary spare tire was screwed on.

A bullet pinged harmlessly off the back of the seat. The make-shift shield was working.

Jack reached down and started unscrewing the nut that held the spare on. It was large and hand-sized, so it required no tool. But Bobby's hand was exposed from underneath his MacGyvered shield.

A bullet pinged off the back of the rover and he yanked his hand back. But he tried again when he realized that the shooter had missed by quite a lot. Apparently, it wasn't easy steering a trike in pitch-blackness while aiming a gun at a moving target at the same time.

Another bullet pinged off the back, but still nowhere near Bobby's hand. This time, he didn't jerk his hand back but kept working. The bolt loosened and finally fell off.

"Back up!" he told Jack. The two boys retreated further into the rover. Then Bobby aimed a kick at the spare tire with his right leg.

The spare fell off and bounced high into the air, becoming invisible in the darkness of the Martian night. When it finally came down, it hit one of the rearward trikes, causing it to swerve and then barrel-roll. The lead trikes, however, were not slowed down by this in the slightest.

Bobby scolded himself. He should have gently *pushed* the spare off gently so as to take out the lead trikes instead of kicking it.

"Did it work?" shouted Carly.

"One more down," said Bobby. "But we didn't gain any time."

"Shit!"

It was time for a desperation play. The trikes were awfully close, now. They would overtake them soon unless she did something extremely clever. It was then that she remembered that the road to Kasei Valles curved off to the right towards the end. By going off road, she could turn a curved route into a straight one, possibly save some time and force the trikes to deal with the off-road rocks.

"Hang on!" she called, and swerved the rover off to the right.

"Whoa! What are you doing?" shouted Jack.

Carly didn't bother to answer. The ride immediately became bumpier, and she had to concentrate hard to avoid the largest rocks, but she was right about the trikes not being able to cope with the off-road terrain. Two trikes peeled off and followed them off of the road. But before long, one of them hit a rock that they couldn't see in time because it had passed *under* the rover, causing that trike to careen high into the air before coming down with a spectacular crash. The remaining trike slowed and retreated to the safety of the rock-free road.

"Daaang!" said Jack. "*That* sure got him!"

"Now we're down to *three!*" said Bobby.

But Carly could quickly see the new problem. Three trikes were still more than enough to stop them, especially when they were armed, and the ones which had stayed on the road were able to surge ahead. Carly's off-road shortcut may have saved them a little time, but not much, and the trikes were still faster. They would arrive at Kasei Valles first – *and* be waiting for them. They would have to run straight at them and hope the Americans could rescue them in time.

*If* they had any air left.

"Turn those lights back forward again," she said to Bobby. "I need to see where I'm going."

Bobby did so, swiveling the lights upward on the bar to face forward again. Jack helped with the other one without Bobby having to say anything.

Carly switched on the rover's radio relay. "C.Q.D! C.Q.D! Kasei Valles Base, come in!"

Only static came in response.

"They're probably still jamming us," said Bobby.

"Maybe," Carly agreed. "But I'm going to keep trying anyway."

They drove along for a few more minutes, the trikes steadily growing farther away as Carly drove towards her best guess at where the American Base was. Then they saw that the trikes were starting to get steadily *closer*. The curve of the road was beginning to bring them back *towards* the rover again, and they were definitely ahead of them now.

"C.Q.D! C.Q.D! This is rover J-10 of the Bequerel Cooperative! Kasei Valles Base, *please* respond!"

Still nothing. Instead, a computerized voice came from her vac suit helmet.

"*Warning, O2 levels are low. Please proceed to the nearest airlock immediately.*"

*Shit!* She wondered how the boys were doing. It didn't take long for her to find out.

"Hey!" shouted Bobby. "I just got an oxygen warning from my suit!"

"I know!" said Carly.

"What?! You *know?!*" Bobby shouted. "How is that possible? We should have several more minutes!"

"It's just an estimate," she reminded him. "We've been breathing harder this whole time."

"Oh, crap! Oh, crap!" wailed Jack. "We're gonna die!"

"*Nobody's* going to die!" shouted Carly. "Just *calm down!* Take a mindfulness moment. Try to relax your bodies. Slow your breathing. Meditate. Conserve what little oxygen you have left."

Incredibly, both boys did as they were told, trying to meditate just like their instructor, Mrs. Pautz, had taught them. It was difficult for them with the bumpiness of the rover, but they managed to relax, somewhat.

Carly didn't have that luxury. She had to stay alert and focused while driving, or else they would strike a large rock and it would all be over. She was fairly certain that the boys would have enough air if they conserved it carefully with their breathing. She only hoped *she* had enough air to make it.

The rover soon encountered the reason why the road swerved off to the right: a rocky ridge that ran northwest to southeast. Not impossible to climb over, but tricky. Carly drove the rover up, up, up… then *over!* The rover accelerated quickly down a steep slope, causing Carly to be deathly afraid. But after a minute or two, the way flattened out, and she took comfort in knowing that they had gone just a little bit faster than the trikes for a little while. Not fast enough to overtake them again, but fast enough to make it a race once more.

And off ahead, she could finally see the lights to Kasei Valles Base. There was no perimeter fence, despite it being a military base. On Mars, distance and the harsh environment were the barriers.

Off to her left, she could see the lights of the trikes approaching as well.

"*Warning, O2 levels are low. Please proceed to the nearest airlo...*"

Carly hit the button to acknowledge her suit's warning and shut it up. Her predicament was difficult enough without her getting interrupted every minute by her own vac suit's damned computer.

"C.Q.D! C.Q.D! This is Bequerel Rover J-10. If you can read us, we are *en route* to you and will arrive in approximately two minutes! We are being pursued by hostile forces, and oxygen levels are low! Kasei Valles Base, if you can read us, *please help us!*"

Carly heard nothing in reply. But she kept signaling.

"C.Q.D! Kasei Valles Base! Please assist!"

Off ahead, she could see the trikes reach the base ahead of her. They lined up between the rover and the Base.

For the first time, Carly slowed down.

"What are we gonna do?" asked Jack. "They're blocking us!"

A bullet pinged off the front of the rover, as if to remind them how dire their situation was.

"*Warning, oxygen levels are now critical,*" said Carly's suit.

*Great. Just great.*

"Keep that seat over your heads, boys," Carly said. "It will protect you."

"What's going to protect *you?*" asked Bobby.

Another bullet pinged off the rover's front hood.

"I think only *one* of those three riders has a gun," she said, ignoring Bobby's question. "I'm going to ram him."

"You're going to *what?!*" Bobby yelled

"*Warning, oxygen levels are now critical.*"

"After I've run him over, I'll try to get near the first airlock I see. Jump off and get to it before they do. Use the passenger seat shield if you have to."

"But..." Bobby started, but Carly's quick action interrupted him.

"*Hang on!*" she called. And hit the accelerator.

"*Warning, oxygen depleted.*"

*Shit! Shit! Shit!*

The rover sped towards the three trikes. They were too far apart for Carly to ram more than one of them. She saw the gun flashes coming from the rider in the center, and so she aimed directly for it.

A bullet pinged off the front bumper. Carly tried keeping her head down to minimize the risk of her being hit, but she didn't dare lower her head all the way down for fear of taking her eyes off her target.

"*Warning, oxygen depleted.*"

Another bullet hit, this time ricocheting off the hood and off the edge of her helmet. It was getting hard to breathe. She could feel it. But she was almost on top of them...

"*Warning, oxygen depleted.*"

In the split second before she hit the center rider, she could have sworn she saw him throw his gun over to one of the other trikes before jumping out of the way.

*No!*

The rover struck the empty trike, and in the ensuing crash, it careened up and to the right. The rover landed on its side, and then rolled upside-down.

Carly was banged up, but she began fumbling for her seat-belt, remembering simultaneously that the boys had no seat belts. They didn't even have *seats!* Were they okay? But she couldn't breathe, she couldn't think, and she couldn't get her damned seat belt off!

Off to her side, she saw a shadow approaching. One of the trike-riders, no doubt.

"*Warning, oxygen depleted.*"

*Yeah, no fucking shit, damned idiot machine! You unbelievably stupid compu....*

For Carly, things went black.

Suddenly, she found she could inhale again, and gasped.

"That's it, kid! Breathe!"

She didn't know whose voice it was, but she had air again. Maybe one of the trike riders was saving her. But no, they were *shooting* at her before. It must be…

Then she saw a man in a vac suit looming above her. On his shoulder was a clearly visible emblem - the unmistakable flag of the Stars and Stripes. From the center of the man's vac suit, a line extended, feeding oxygen into Carly's helmet. Whoever it was must have also cut her out of her seat belt.

"*Missiles!*" she choked out. "*Missiles!* They're headed to Musk City!"

"We know," said the man. "Your brother told us a few seconds ago."

*He did?* "Are he and Jack…?"

"Yeah, they're okay. They jumped off right before you rolled over. Can you stand?"

"I'll try," she said, and found that, with the man's help, she could indeed stand. But her torso felt badly bruised. She quickly looked at the clock on her wrist-pad, and let out a small cry.

"What is it?" asked the man.

"We're too late!" she said. "We had to get here over two minutes *earlier* in order to warn you about Musk City! But the missiles must have *hit* by now! Oh my God! All those people!"

"Don't worry about that, now," said the man. "You did all you could. For now, you're safe." He paused, then added, "I'm Commander Gene Lister, by the way. Third in command around here."

"Carly Mancuso," she weakly said, her voice trembling, then remembered her manners and shook his hand. "Thanks for saving my life."

"Don't mention it," he replied. "Let's get you inside."

"Where are the Sikhs?" she asked as they started walking to the nearest airlock.

"You mean those guys who were chasing you?" said Commander Lister. "Most of them weren't Sikhs. But the three that were in front of the base surrendered to us right away after you hit that trike. We were waiting for them."

"You were?" she asked. "You mean, you eventually got our transmissions?"

"We got *all* your transmissions. We just couldn't *reply*." He smiled when she gave him a quizzical look. "They can jam *your* communications equipment, but *nothing* jams ours.".

"Hey, Carly!" said Bobby, bounding up to them. "Did you see? We won! We *beat* 'em!"

"We didn't," Carly replied. "We were two minutes too late."

"Well, don't be too sure," said the Commander. "I have a hunch about it. You'll see what I mean when you get inside."

Jack was already inside the airlock when they arrived. "Mr. Commander, Sir?" he timidly asked, "Are you going to be able to rescue our families?"

"We've already sent a team," he answered. "Don't worry. We'll have you home soon."

Two more officers joined them in that particular airlock, and the outer door closed. When the inner door's light turned green and opened up, the kids all saw the inner workings of Kasei Valles Base, KV-2141 officially nicknamed "KaVes," as the American military always reduced the names of their outposts to a simple designation. Everyone removed their helmets, and Carly, Bobby and Jack were never so relieved to be breathing recycled air once more.

"Ah, Commander," said a tall officer who was clearly the man in charge. "These three kids are all well, I assume?"

"A bit tousled, sir, but they'll be all right," said Lister. "Kids, this is my commanding officer, Colonel Maynard."

"Greetings," the Colonel responded. "I want to thank you all for some pretty quick thinking. You took six out of nine hostiles out all on your own!

That's impressive! If any of you wish to join the United States military someday, I'll be proud to sponsor any of you."

Carly spoke for them all. "That's much appreciated, sir. But I'm still very worried about Musk City. Is it *really* destroyed?"

The big officer beamed a broad smile at her. "Well, young lady, that's a question which I expect you might enjoy the answer to. Corporal? Let's hear that reply we received from Musk City just now."

From a console far behind the Colonel, a young soldier said, "Replaying now, sir."

They all could hear the sound of a recorded voice, *"Thank you for checking in KV-2141. We're happy to say that we're all fine, here. Thanks so much for the early warning."*

Carly gave Commander Lister a puzzled look. "Early warning? *What* early warning? We got here too late."

"Well, that's the really interesting part," Lister replied. "I assume you've heard about our new matter-energy converter, the 'Scotty?'"

"Of course," Carly replied. "That's why we came here. We knew it could warn Musk City instantly."

"Well, it does a bit more than send instantaneous communications. It can also send communications *back* in time. Space and time are the same continuum, you know."

"Careful, Commander," warned the Colonel. "Remember, only *some* of this has been declassified."

"Yes, sir," Lister responded.

"Cool!" said Jack. "You mean the Scotty is a *time machine* too?"

"Perhaps it will be someday," Lister answered. "We've experimented with it a little, and we're getting better at it, but so far, we've only had success at short range."

"Speaking of which," said the Colonel, "XO? Have the Scotty team transmit a warning message to Musk City twelve minutes ago. On second thought, make that *fifteen* minutes."

"Yes, sir!" came the reply from the XO, a dark-haired white woman almost as tall as the Colonel.

"You mean," said Carly, "You can send a message back in time to change history so that the missiles never hit?"

"Not so much *change* history," the Commander explained. "More like *fulfill* it. You see, when you have the ability to send things back in time, it begins to do some funny things. Like this event just now. We heard the Scotty communication from Musk City that thanked us for the early warning we hadn't sent. Therefore, we knew we must be about to send one, but send it back in time."

Bobby scratched his head. "That's really strange."

"Tell me about it," said Lister. "The missiles were actually shot down *before* you arrived with your warning about them."

Carly looked even more puzzled. "So, if we arrived *really* late, would the missiles have actually hit?"

Lister shook his head. "Girl, I just don't know. At this point, it's a question better left to philosophers."

"I kind of feel bad for the people who wiped out chasing us," said Jack. "Sure, they were trying to kill us, but we weren't out to hurt anybody."

"You didn't kill anyone," said the Commander. "The trike riders who wiped out were marooned, but still alive. We're picking them up right now."

"How do you know?" Jack asked.

"Communications," said Lister. "We can hear them all, remember?"

"Is that an extension of the Scotty device?" asked Carly. "You can use it to get around any jamming?"

In response, the Commander merely winked.

"Do you know why they attacked us?" asked Bobby. "That's the one thing about all this we couldn't figure out."

The Commander nodded. "That happened because of some tricky politics on Earth. Have any of you heard about the Iosef Irfan case?"

All three kids shook their heads. Lister continued:

"It's the case in the U.N.'s New International Court of Justice that outlawed proselytizing children under the age of thirteen."

"Oh, yeah, I remember now," said Carly. "Some kid genius sued his parents for the right to not be forced into Islam and won. Right?"

"That's the one. And now all of Earth's religions are up in arms over it," said the Commander.

"So what?" said Bobby. "Let them indoctrinate their kids when they turn thirteen. If their religion has any truth to it, it should be no big deal."

"Oh, Bobby," Carly chided. "You don't know anything about religion, do you?"

The big Commander smiled at this. "She's right, you know. That's how religion typically spreads. It almost never convinces an adult mind to join. Not that it's impossible, it's just unlikely. Religion relies on indoctrinating the very young who have no choice in the matter. A child is most easily forced into a religion between the ages of three and eleven. Wait until after then, and the child almost never becomes religious." He tousled Bobby's hair, then added, "That's why they're so pissed off about it. They know if they can't force their kids into their religions at an early enough age, their religions will die."

"Ooohhh," said Carly as realization dawned. "So *that's* why they're leaving Earth. They can't force their kids into their religion on Earth anymore, so they're going to *other* planets to do it! They're leaving Earth's jurisdiction."

It made perfect sense to her. The *one thing* that could drive the otherwise peaceful Sikhs to violence was the potential destruction of their religion. Maybe even their culture with it.

"Exactly," said Lister. "In a couple of decades, most of Earth's religions will have abandoned Earth in favor of the outer planets."

"Why wouldn't they just break the law?" asked Jack.

"Undoubtedly, some will," answered the Commander. "But people who live in big cities or major democracies wouldn't be able to get away with it for long. No, there's a mass exodus coming. And it just tried to take over Mars. It failed, thanks to you three. But they'll probably try again."

"And keep trying after that too, I suppose," said Carly.

"Undoubtedly," Lister agreed.

"I remember Carly mentioning that there were more colony ships on their way here from Earth," said Bobby. "Ones that contained more religious people. They were probably counting on this attack being successful. What's going to happen to them now?"

"They might be asked to return to Earth," Lister replied. "At the very least, they'll be held up in orbit for a good, long while."

Carly had an unpleasant thought. "I'm not going to like having to explain to my dad about crashing the rover."

"Don't worry about it, kid," said the Colonel. "You saved Mars! I'd say that was worth a smashed rover or two."

"I hope you'll explain that to my dad," she told him.

"Don't worry, I will."

## Chapter 4: The Twelve Monkeys Effect

If you could go back in time and change history, would you?

Pavel Entwistle could. So, Pavel Entwistle did.

Or, rather, he tried, and failed, because he found something so completely unexpected it was like dropping an anvil and seeing it fall up.

I know. Because I was there. My therapist says writing all this down will help. I'm not so sure, but I guess it can't hurt.

When the Scotty was first invented, it was conceived merely as a transportation device, hence the "Star Trek" inspired name. But when they played around with the technology, they discovered that it could be many other things too. It could be a spy device, a communicator, a replicator – and yes, even a time machine. Because space and time are the same continuum, materializing things instantly across vast distances of space also means materializing them across vast distances of *time* as well. Scientists experimented with the device and began materializing things into the past and the future with increasing degrees of success. Naturally, it wasn't long before a Temporal Bureau was created and charged with policing the timeline. Espionage units desperately tried to prevent the technology from falling into the wrong hands. Forensics teams began working with the Bureau to solve cold-case crimes. Historians cued up to learn crucial details about the past. And, of course, "time cops" were trained, deputized, and sent out into the field.

Entwistle was just such a time cop – charged with preventing others from doing exactly what he later attempted himself. After he went crazy.

In fact, all time travelers go crazy. It's a side effect of time-travel.

It's why I went crazy, too.

Unfortunately, by the time Entwistle went rogue, so many other time cops had gone nuts that there weren't any left to go after him. Entwistle had been the last one. Or at least, the last one left who wasn't hospitalized. The Temporal Bureau needed to find a quick, discreet replacement before other, higher bureaucrats decided to shut them down – someone young and naïve enough to take on the job.

That's right, me.

For those readers who might happen to *not* be my therapist, my name's Angie Elsinore. I was a historian, not a cop. I say "was" because I'm out of the whole business now. I knew nothing about policing time, the real nature of what the Scotty did, or how it worked. I was just excited about being chosen for a secret government program that would allow me to meet Billy the Kid in person. Shit, I was a fool.

I got pulled into the program after being referred by my boss, Dr. Martin Scarbury, head of the History Department at Cornell, whom I also happened to have a crush on. I doubt he knew what he recommended me for. Maybe he wanted me out of his hair. Or maybe he just didn't want me to gain tenure. Whatever his motivation for getting rid of me, it worked. He referred me to someone at DARPA, who referred me to the Scotty Research leader, who referred me to the director of Joint Operations, who introduced me to Colonel Ajith Acharya, the Deputy Director of the Temporal Bureau, who lived in the house that Jack built. By that point, they'd informed me I had the opportunity to witness historical events *in person*, and I was hooked. I chose the Old West because that was always my favorite historical period.

I was allowed to bring along one other person, so I took my intern, Katie Ott. She was a drama major, constantly prattling on about being an "aspiring actress." You know the type; young, pretty, naïve, untouched by the massive Hollywood disappointments and drug pushers that inevitably slap star-struck dreamers like her in the face. She believed studying history would better prepare her for costume dramas, so the prospect of seeing what the Old West was really like excited her to no end. Poor girl. I dragged her into this. I'd rather have hired any *other* intern, but… she was the only person who answered my job posting.

Marlin Kettrell, the Director of the TB at the time, was as kind and understanding as your average wolverine. When Acharya introduced us to him, Katie and I were already in costume (we'd gotten a little too excited) and the mere sight of us sent him off on a tirade. He belittled us for how gaudy we looked, said we looked like booth girls at a steampunk convention, said we would be mistaken for harlots, etc. etc. I was mortified, but kept my cool.

"What we're wearing *is* period authentic," I insisted. "And we're *supposed* to attract people's attention so that they will be more likely to talk to us. Sure, dressed like matrons we might blend in, but as soon as we would start asking questions about people like William H. Bonnie and Wyatt Earp, people would begin to get suspicious. Strumpets, on the other hand, would be expected to chase after outlaws and lawmen. It's stealth by extravagance."

I don't think he bought it. But he calmed down, somewhat.

"What you and your assistant did, doctor, was let yourselves get carried away by our period authentic wardrobe," Kettrell replied. Then added with a sigh, "But you aren't the *first* time-travelers to do that."

I said before that I kept my cool. That's not entirely true. When he called us "time-travelers," I did a little flip for joy inside, and I'm certain it showed on my face.

"Now as it is, I'm going to let you do your historical research excursion," he continued. "However, I'm afraid it needs to be put on hold while you do something for us first. There's an emergency, and we require your assistance."

"Assistance? From *us?*" I was surprised but shook it off. "What sort of assistance?"

"One of our time agents has gone missing," said Acharya, showing a picture of the agent in question via his tablet. The picture showed a round-faced man with salt-and-pepper hair. "Pavel Entwistle. Up until this incident he was our most reliable operative. He dug the sub-dermal tracking beacon out of his arm and abandoned his Washington D.C. mission in the year 1987. What he was doing there is classified, but irrelevant. What we need you to do is simply go to 1987, find him, and bring him back."

"And that's it?" I asked.

"That's it."

It seemed to me like going through the 1980's was an awfully long detour to get to the 1880's. So, I balked. "I don't think this is really something we're up for," I eventually said. "I mean, I get it, you're in a jam, but I still think you'd be better off with somebody else. I mean, don't you have *anybody* else who can go get this guy?"

"Oddly enough, no," answered the Colonel.

"Really? Huh," I said. "Okay, so here's a really dumb question. This is supposed to be a time agency, right? You can send somebody back to get this guy at any time. So, you should technically have, like, all the time in the world to train someone new. If you don't have anybody now, why not simply wait until you do? You don't necessarily have to send *us* to go get him."

Kettrell quickly stepped back into the conversation, looking slightly nervous. "Yes, Doctor Elsinore, we could wait for a new agent to be trained. But that means the congressional subcommittee which oversees this agency might eventually learn of our mishap. It would be…" he paused, looking for the words, "*prudent* of us to resolve this situation quickly and, more to the point, discreetly."

"Ah, I see," I said. "You need us to cover your asses right away."

"In a word, yes," Acharya admitted. "But rest assured, we'll also give you adequate compensation for your trouble. You'll be given the standard time-agent pay for a single mission. I think you will find that sufficient."

"What is the standard pay?" I asked.

"Half a million," he answered. "That's for *each* of you, of course."

Okay, I definitely lied before when I said I kept my cool, because I was struck speechless.

Fortunately, Katie covered for me. "Well, I suppose," she said, trying unsuccessfully to sound nonchalant. "I mean, if it's an *emergency* and all…"

I thought about that a moment. Something nagged at me like – well, like a *nag*. The money was awfully good. *Too* good, that was the problem. It was almost as if they didn't want us to look too closely at what we were signing up for by blinding us with gold. 'Standard pay' my ass! Finally, I asked, "Why would Entwistle go rogue?"

"We're not sure," said Kettrell. "Our working hypothesis is that he's trying to commit suicide."

"Why on earth would he do that?" asked Katie.

Kettrell again looked surprised. "Can you think of a more painless way to go?" he said. "Alter your parents' history and you simply fade away into nothingness, not even realizing you ever existed."

"I think what she means is," I said, "why would he want to commit suicide in the first place?"

Acharya stepped in again. "Agent Entwistle probably suffers from something which we call omphalos psychosis. It's a side-effect that comes from using the Scotty transporter, but we do provide medications which help treat it. We believe that this agent of ours neglected his meds and succumbed to his psychosis as a result. Suicidal tendencies are a well-known symptom of such a condition."

"And if he erases himself from history, he will have altered the timeline," I completed his thought for him.

"Exactly," Kettrell agreed. "Billions of dollars and the cooperation of hundreds of governments have gone into creating this agency. If someone has successfully altered the timeline, and it turns out to be one of our own, no less, it would be a spectacular failure. No government would be certain of security. Global panic would ensue. Entire nations would succumb to chaos, including and especially *this* one. We must not allow this to happen!"

I pondered that. He had a point, but that was still one hell of a barbell to throw onto *our* tiny shoulders.

"Okay, here's another dumb question," said Katie. "If he erases himself from history, how would you even know? I mean, how could *anyone* know?"

Marlin (Oh, my god, he's a *fish!* Why didn't I notice before that his first name is a fish?) and the Colonel exchanged a pair of uncomfortable looks before Acharya finally volunteered the truth. "Technically, we probably *wouldn't* know. But…"

"We've never had an instance of temporal alteration before," Kettrell interrupted him.

"That you *know* of," added Katie.

"That we know of," he agreed. "Until this mishap, our policing of the timeline has been perfect. Perhaps it takes some time before the altered timeline catches up to us in the present. Or maybe the altered timeline exists as a brand-new parallel universe. Who knows? We honestly aren't sure." He paused. "But either way, it is an *imperative* that the nations of the world feel secure that this sort of thing cannot and will not ever happen. That's why we have to fix this."

"Discreetly?" I asked.

"Discreetly," the Colonel agreed.

I exchanged another look with Katie, then turned to face the Big Fish. "Okay, my turn for another dumb question," I said. "If this agent of yours got impala, um…"

"Omphalos psychosis," Kettrell corrected.

"Whatever. If he got this whatsis-condition from going through the Scotty transporter, what's to prevent *us* from getting it?"

"Nothing," the Fish replied. "You will undoubtedly contract the malady, just as Entwistle did. All time agents do."

My jaw not only dropped, it dropped everything *else* it had been doing and stared wide-eyed along with the rest of my face. "You might have told us this beforehand!" I protested.

"You needn't worry," the Fish continued. "We will provide you with medications, just as we did for him. You will be able to lead normal lives, so long as you take your pills regularly."

I was aghast, but slowly nodded. I'd already decided that, whatever the risks, I was going back in time no matter what. I turned to Katie, and the look on her face seemed to indicate that she was of a similar mindset.

She turned to Kettrell. "I think I understand you," she lied. "When do we leave?"

"Today," he answered. "In fact, the sooner, the better. Right now, go get changed. We'll have your equipment ready for you when you get back."

So that was it. It was the 1980's for us. Katie and I changed clothes, making ourselves a little bit less *Young Guns* and a little bit more *Desperately Seeking Susan*. Then we were given a crash-course on the three main rules the Temporal Bureau was established to enforce:

One: no one may steal knowledge about the future.

Two: no one may spy on anyone in the present.

Three: no one may alter the past.

"On pain of *death*," Acharya emphasized. "Make no mistake, if you can't retrieve Entwistle, your orders are to kill him."

I was taken aback at that. "Wait, you're asking us to *kill* a man who wants to commit *suicide?*"

"We're asking you to protect the *timeline*," Acharya insisted. "The absence of Entwistle's birth could have ripple effects which could be disastrous to future events."

"Maybe so, but we're academics, not soldiers," I said. "We're not trained to kill."

"You probably won't *have* to kill him," interjected Kettrell. "If he wants to kill himself, fine. Let him do so using conventional means. But if he wants to do so by disrupting the timeline, you are authorized to protect history by any means necessary. You'll only be fulfilling his wishes if you kill him, anyway.

I seriously began to wonder what sort of shit I'd just stepped in. Looking back, this was one of the first real indicators that something about this whole goddamned situation didn't quite smell right.

We received the appropriate tools, the first of which were tracking patches which would allow Entwistle to be recalled. All we had to do was throw one at him. If it hit anywhere on his body, his own DNA would activate the device. It would stick to him and he would be whisked home. Poof! Just like that.

We were given DNA sniffers, which could detect Entwistle's unique genetic pattern. They were disguised as some sort of period-wear called a "Swatch." (Ask your grandma. I did.) If Entwistle's DNA had passed anywhere close by within a few days, the little wristwatch would give a small 'beep.'

We were issued period-specific walking-around money, several hundred dollars. Then we were both injected with tracking beacons of our own so they could keep tabs on us. "Trust me," said Kettrell, "it won't hurt much."

He lied. The beacon hurt like a son-of-a-bitch for at least two minutes. That asshole.

"The trackers double as communication devices," the Fish said. "Squeeze it and talk into your wrist. It's calibrated so that we'll be able to hear you, now, in this present time."

Then we were both given nanodart guns. After being told to grasp the handle firmly, Acharya pushed a button on the side of each weapon. That keyed them to our DNA so that they couldn't be used by anyone else. Fire a dart at something, and the nanites dissolve all organic material for about 30 seconds, making sure the item, whatever it is, isn't a futuristic artifact to be left behind – even if it's a human body. Accidentally lose the gun, and it would self-disintegrate after about a day.

Finally, they gave us the pills for our omphalos psychosis. We were to take them immediately after transport, and then once daily thereafter.

Ugh, it hurts me just writing that, but I'll explain later.

Katie and I were placed on disapparation pads, and the next thing we knew, we were in Minneapolis of 1987.

Why Minneapolis? Because that's where Entwistle was born.

It had taken only a fraction of a second for everything around me to change. My first realization was that I was closed in on four sides. There were windows surrounding me. I eventually noticed an old-fashioned telephone receiver nearby, the kind that took coins. I'd never seen a phone like that before, much less a phone *booth*, so it took me a moment to realize that I was inside one. I also had no idea how to get out.

Eventually, I figured out that you have to pull on the door, not push, and slid it aside. I then came to my intern's rescue, who was pounding on the glass in a furiously futile effort to force her way out of a similar phone booth right next to mine. I pushed it inward at the center, freeing my captive employee.

"Shit!" Katie cried. "What the hell *is* that thing? Some kind of glass coffin?"

"Telephone booth, I think," I replied. "I read about one in an old Superman comic years ago, but this is the first time I've actually seen one."

"A telephone booth? But my great uncle Eric told me that they'd all disappeared after the 1970's."

"It's 1987, so there must still be some old ones left." Indeed, the two booths we'd just exited from were the first two in a row of six.

I withdrew my vial and shook two pills out. I picked one for myself, and handed the other to Katie. "Here," I said. "For the omphalos psychosis, don't forget."

"I know, but I can't take that without water. Let's find a drinking fountain."

"Let's also find out where we are," I added, and was surprised we hadn't been told beforehand where exactly in the city we were going to appear. The Fish and the Colonel must have been in a more desperate hurry than I'd thought if they'd forgotten such an important detail.

We were inside a somewhat triangular-shaped public space with a high ceiling, many windows and a great many benches. In some of them, assorted people were sitting alongside bags of irregular luggage, reading, talking or just looking bored.

"Oh! Look," cried Katie, pointing at a large sign on the upper portion of one wall. "It says, 'Greyhound Lines.' We must be at the race track."

"No, we're at the bus depot."

Katie looked confused. "What do buses have to do with greyhounds?"

"Greyhound was the name of a nationwide bus company. They don't exist anymore, but they just about dominated the market during this period."

"Huh," she replied. Then it sank in. "Oh, *greyhound!* I get it."

I looked daggers at her, but I was never very good at knife-throwing. Getting back to the problem at hand, I said, "We need to find a map. Get our bearings."

"While we're looking, maybe we should use the sniffers," suggested Katie. "Could be that our guy arrived through here."

I wasn't sure which was more surprising: that Katie came up with a pretty good idea, or that I hadn't thought of it first.

After ranging all over the area, we found our Swatches remained silent. Wherever Entwistle was, he didn't come through there recently. We did, however, find a drinking fountain which allowed us to swallow our pills. We also found a giant, illuminated display-map showing the Minneapolis downtown area, with a bright red arrow labeled 'You are here,' pointed at the center.

"This map only shows the central city. We'll need a lot more than that."

We found a newspaper vending machine, and saw that it was Thursday, September 10$^{th}$, 1987. A clock on the wall read 9:45. At a booth labeled, 'Information,' I purchased a map of the greater Twin Cities area for $1.75, and a nearby rack provided free maps of all the bus routes and schedules. After sitting down and pouring over the information, we determined where we were, where we had to go, and which bus routes we needed to take in order to get there. We already had the addresses of Entwistle's parents.

"Let's start with his mother's place," I said.

The first thing we noticed when we stepped outside an acrid and stale scent that smelled strongly of petroleum fumes from cars which looked so bulky and square-shaped that they scarcely seemed like automobiles at all. There were some pedestrians, but not that many. Apparently, most people stayed inside the network of skyways connecting the city.

"God, does it always smell this bad?"

"Most cities were much worse," I said. "I doubt any of the people around here even notice it."

"But how can they not? It's disgusting!"

I didn't say so, but I felt sure that it was only disgusting to people who were used to the clean smells and purposeful fragrances found in the cities of 2075. I was equally sure that if Katie found *this* smell disgusting, the scents of pig manure and horse piss found in the streets of every town in the Old West would surely suffocate her.

We'd exited the bus depot near the southernmost intersection, which was confusingly where 9$^{th}$ Street and 10$^{th}$ Street intersected, and realized that we'd gone out the wrong doors. So, we walked up 9$^{th}$ and then went left where 8$^{th}$ and 7$^{th}$ Streets also converged, making a befuddling situation even worse. At this point I wondered if there were *any* right angles to this city. Fortunately, the metro bus stop was nearby, and a short walk west down 7$^{th}$ allowed us to find our way.

Along that stretch, we passed by a man lying sprawled on the pavement. His facial features were Native American. He was also grotesquely fat, which made his too-small, torn, and filthy white t-shirt ride up on his torso, and he stank of sweat and piss. Whether he was drunk or dead was anybody's guess. As we overtook him, other people casually passed him by, apparently oblivious to his presence. Katie started to go over to him, but I caught her by the arm.

"But he needs help!" Katie protested.

"No! We have to interact with the locals as little as possible, remember?" I scolded. She put up a fight over it, but eventually realized I was right. If empathy and social programs were lacking in this era, we had no choice but to go along with it.

At the bus stop, we awaited route 5E which would take us south. It was a very uncomfortable wait. Alcoholics and mentally challenged people seemed to be everywhere, and a disturbingly large number of them were Indians. I didn't understand that at all. Every First National I'd ever met in 2075 was wealthy and smart. Hell, *I'm* half-Ojibwe, and I've led a pretty privileged life. What could have gone so wrong during *this* era?

We were stared at, and three times got solicited by unshaven panhandlers with horrifyingly bad breath, twice by a man so befuddled that he seemed to have forgotten he'd already asked us once before. An old woman who'd been muttering something caught my attention because I thought she'd spoken to me, but when I asked what it was, the woman merely replied, "Oh, sorry, I was just talking to my spiritual friend." I didn't inquire further. The "spirits" she was consulting with probably weren't the holy kind.

Finally, after three buses arrived showing the wrong number, the 5E arrived. We felt relieved to be able to get off the streets, but that relief was quickly dashed as we boarded and found that there was no place to sit. Every seat was filled with people possessing unhappy, jaded faces staring at us, all of which had skin hues much darker than our own. Racism was virtually dead by 2075, but in this era, we could practically feel, through their expressions, that it was very much alive.

We decided to remain standing, holding onto the overhead bars inside the bus for support. Several other people had decided to do the same, and so we ended up standing midway up the aisle. But sexism was every bit as much of a reality as racism, and we could practically feel ourselves being leered at by every pair of male eyes present. I wanted desperately to cross my arms in self-defense so as to better hide my profile, but couldn't do so while forced to cling to the bars overhead for support. All I could do was stand there helplessly while the jostling motions of the bus caused our bodies to put on an unintentional cabaret show for all those men who refused to avert their eyes.

It was some time before the discomfort of the situation was relieved. The bus proceeded southeast down 8$^{th}$ Ave. before turning south onto Centennial Place and then Chicago Avenue, going past some sort of ridiculous fundamentalist Bible college along the way. During that stretch, even more people climbed aboard the already too-full transport, forcing us to stand even further towards the back. Then, very slowly, the bus began to empty itself of people as it went further and further south. We were eventually able to find a pair of seats next to each other, and by the time they passed a large cemetery on our left, the bus had become quite empty, and we could finally breathe a sigh of relief.

Entwistle's mother lived in the same neighborhood as his father – an area south of Veteran's Memorial Park and west of the Minneapolis-St. Paul International Airport. We were able to visit both addresses relatively quickly after stepping off the bus, yet at both locations, the sniffer remained silent. Pavel had not been there, or at least had not been there yet.

Katie suggested that we knock on the front door and ask about him, but I dismissed that idea. Pavel had yet to be born, after all, so asking questions about him before his parents were even married would simply be awkward and confusing.

We boarded a second bus and visited the airport to see if Pavel had come that way. This was pre-9/11 era, so we were able to explore every single concourse without having to go through any check-points, but our sniffers remained silent. I was beginning to wonder if the damned things even worked.

"Where could he be?" asked Katie.

"Maybe he didn't come home," I speculated. "Or maybe he simply offed himself in D.C."

"Does that mean we have to go all the way over there to find out?"

That thought was almost more disturbing than the one I once had three weeks after sleeping with Gary Olaf – and realized I was *late*. "I hope not. It would really suck if we went all the way over there only to just miss him as he was coming here. It might be better to stay here and find out if there were any suicides reported in the nation's capital."

"How? The Internet is still ten years off."

"No, the Internet exists at this time, but it isn't being widely used. You're right, though. We'll have to look at a D.C. newspaper. The Washington Times, perhaps. A library would have such newspapers, but only a downtown library would be big enough to have access to something from out of state."

Katie sighed. "Downtown again?"

"Downtown again."

We boarded the bus again, went back up Chicago Ave and transferred to the 5E going northbound. I *really* didn't relish the idea of being back among rude crowds and panhandlers again, but at least this time, we boarded at a point where the bus was mostly empty.

We were looking at the map, working out where the downtown library might be located, when a tall, fat man, sporting long, blond hair and a cowboy hat, boarded the bus and passed by us on his way to finding a seat. He looked clearly drunk. But no sooner had he passed by us than my Swatch began beeping. It startled us both.

"What just happened?" Katie asked.

"That guy!" I whispered. "The one who just passed us!"

"Who? The *Cowboy?*"

We very nearly both turned to look at him, but I caught Katie's arm, and we both stopped. "No! We *can't* let him notice us," I said. "Just give a quick glance. Then tell me what you see."

Katie nodded. She casually peered over her shoulder, gave the man a quick glance, then turned back around. "He sure doesn't *look* like Pavel," she said.

"Could he be in disguise?"

"That must be one *hell* of a disguise, then!" she replied.

This time, I turned my head for a quick peek. "You're right," I said. "It's somebody else."

"Then why did the sniffer go off?"

I thought about that for a moment. "Could be that he met Pavel recently. Maybe he bumped into him, and some of his DNA got on him."

"Or not," suggested Katie. "There are some pretty good disguises, even in this era. And *that's* assuming Pavel didn't smuggle a disguise kit with him from our own time period. But maybe we could find out for sure." She held up one of the Velcro-like tracking patches Acharya had given to us.

I had misgivings about that idea. If we hit the cowboy with that patch, and he turned out to be Entwistle, he would disappear right in front of everyone on the bus. Then I took a look around. Everyone was mindlessly staring out the window or reading books or newspapers. They probably wouldn't notice anything, and even if they did, who would believe them? I therefore nodded my approval, and we watched for our opportunity. We would have to wait until the man arrived at his stop, then toss the tracking patch at him as soon as he went by.

We had nearly reached downtown Minneapolis again before the apparently inebriated buckaroo finally stood up. He pulled on the cord to make the driver pull over at the next stop, then staggered unsteadily into the center aisle. When he shuffled past our seat, the sniffer-watch beeped again, and Katie tossed a tracking patch at him, hitting him squarely in the back. The patch bounced off of him harmlessly, then landed on the floor.

We exchanged wide-eyed looks before quickly getting to our feet. We had to follow him! He wasn't Entwistle, but he was the only solid lead we had. We tailed him to the front of the bus and then exited shortly after he did.

The man staggered a little bit when he walked, but seemed to have some idea about where he was going. He walked due south back down Chicago Avenue, as though the stop he'd gotten off at had been too far from where he'd intended. We waited a moment, loitering for a while before starting after him.

We followed him south for a block and a half before we saw him turn and look over his shoulder. He saw us. I was certain of it. But did that mean anything? Did he even care? He seemed to stop staggering quite so much after that, almost as if he was aware of being watched. When he came to the next corner, he turned left and disappeared behind a building. We trotted over to the corner as quickly as we dared and then found him again after turning the corner ourselves. He was walking eastward. We followed him again, but then he looked over his shoulder once more. This time, he locked eyes on us. There was no doubt he'd spotted us this time. He quickened his pace.

We continued after him, but had a hard time keeping up. The cowboy had very long legs and so a brisk walk for him was almost the equivalent of a slow jog for us. Even with his gait unsteady from drink, he was nearly outpacing us. We had to alternate between a fast walk and a canter just to keep from losing ground. This went on for another block before the cowboy turned around and glared at us again. We nearly froze, but managed to try and look as though we'd been walking normally – a useless charade since it was quite clear we'd been keeping pace.

He began to run.

"Shit!" I breathed, and we both dashed after him, all pretense of subterfuge abandoned. We were both wearing sneakers with our 80's costumes, which aided us in running, but the cowboy was simply too tall and too fast. He quickly put almost half a block's distance between us, then disappeared to his left around the corner of the next intersection. By the time we got there, he was nowhere to be seen.

"Damn it!" wailed Katie. "We lost him!"

I looked around for a moment while I caught my breath, then brightened. "Maybe not," I replied. "Look over there."

Katie followed where I was pointing, and saw a sign which said, 'Tom's Terribly Terrific Tap.' Realization dawned and her face lightened. Our person of interest was a drunkard, but would he be so obvious as to hide inside a bar? Maybe. It was worth a look.

We saw that the sign hung over a cracked, glass door. I pulled it open, and we went inside. It was a darkened place, where the only real illumination came from behind the bar and from a lamp over the lone pool table. To our right was a long bar counter, and at its far end was a hulking figure leaning over a mug of beer. Even in the dim light, it was easy to make out the long blond hair of our quarry. The cowboy hat was lying on the counter next to him. It was definitely our guy.

Without speaking, we silently positioned ourselves slightly behind the man. Neither of us had a weapon, other than our nanodart guns, but at least we were in a public place. Even with only two or three other customers inside, it was a good bet that the cowboy wouldn't want to be seen striking women in a bar. We sidled up to the bar and confronted him from both sides at the same time.

The cowboy glanced over at me to his left as my watch beeped again. He noticed me, started at recognizing who I was, then spotted Katie to his right. His head whipped from one side to the other, looking at each of us, and his eyes widened as though he were a caged animal. But this expression quickly faded into one of sour indignation.

"Christ!" he spat. "*You* two again! Who the hell are you? Why are you following me?"

"We're looking for *this* man," I told him, holding a photograph of Pavel Entwistle out for him to see. "Know where he might be?"

"Never seen 'im."

"That's a lie," said Katie.

"Yeah? How would *you* know?"

Katie's response was an exasperated look which seemed to say, 'Really? Are we going to play this stupid game?'

Honestly, I couldn't have been prouder of my employee, because the ruse worked.

"Yeah, okay, fine, I bumped into him today. So what?"

"You did a lot more than bump into him," I said.

"Is *that* right?" the cowboy growled.

By this time, the bartender had noticed what was transpiring and came over to investigate. He was a large man with a loose, flabby body and a bald head. "Problem, Leroy?"

"Just a couple of floozies, Tom," the cowboy replied. "No big deal."

The bartender gave us a once-over. He was a redneck too, judging by his sideburns and plaid shirt. "Floozies, huh? Either of you girls got an I.D.?"

I froze. We were both in our twenties, easily legal drinking age to be sure, but our I.D.'s were from the year 2075. Any bartender would think they were fakes, and ridiculous ones at that. *Why hadn't Fish thought to give us fake I.D.'s?*

Leroy spotted our hesitation and decided to press the advantage. "Yeah, they're probably underage. Better throw 'em out."

"I've a mind to throw *you* out with 'em!" bellowed the barkeep. "Two weeks out of jail, and you show up with a huge wad of cash and these two hotties suddenly show up with you? I don't know what kind of drugs you're dealing, but I sure as shit don't want that nonsense going on inside my establishment!"

"Jeezus, man, I haven't been dealing drugs. You know that."

"That's right, he hasn't," Katie said. "But he's been involved with someone who *has*." She looked to me for support.

I took the hint. "Yes! And his parole officer wouldn't like the fact he's been hanging around with a person like that."

"Might even think it's a parole violation if he doesn't help us catch the guy," Katie added.

"Maybe even tell the judge that he hasn't been properly rehabilitated and suggest that he go back to the slammer," I added.

"Which is why he's going to tell us all about this person instead."

"And where to find him."

Leroy had resumed the frightened animal look, his head swiveling side to side to face each of us as we spoke. But with our double-teaming done, he relaxed into a fatalistic slump. After a few seconds, he heaved a sigh and stood up off of his bar stool. "Shit. Tom, can you give me a minute while I go outside and deal with these bitches?"

The bartender grimaced at him. "Better make it a *long* minute," he replied.

That remark made the cowboy pause, after which he seized his beer mug and promptly drained its remaining contents in a single gulp. Apparently, he believed that once out the door, Tom would be disinclined to let him back in. He picked up his hat, placed it on his head and walked unsteadily towards the door as we followed him out.

"Okay," he said as soon as we were all outside. "Are you chicks cops or something?"

"Or something," I said. "We're just trying to find this guy, that's all."

"Really. Why the hell is he so important to you?"

I paused. I hadn't considered coming up with a cover story about why we were trying to find Entwistle. Fortunately, Katie came to my rescue. "He knocked up a friend of ours," she said. Then, after a pause, added, "Look, he's not in trouble or anything. We just want to find him. He doesn't even know he's the father of the baby."

Leroy took that in for a moment, then shrugged, apparently satisfied. "Okay, fine, let's get this over with. What do you want to know?"

"Well, where he is, for starters," I said.

"No idea. He didn't tell me where he was going."

"When did you see him last?"

"Not sure. 'Bout an hour ago. Or two. Maybe."

That was good news. It meant the trail was fresh. "What was your business with him?" asked Katie.

He shuffled his feet, as if he didn't like the answer he was about to give. "There's this church pantry that gives out free food to homeless people over near the river. I was standing in line over there this morning. Breakfast, you know? And this guy just walks right up to me. Maybe because I was the tough-looking one or something, I dunno."

"What did he want?" Katie prodded.

"Well, he asks me if I'd like to make a lot of money, right? And I say, 'sure!' So he pulls me aside and asks me to help him buy a gun."

I felt my eyebrows shoot straight up at this. "A gun?" I asked.

"Yeah. Something strings-free, no background checks or nothin,'" he added.

That seemed to make no sense at first. Entwistle would already have a nanodart gun as part of his time-agent arsenal. Or would he? Now that I thought about it, the nanodart gun was probably being tracked by the Temporal Bureau and he had to get rid of it. He therefore felt the need for a conventional firearm.

"And you got this gun for him?" I asked.

"Oh, hell, no," he insisted. "I don't let myself get mixed up in shit like that. All I did was show him where to go. After that, he was on his own."

"Where *did* you tell him to go?" asked Katie.

"This place called Lakeland Guns & Ammo. It's just north of Chicago and Lake, not too far from here. That place will sell you a decent handgun under the table, if you pay enough." He smiled broadly. "And if you know the right people."

"People like you?" I asked.

"Sure. The owner's my cousin." The smile faded from his face as a thought occurred to him. "Uh, you were just kidding about telling this stuff to my parole officer, right?"

"You said the place was back down Chicago Avenue?" I pressed, ignoring his question.

"Yeah," Leroy answered. "The guy even made me go there with him in his car. But you should be able to find it without too much trouble. Just go back to Chicago, turn left and go south a few blocks. You can't miss it."

I turned to Katie and saw she had the same wide-eyed expression. He had his own car! No wonder the sniffer didn't detect anything at the major transit centers. That meant he had an impossible advantage over two women traveling by foot and mass transit. We could never hope to catch up with him. Unless…

"We have to find out where he's going," Katie told him. "Can you come with us to the gun shop and help speak to the owner for us? We'll pay you."

This seemed to take the cowboy aback, and he gave her a quizzical look. "How much?" he finally asked.

In response, Katie pulled out the period money the Temporal Bureau had given her from her denim jeans. She looked at it momentarily, then handed the folded bills over to him.

I was aghast. "Did you just give him *everything* we have?"

"Yeah," she replied. "Why? Think it's enough?"

It apparently was, because the cowboy's eyes grew wide and he pocketed the bills with gleeful delight. "Okay, sure I'll help! Follow me, ladies! I'll take you right over there. You know, you can never have a better person to help you track somebody down than me. I was an Army Ranger. I can find *anybody*. And I've got *contacts*, man! My other cousin is even a cop. Don't you worry, I'll sniff out that deadbeat dad for you in no time."

On and on he went, bragging about how easily we'd find him, and how good it was that he was our guide. I, on the other hand, was not at all happy about the situation. "We might have *needed* that money!" I scolded in a harsh whisper. "Now we're broke!"

"Not really," Katie answered. "If we need more, we'll just contact Acharya and have him Scotty some more to us."

That surprised me. I hadn't considered that.

It only took fifteen minutes for us to walk to Lakeland Guns & Ammo, although it seemed much longer with Leroy yammering on about how fantastic he was at tracking people down. The store itself wasn't all that impressive. It was little more than a painted-over concrete wall with a single, recessed glass door in the middle which had black-painted, rusty iron bars protecting it. Oddly, it had a crack in the lower part of the glass similar to that of Tom's Terribly Terrific Tap. The only difference was that this glass had wire mesh to reinforce it.

"Hello, ladies!" said the impressively large white man behind the counter. "How can I help you?" He seemed quite presentable, despite wearing a Megadeth t-shirt. But when he caught sight of Leroy, his smile vanished.

"We're looking for *this* man," I said, holding out Entwistle's photo. "Have you seen him?"

He didn't answer. Instead, he gave Leroy an expression which seemed to say, 'Dude, what the fuck?'

"It's okay, Jim. They're not cops."

He eyed us both over skeptically, then shrugged. "Yeah, I suppose not. Two girls like you? You certainly don't look like cops, and I don't buy into that Cagney and Lacey shit."

I had no idea who Cagney and Lacey were, but I surmised that they were female detectives from some period-relevant television show.

"But you realize," he continued, "I can't discuss any of my customers. Confidentiality, you see? I'm sure you understand."

At this, Katie again launched into her sob story about her poor friend who'd gotten pregnant, and our simple mission to find Pavel and tell him that he was a newly minted father. For such a ridiculous story, she did a pretty good job of selling it, and a few timely tears went a long way in making it seem realistic. In retrospect, she might have sometimes sucked as an intern, but she *was* a pretty damned good actress.

The redneck behind the counter apparently bought it. "Look, lady, he didn't say where he was headed. All he did was ask if I had a White Pages. I told him there was one in the telephone booth outside. Then I saw him go out there and look through it. He tore a page out and took off. That's all I know."

"He tore out a page?" I asked.

"Yeah. Kind of a rude fucker. Then again, most of my customers are."

"What are white pages?" asked Katie.

Jim laughed heartily. "Girl, what rock did *you* just crawl out from under?"

"Farm girl," I quickly covered for her. "Used to be Amish," and then shot her a glare which could have killed Medusa. I took her by the shoulders and practically jerked her over towards the door. Then, putting on the friendliest face I could manage given my current state of mind, I called back to Jim, saying, "Thanks for all your help, sir! We really appreciate it!"

I only caught a glimpse of the pair of bemused faces watching us walk out the door.

Once outside, I scolded my partner. "Way to go, genius! You nearly blew our cover in there!"

"Hey! I got us some information, didn't I?"

"Yeah, you got us a clue, I'll give you that," I said, heading over to the telephone booth Jim had earlier pointed out. "Now we have to see if that clue is worth anything." I got into the phone booth and pulled Katie inside along with me. "Shut the door," I ordered.

"Aww," Katie groaned. "I really *hate* these things." But she pulled the door shut anyway. Apparently, 1987 had a *lot* of old phone booths hanging around, at least in Minneapolis. It was cramped with both of us inside, and the afternoon sun made it hotter than a greenhouse.

I pulled up a large book in a metal casing from beneath the telephone. It had been hanging there next to a similarly bound volume which was colored yellow. "We have to find out which page Pavel tore out. That should help us determine where he's going."

Katie watched what I was doing, and it suddenly dawned on her what she was seeing. "Oh! It's a book full of phone numbers and addresses! And it's *white*. White *pages*. I see!"

I was too focused to be annoyed. "Yes. White for residences, yellow for businesses."

"That must be why they're called White Listings on the Netstream. I always wondered about that."

I kept flipping through pages until I found what I was looking for – the small remnant of a page which had been ripped away. "There!" I said. "That must be the page he tore out."

"But if he tore it out, how can we find out where he went?"

I was about to answer her when we were interrupted by a knocking sound. We turned around and saw that it was Leroy. He was standing outside the closed phone booth door, looking in at us. Apparently, he wasn't about to let an opportunity for more beer money simply walk away.

"Hey!" he shouted. "Do you ladies still need help? I know the make and model on the guy's car, you know. I might even remember the license plate…"

I held up my index finger, silencing him. Then turned my back to him and picked up the telephone receiver as if I were about to make a call.

"You're going to call somebody?" Katie asked.

"Yes. But not with this thing." I took the receiver off its cradle, pretending to use the telephone while lifting my left wrist up to my mouth. An odd, single-note tone was coming from the telephone receiver, which I found distracting. I hadn't expected that. "Acharya? Colonel, are you there?"

"*Yes, I can hear you*," came the answering voice from my wrist. It had an odd, muffled tonal quality which made it seem quite macabre.

"I need a cross-reference," I said. "Entwistle was here, and he tore a page out of a telephone book. It was page 1177 to 1178, from the Twin Cities municipal White Pages directory for…" I flipped the book to its front cover "…1983 to 1984."

At least, I said something *like* that. To be honest, I don't remember such details so well. I'm guesstimating for the purpose of telling this story.

"We need to know if any of the names and addresses on that page are a hit for people in Pavel's background. That way we can figure out where he's going."

"Angie! That's brilliant!" Katie exclaimed.

"*Give us a second to see what the database comes up with,*" Acharya replied.

"Hey!" said Leroy, knocking on the door again. "You're not fooling me! I see you talking on the phone, but you didn't dial any numbers!"

*Shit!* But I had no time to deal with that now. I braced my foot against the middle joint in the door so the cowboy couldn't try to push his way in, and waited for the Colonel to answer.

"*Okay, here it is. Oh, no. This is bad. This is very, very bad.*"

"What? What's bad?" asked Katie.

"*Your phone book reference come up with one hit. But it's for the family surname of Moriston.*"

"Why is that bad?" I asked.

"*Entwistle was married once. But his wife and five-year-old daughter died in the year 2050. They were murdered by a serial killer named Andrew Moriston, who was then aged 70. He was alleged to have committed at least thirty other murders over a span of four decades. He was caught and sentenced, but died in prison soon afterward. Now listen: In the year 1987, Andrew is only five years old!*"

I exchanged a look of horror with Katie as the realization slowly dawned on us. As if we needed any help in putting the pieces together Acharya said, "*He hasn't gone rogue to commit suicide. He's going to commit a murder!*"

Leroy pounded on the glass. "Hey!" he shouted.

I again lifted a finger to silence him, but it wasn't my index finger.

"We need to get to the Moriston address as quickly as possible," I said into my wrist, not bothering with the pretext of the telephone this time. "He has at least a two-hour head start on us, and he's driving a car."

"*The address is in the nearby suburb of Roseville. We can Scotty you directly there from your current location, and put you back by 90 minutes to compensate for the head start. You should be able to intercept him when you get there. Are you alone?*"

Katie and I looked outside the glass at the inebriated cowpoke whose expression was increasingly one of exasperated, red-eyed desperation. Simultaneously, we both lied, "Yes!"

*"Then stand by. We're transporting you in three... two... one..."*

That cowboy must have needed another drink after he saw us disappear right in front of him.

We materialized inside a hallway with four doors situated nearby. Two of them were open, revealing a bedroom and bathroom. The other two were closed. The hallway ended abruptly behind us, and ahead opened up into two larger rooms separated by a central wall. From the room to the right, we heard the muffled sounds of someone sobbing.

I pulled out my nanodart gun while Katie readied a tracking patch. We looked at each other, nodded, then crept towards the room where the sounds were coming from. Slowly, we emerged from the hallway and into the room. It was a modestly large living room with two davenports and an unlit fireplace in the far corner. Two people were lay on the floor in front of the davenports, tied up with rope and gagged with duct tape. One was a dark haired, and the other a curly-haired boy. Mother and son, presumably. Both had eyes wet with tears and wide with fear. Where was the father? At work, most likely. When the mother saw us, she tried desperately to cry out, but it was already too late.

"Stop right there!" came a voice from the other room, and Entwistle emerged from his hiding place, the Colt .45 in his hand, his sweating face showing maniacal malevolence. *Damn.* For all our caution, we hadn't even considered checking the other room first.

"So, *you're* the ones the T.B. sent to come get me." He looked us over. "They must really be getting desperate. Drop the nanogun, then drop your purses. And *you,*" he pointed the gun directly at Katie, "don't even *think* of throwing that tracking patch. Toss it behind you. Right now!"

Katie gave the balled-up patch a nervous toss over her right shoulder. Then we both let our purses fall from our shoulders. I slowly placed the nanodart gun on the floor, then backed away from it.

"Good. Now, into that corner by the front door," he ordered. "And *stay* there. You're about to witness justice."

"Justice?" I asked. "What justice? He's just a kid."

"A kid who will grow up! And then he'll fucking kill thirty people!" Pavel roared. From the floor, Andrew's mother spilled out a fresh batch of muffled sobs.

"I know," Katie said, her voice soothing. "I know about your wife. I know about your daughter."

"You don't know *shit!*" he spat back, waving his gun threateningly for emphasis. "Don't you even *think* to presume to know what I went through! I didn't even get the satisfaction of seeing the fucker executed! He had to go and die in jail of natural, goddamned causes." For just a moment, he lowered his gun, and raised his eyes up to the ceiling, as if addressing God, the universe, or whatever powers might be. "Why did he have to be so *old*?"

Angie, sensing what she hoped was a soft moment, said, "But the potential consequences of changing…"

"Oh, *fuck* the consequences!" he yelled, raising his gun again. "Tell me, lady, if you had the opportunity to go back and kill Hitler, or Ted Bundy, or Jim Jones, wouldn't you have a moral obligation to do so? Wouldn't you be just as evil as those people if you didn't take that opportunity? Wouldn't their blood be on your hands?"

"And what would the unintended consequences be of doing that?" I countered. "Who's to say that the absence of Hitler or Ted Bundy wouldn't accidentally unleash an even greater evil upon the world later? And what other sort of unforeseen consequences might there be if you kill this boy, here?"

"I don't care." The calm demeanor with which he said it was more powerful than all the shouted words he'd uttered before. In an instant, he'd gone from moral altruism to flippant apathy. That dime he turned on must have spun like a top.

"Listen," I said, "Your reasoning might be tainted by omphalos psychosis. We brought some medication with us. If you still feel the same after taking…"

"They're *sugar* pills, woman!" he shouted, training the gun on her. "Crunch down on one with your teeth if you don't believe me!"

My eyes grew wide, and Pavel grinned with satisfaction.

"Oh, yes!" he went on. "They *lied* to you. They lied to me, too. Hell, they lie to *everybody*, those fucking bastards at the Temporal Bureau! Do you even *know* what omphalos psychosis is? *Do* you?" He paused, lowering his gun, then answered his own question. "You go through the Scotty transporter without really going through it at all. The old you actually dies, and a copy of you gets made with all your memories implanted. Realizing that the 'real' you is dead is enough to fuck anybody's mind up. At first, they thought that's all omphalos psychosis was – just something in your head. So they figured that if they simply lied to the people who used the Scotty, that would fix it. Give the subject a placebo and everything would be just fine. Real disease, fake cure. But it's even worse than that. There's something called *Scotty dementia*. Whenever you make a copy, there are always little imperfections that get passed on. No big deal with the meat portion of your body, that simply heals itself. But the damage done to the *brain*, oh, well, now that's permanent! Put a person through the Scotty enough times, and shit starts to happen. Personalities change, inhibitions get lowered, manic and reckless behavior becomes manifest. The Scotty permanently *fucks* you up in the head. It always has." His stare bore into me. "But they didn't bother to tell that to your pretty, little faces, did they?"

The look of horror on my face was all the answer he needed.

"Well," he concluded. "No more lies. No more bullshit." He cocked the gun and took aim at the boy.

The child recoiled and tried to scream, wiggling away like a helpless worm, but only succeeded in backing himself into a corner. His mother screamed into her gag too, desperately working against her bonds to get to her boy before it was too late.

"If I can't have my sanity," Entwistle said, "at least I can have my wife and daughter back."

"No, *don't!*" I cried as the hammer fell.

'Click!'

There was no bang. The gun had misfired.

"What the hell?!" He pointed and pulled the trigger again.

'Click!'

"Aw, come *on!*"

'Click!' 'Click!' 'Click!'

"What the fuck is the matter with this thing?" He pointed the gun at the fireplace and pulled the trigger.

'BANG!' The bullet shattered the glass of the fireplace doors. It seemed as though everyone's nerves had shattered with them.

"No!" Entwistle whispered.

He pointed the gun back at Andrew, and pulled the trigger again. Again, it clicked.

"*Noooo!*" he roared and clicked the useless trigger at the boy again and again. In frustration, he aimed at a nearby lamp and fired. The loud shot exploded it into shards, and he went into a fiery rage.

"FUCK!" He pointed again at the boy and went into a frenzy of pulling the trigger over and over again as nothing but useless clicks resulted from the gun. He roared out an anguished howl of rage as he vented his frustration by firing successfully at the ceiling, then the floor, then the fireplace again, a loud bang erupting each and every time the gun was aimed anyplace *except* the boy. Again, he erupted into a long series of unsuccessful clicks aimed at Andrew, and then finally fired one more bullet which destroyed another lamp. Letting out a scream of rage and frustration, he collapsed onto the floor, sobbing and howling in fury and tears.

I watched the weeping man for a long time, unsure of what to do. Finally, Katie quietly whispered, "What – just – happened?"

"It's *history*," I answered. "History must be meant to happen a certain way. It's *impossible* to change it. So, if you try…" I paused to find the words, "…it fights back, somehow."

From the floor, Pavel responded with a wail. He'd heard me, and he knew it was true. Perhaps he even suspected this sort of thing from his experience as a time agent. And it made sense. All the paradoxes that would happen if one went back in time and killed one's own parents were now solved. The Universe would simply never allow that sort of thing to happen. There could be no temporal paradoxes.

Twelve Monkeys. That's what it was. The Twelve Monkeys effect. If you don't know, it's the title of an old Terry Gilliam movie about a guy who goes back in time, but in trying to stop a disaster, actually helps it happen. I mean, the reference fits as well as anything.

"So, what's the point of the Temporal Bureau, then?" Katie asked.

"There isn't one," I answered. "Except government bureaucratic tomfoolery. They got hold of this technology and put a series of overpriced protections around it before they even understood how it really worked."

I went over to where Entwistle was kneeling on the floor, almost as if he were in a praying position. I kept a respectable distance since he was still armed, but felt he was reasonably safe now that he realized his plans were predestined to fail. I crouched down in front of him, bracing my weight on one knee.

"Pavel?" I asked. But he didn't seem to know I was there. "Agent Entwistle?" I said a little louder.

This seemed to get his attention. He rose up, remaining on his knees, his face wet, his eyes reddened. Those eyes looked right at me, a picture of hopeless anguish.

"Come back with us," I said to him. "The Agency is nothing, now. It's all over. And they'll understand why you tried to do this, I'm sure of it. They have no reason to prosecute you."

He swallowed hard before answering, then croaked out, "They *never* understand." He then put the gun to his temple and pulled the trigger.

The resulting bang made me jump. The opposite wall was instantly spattered with blood and brain. Lying next to her son, the mother's eyes rolled back in her head and she passed out. The child stared wide-eyed at the bloody mess, screaming muffled screams repeatedly into his gag.

It was a long moment before anyone did anything. Katie stood frozen, unable to move. I was much the same.

The boy suddenly stopped screaming. I looked at him and saw that he was staring wide-eyed at Pavel's bloodied body. The look on his face was a mixture of horror and fascination, as though he were seeing something beautiful while falling from a great height.

The muscles in my crouching legs started to ache. Slowly, I stood up and went over to where Katie was. My intern was still staring at Entwistle's body.

"Katie?"

She started, as though she'd been suddenly roused from sleep. "Huh?"

"Get your things."

She didn't seem to understand at first, but then it clicked. "Oh. Right." She went and picked up her purse. I did the same, remembering to also collect the tracking patch Katie had thrown, as well as my nanogun. I went to an area of the room nearly between where the boy lay and where Entwistle had fallen. Looking straight at him, I said, "Andrew?"

The boy responded immediately, meeting my eyes with his. Perhaps he wondered how I knew his name.

"Close your eyes," I told him. And remarkably, he did.

I pointed the nanogun at Pavel's body and fired a single dart into it. There was a slight hissing noise as a dark patch began to slowly spread over the corpse. Then it began to crumble away from the inside out, releasing something into the air which looked like steam. In seconds, nothing remained but an odd-looking pile of dust.

"Why did you do that?" asked Katie.

"No artifacts left behind to pollute the timeline," I answered. There would still be a blood stain on the wall, but the police wouldn't be able to connect that with anyone. Then I went over to the mother and loosened the ropes which bound her wrists and feet. When she woke up, she would be able to call the police. Then I looked back over at the boy, and saw that he had opened his eyes again. He was staring *right* at me – a kind of blank stare that was utterly emotionless and probing. I knew everything he was seeing was being burned into his memory. Something in his eyes made me recoil, and I decided not to untie him. Let his mother or the police do that.

And then it dawned on me. Andrew would become a serial killer because the events of this day traumatized him. In seeking to destroy a serial killer, Pavel Entwistle had instead created one. Incredible.

"Back door," I said to my intern, and Katie did not argue. We both quietly went into the other room and exited out the back way.

Outside in the autumn air, we saw that the back yard was surrounded by trees and shrubbery. There was no chance of being seen. I squeezed the tracker and spoke into my wrist. "Colonel?" I waited for a response.

"*Yes, I'm here*," came the voice from beneath my skin.

"Subject has committed suicide by conventional means." I paused, trying to find the right words, then simply said, "Mission complete. Take us home."

Around us, 1987 faded away.

So that's it. I've written it all down. I don't feel much better, to be honest. But then, I don't think anything would really have worked.

I'm not sure how history managed to prevent Pavel's gun from firing at the boy. Perhaps some quantum mechanical principle was at work. Let the physicists figure that one out. Personally, I'm convinced that I felt a *presence* intervene. Oh, I know, I know, that's not very rational. I know it's probably just my imagination, but it almost felt like an invisible hand stopped Pavel's gun. What was it? The hand of history? Of providence? Is this, at long last, the scientific proof of God we've always coveted?

Who knows? Thanks to omphalos psychosis, I'm not exactly sane enough to ponder it. And Pavel was right, the medications were just sugar. I was lied to, and now I'm nuts. So here I sit, scribbling my memoirs from inside a loony bin, like some strange cross between H.G. Wells and J.D. Salinger.

Then again, my therapist just told me that there's a new Scotty-based treatment out there which tamps down the brain's fear response and cures omphalos psychosis. That means I might cross the street more recklessly, but I'll be able to leave here and lead an otherwise normal life. Someday.

Also, someone is bound to take an academic interest in my first-hand account. As a historian, that's all I ever really wanted – to make a meaningful contribution to the understanding of history. In a way, I've accomplished that.

That's sort of like a happy ending, right?

# Chapter 5: Space Camp Europa

**[JSC Video Record, 137569-A, April 9, 110 A.T. (the year 2079, Gregorian).]**

Oh, we're recording? Okay. Well, I guess I should start by saying that being an astronaut wasn't all it was cracked up to be. Believe me, I know. I did everything I could to keep from becoming one, and ended up in outer space anyway.

The story you are about to hear is true. The names have not been changed, innocent or not, on the general principle that if I'm willing to endure the ridicule, so should they. Now, I'm supposed to be telling you nice recruits out there about my experiences and how much fun it was to be in outer space, but – ah, fuck it. I really don't want to talk about that, because, truth be told, it wasn't all that much fun. I'm sure to get in trouble for telling my story in my own way, but I simply don't give a shit. I'm recording whatever the hell I want to. Anyway, they'll probably just cut out the parts they can use and splice together whatever they need out of it. You won't get to see the unedited version. Well, so be it. Fuck 'em.

You see, the major problem with space travel is, there's too much damned *space*. If you want to go anywhere at all, you'll likely be dead before you even begin to get there. Oh, you could burn up a ridiculous amount of fuel in order to try to get there fast enough, but you'll still likely die before you arrive, if not of old age, then at least of sheer boredom.

Well, at least these days, there's a way around that nonsense. It's a nifty device called the *Scotty*. You've undoubtedly heard of it. It transforms matter into energy and energy back into matter again, just like on Star Trek. With it, humanity is finally beginning to explore the stars in real-time, just like we always dreamed. On Earth, you get turned into energy, and then in your target destination, somewhere in outer space, Alpha Centauri, say, energy gets transformed back into you. Sounds simple in theory, but in practice, it's almost as bad as space travel the old-fashioned way. But I'll get to that later.

First, I need to tell you a little bit about Billy Euanker, pilot extraordinaire. (That's me.)

I suppose it began when I was approached by a government "recruiter" of some sort. He was a gargantuan man whose suit was such a tight fit that it looked as if someone had inflated his body without bothering to check the gauge. He introduced himself as Bobby Bighorn. "Mr. Euanker," he asked me, "how would you like to become an astronaut for fifty thousand dollars?"

"I don't have fifty thousand dollars," I told him. "But I suppose I could borrow some money from my dad."

He showed no reaction whatsoever at my lame attempt at humor. "We want to pay *you* fifty thousand, Mr. Euanker."

"Sure, go ahead."

"And send you into outer space."

"Yeah, not so sure about that last part."

"The government has particular need of your talents, Mr. Euanker. Your country needs you."

I was no fool. By 'talents' he meant the genetic quirkiness of my brain. I'm one of only two people who ever survived having a base-jack installed in his cerebral cortex, and the other guy went catatonic. That means I'm the only one who can fly remote vehicles by thought, even through electromagnetic disturbances. This comes in handy during storms or in certain dangerous situations, so this wasn't the first goon sent by a bureaucrat to come fetch me.

"Yeah, um, no thanks," I told him. "The government owes me one. In fact, it owes me several."

"Mr. Euanker, I need to inform you that if you decline to volunteer, I am empowered to take you into custody under the Selective Services Act, as detailed in Section 50, Subsection 201 of the United States Legal Code."

I stared up – *way* up – at this tower of a man, and didn't flinch. Of course, neither did he. He was certainly big enough to take me by force. Hell, he could probably just sit on me until I passed out. "In other words, if I decline to volunteer, you'll draft me."

"That is correct."

"Then how is it volunteering?"

"I really don't care about the semantics, Mr. Euanker. One way or another, you're coming with me."

So that was it. I was becoming an astronaut, whether I wanted to or not. I was taken away, shoved in a car, and driven off, with little more than the shirt on my back and a few dollars in my wallet.

I was taken to Houston, Texas, where the Johnson Space Center was located. NASA may have been replaced by ISA, the International Space Agency, but like the United Nations, America pretty much ran the show. The moment I got there, I was dumped into a meeting room of some sort, all chairs and no tables, along with several other people. We were given no formal introduction to each other, except hearing some little administrative troll issuing us berthing assignments. He did so by going through the names alphabetically, issuing bunks and locker numbers as he went. Since my last name begins with an 'E,' he came to mine relatively quickly. "Mister William Ewe-Anchor?"

"Actually, it's pronounced, 'Wanker,'" I corrected him. Several sniggers could be heard throughout the room.

He stared at me blankly. "William Wanker," he said, dryly. "That's *really* your name, is it? Willy Wanker?"

More sniggering was heard.

"Not Willy, sir."

"Not Willy?"

"No, sir. Not Willy Willy." I sighed, then corrected myself. "I mean, not *really* Willy." The sniggers got noticeably louder.

He tried to sound authoritatively sarcastic. "Oh, *Willy?*" He blushed. "I mean, *really?*" The sniggers became outright cackles.

"Yes, sir. Everyone calls me Billy."

"*Billy* Euanker. Not much better." He tapped his pad a few times. "Berth six, lower bunk, stowage locker eleven."

Not surprisingly, I was known thereafter as Billy 'Bater.

Now ensconced in my Spartan living quarters, given essential toiletries and some uniform clothing items, I felt as plucked and bagged as a harvested nut. I'd been tossed in with an assortment of other nuts, most of whom had shells just as hard as mine. There was a black walnut named Bruce, a Brazil nut named Paulo, a seasoned cashew named Satchel, and a tall Norwegian-looking man named Bjorn, a true almond. It being an equal-opportunity space program, there were also several women. There was a hazelnut named Barbara, a macadamia named Latona, a Korean pine nut named Min, and little Kimmie – definitely a peanut. There was also a middle-aged brunette named Tawney who I strongly suspected was a well-salted pistachio. Then there was me – a chest-nut if ever there was one. Five women and five men in all. Herding us all together was the administrative assistant – the same little troll who'd issued us our berthing assignments – a nerdy man whose last name was (I shit you not) Filbert. Together we made quite a party mix.

Of course, every assortment of mixed nuts requires a nutcracker, and ours came in the form of our commanding officer, a large German man (apparently on loan from the European Space Agency) with the entertaining name of Griest Rohler-Behring. Colonel Behring, as he called himself, told us that his nickname was 'Ball.' "As in 'Ball Behring,'" he said in his thick, Teutonic accent, chuckling to himself at his witticism. Naturally, behind his back, we all called him, "Over."

We first met him after we'd gotten settled into our berths. He entered authoritatively and bellowed out, "Atten-TION!"

This produced an immediate response, which was for everyone to do absolutely nothing. A few people might have looked absent-mindedly in his direction for a moment, after which they simply returned to whatever lazy activity they had been occupying themselves with beforehand.

He let out a deep sigh and took a different approach. "My name is Colonel Behring. Welcome to astronaut training. Now, I Would greatly appreciate it, as a favor to me, if everyone lined up at attention next to their bunks. Oh, and, I might add, anyone who does not do so will be put in solitary confinement."

Well, we weren't military, and we weren't about to become military, but we grudgingly hauled our asses up and stood more or less at attention anyway.

"That's better. Now, the traditional astronaut training process has always begun with two full years of basic training, followed by a selection process which takes nothing but the upper 1% of graduates. All of you, however, will be undergoing an accelerated program which will train you in merely four months. That means you will be very busy after today, so be forewarned. I am uploading tomorrow's itinerary to your Ex Drives. I expect everyone to follow it punctually. Mr. Euanker?"

A few sniggers spurted out again at the sudden mention of my silly-sounding name. At least the pompous ass pronounced it correctly. "Yes, Colonel?"

"You are the only one who does not have an Ex Drive. Why not?"

He was right, of course. I'd never had an external hard drive implanted into my brain. "Medical reasons, sir."

"Medical reasons? What are you, allergic to neuroelectrodes?"

"No, sir. I have posterior corpus colossal hypertrophy."

"You have what?"

I launched right into my well-practiced explanation. It was a speech I, unfortunately, had to give rather often. Every time I'd gotten handed a new job (or been forced into one), some dolt who happened to be in charge always wanted to know why my brain didn't have the so-called advantage of being hard-wired into a computer. "Well, sir, basically it means that the left and right hemispheres of my brain are far more interconnected than those of other people. I'm actually quite mentally gifted. But that also means that having an Ex Drive installed might lobotomize me."

"I see," he said, even though he clearly didn't. "Well, Euanker, we simply can't afford to take the time to train you slowly. These other recruits will be able to save information instantly to their Ex Drives, and that ability is essential. We can't wait around for you to catch up."

"You won't have to, sir," I answered him. "I have a photographic memory, and can do most things people with Ex Drives can do."

"Oh, really?" he said, skeptically. "What's twelve thousand, nine hundred and seventy-seven times forty-two thousand, nine hundred and seventy-six?"

"Five hundred and fifty-seven million, six hundred and ninety-nine thousand, five hundred and fifty-two," I answered instantly.

His eyes narrowed on me. "What's the capital of Estonia?"

"Tallin."

"Quote to me out of the book of Revelation, chapter twenty-three, verse four."

"Revelation only has twenty-two chapters."

He lifted an eyebrow at me, clearly impressed but trying to restrain himself. "Well, we would still have to give you hard-copy for you to study. We simply don't have the time or wherewithal to bother with all that."

"Begging your pardon, sir, but are any of your other recruits equipped with a base-jack?" I tilted my head to the right so as to show him the access portal behind my left ear.

Now he lifted *both* eyebrows. "No. In fact, I've never *seen* anyone with a base-jack before."

"I'm the only one. And I believe you require someone with a base-jack for the upcoming mission, do you not?"

His eyebrows slowly lowered as a cold look of realization descended down the slope of his face like a rolling snowball, and the resulting avalanche of capitulation crashed down all around him.

"I'll have tomorrow's itinerary printed out and brought to you," he said.

"Thank you, sir."

*Thank you, sir?* What an *idiot* I was! I've always been proud of my genetically quirky brain, as well as my base-jack, and had, in that moment of weakness, let that pride keep me mired in space camp. What was I thinking? Shit, I could have simply *agreed* with Colonel Over Behring about my lack of an Ex Drive being a disadvantage and gone straight home! But no, I just had to score points on the guy in charge. Heaven knows why I'm so proud.

Without an Ex Drive, I'm still seen as a complete retard, genetic smarts or not. On the other hand, I might simply have gotten sent home only to enjoy my freedom for barely a few hours before they realized their mistake and sent Bobby Bighorn to come grab me again.

The itinerary, it turned out, was mostly physical training for the first several days. We got up at the crack of dawn to wolf down an abbreviated breakfast and then jog for three miles. This later became four miles, then five. We would afterward go through some ridiculous obstacle course, finishing with a round of push-ups, sit-ups and chin-ups, with one or two people usually doing some throw-ups for good measure. Usually, the person doing the vomiting was Bjorn, the almond. Since his last name was Barclay, he was soon nicknamed Barfy.

After a week of that nonsense, our training began to include classroom instruction. My classmates were able to simply upload their lessons, then do hands-on practice with vehicle and space-station systems. I had to speed-read it all, then be the last one to do anything after they'd all finished.

It was in the process of this phase of training that we learned what we were being trained for, and where we were eventually going: *Europa,* the second-closest moon of the planet Jupiter, and the most interesting of the Galilean satellites. It was a moon known to have liquid water beneath its icy surface, and was therefore an ideal candidate for potential extraterrestrial life.

Still, this made me wonder a bit about our collective predicament. Why was such a motley bunch of people recruited for such a landmark mission, and not a more traditional, cohesive unit? Why such an accelerated training program? And why was the discipline so lax? Not once did Colonel Behring get in our faces and yell at us. All he ever did was threaten solitary, and this usually seemed motivation enough, even though the compliance was often grudgingly given. And why would such a high-ranking officer be assigned to train a bunch of simple recruits? What was the deal, here?

I could understand why the Colonel never yelled at *me*. He must have reviewed my medical records after his initial mistake my first day and realized that my quirky brain also had something called amygdaline hypoplatia. Basically, that means that I can't experience fear. No, really. Nothing scares me. I'm not afraid of heights, nor spiders, nor snakes, nor having a loaded gun pointed in my face. The Colonel could threaten me all he wanted, and my blood pressure would never rise. If he wanted my pulse rate to go up, he'd have to put a sexy woman in a bikini in front of me. Hence, no yelling. But why did he treat the others the same way?

I finally figured it out in our third week of training. This was when they began to incorporate military water and land survival training – something Over Behring said we would need in the event of an unplanned landing back to Earth. A swim test was the first thing required for this. We had to swim three lengths of a 25-meter pool, free-style, then tread water for ten minutes. By this time, I had befriended Bruce Chumley (or, "Chum," as we all called him), the man who slept in the bunk above mine (perhaps because walnuts and chestnuts go so well together). It was he who raised the objection to this particular phase of our training.

"Colonel, why do we need to prepare for a splash-down landing back to Earth?" he asked. "I thought we were going to be traveling using the new Scotty transport. Won't we simply re-materialize back on the planet's surface?"

The big German was clearly prepared for this. "Mr. Chumley, The Scotty is a new piece of technology. If something should go wrong, you will need to return to Earth from Europa the old-fashioned way, or not at all. And the only thing which will keep you alive is what you learn here. So please pay attention."

He did. We all did.

"Everyone must enter the water simultaneously, then swim three lengths. And do *not* urinate in the pool."

There were a lot of chuckles at this, but the warning turned out to be wisely given. The water had been treated with a trace chemical which turned blue in the presence of urea, and no sooner had we jumped in than Satchel Lister, our seasoned cashew, started leaving swirling blue clouds in his wake. He was an older man, and probably couldn't help himself. He was fished out by two lifeguards who used an enormously long hook to drag him out of the water and was subsequently put in solitary confinement. Poor guy. We didn't see him for a few days after that. It was only later that we learned that he was subjected to this test repeatedly during that time. Out of solitary he would come, was told to jump in the water again, and again he left blue swirls. Finally, repeated trips to the bathroom, a visit to a sauna to sweat out as much water as he could beforehand, and twelve hours of no fluids got him through the test. He nearly dehydrated, but he got through it. And if you think that such an ordeal made us merciful enough not to nickname him Satchel *Pisser*, you'd be mistaken.

Meanwhile, our own aquatic adventure involved laps and treading water, but this was only the beginning. We had to jump into the water from a platform which was twelve meters high – about forty feet, or two meters higher than an Olympic high-diving board. This did not necessarily simulate a traditional splash-down which an astronaut would experience, but it was still a traditional part of the training program, according to Over Behring. Two by two, each of us went to the edge of the platform and jumped off, landing feet first into the water. None of us showed any hesitation, nor did anyone experience the fear of heights which so many people do when jumping off a high-dive.

And that's when I figured it out. *None* of us could experience fear! Bruce and I were the next to last to go over, and when we surfaced and exited the pool I asked him, "Hey, Bruce, are you fear-deficient?"

"Yeah!" he admitted. "How did you know?"

"I have it, too. You weren't afraid when you jumped in. In fact, I don't think anybody was."

Sure enough, subsequent conversations with others revealed the same thing. We were all genetically deficient in fear response. That explained why Behring wasn't trying to scare us – he knew he couldn't. It also explained how such an oddball set got thrown in together. Amygdaline hypoplatia is a very rare genetic trait.

It got us talking. It was obvious why the government would want fearless astronauts, but why was it suddenly so desperate to have astronauts that were outright *devoid* of any fear?

We didn't have an answer which made sense until Satchel Pisser finally came back from his water-torture a few days later. "Omphalos psychosis," he told us. "That must be it."

"Ompala-what?" I asked. "What's that supposed to be?"

"It's what happened when the first few people tried the Scotty," he said. "It was briefly on the news, but they hushed it up afterward. Basically, when the Scotty transports someone, the original person technically dies, and a new person who is an exact copy of the old gets created. If that person has a normal brain, the knowledge that he is only a copy of recent origin will trigger an existential fear response which drives him insane."

"You're making that up," Bruce accused.

"Nope," he replied. "God's honest truth. Even the Scotty's inventor went nuts."

Like an unwelcome hangover, it dawned on us what had been happening. "Of course!" I said. "Having no fear means a person won't wig out afterward. That makes them the ideal Scotty candidate, and therefore the ideal astronaut."

"And it means we're all stuck with this to the end," said Satchel. "We can't quit, and we can't get kicked out. I mean, look at *me*. They wouldn't even dump my ass when my finicky prostate couldn't keep me from pissing in the pool."

He was right, of course. But now, armed with this new knowledge, we reveled in the freedom to be complete assholes. Over the next several days, we broke every rule in the book, just to see if we could get thrown out. We started saying no to Behring's orders, sometimes even to the point of telling him to go fuck himself. Most of us blew off our PT assignments entirely. Once, while he was insisting we do our daily run, we did – in the *opposite* direction. On another occasion, Satchel took a piss in Behring's office as a sort of private revenge for what he'd gone through in the pool. But sure enough, none of us got tossed out. Finally, with nearly all of us in solitary most of the time, Behring shifted tactics. He hauled us all out and addressed us directly.

"Okay, it's quite clear that you've all figured out why we need you, and you *specifically*, for this training program. And you have all begun to take advantage of the fact that you are indispensable. Well, so be it. I see no reason to argue with you about the matter. I've used a stick, but now that stick is apparently no longer effective. So, from now on, I will also use a carrot. All those who cooperate with our training regimen will be given recreational privileges every evening. With these, you will have the luxuries of an allotment of booze at local taverns, various forms of entertainment, and a hotel room where you may sleep privately, either with yourself or someone else if you so choose. But you *will* follow orders to receive all this, and believe me when I say that you will follow them *to the letter*. Also, the other alternative still applies. Continue to be defiant, and your nights will be spent in solitary."

Well, I needn't say that this got us all cooperating fully with the Colonel, although a few of us were in favor of being even bigger ass-pains just to see what other goodies we might be able to squeeze out of the system.

Bereft of being defiant in the training room, many of us took to being defiant in the bedroom. Most of us guys took advantage of our odd status as forced conscripts to score points with any women we met at the bar. Believe me, nothing's a better pick-up line than waiting for a woman to ask the inevitable question, "So what do you do?" and then tell her that you're an astronaut. Any skeptical reactions could be met with the 3-D laser-imprinted Johnson Space Center I.D. badge. Quite a few of us got lucky that way. But the women in our group did their share of fooling around, too. I think Bruce slept with every woman in the program, and several more besides. The stud. Even Satchel Pisser got it on once or twice, although whether or not he had to resort to Viagra 2.0 was a matter of conjecture.

I remember that while we were all at our usual watering hole one night, I overheard hazelnut Barbara and macadamia Latona gossiping about Paulo, the Brazil nut. He was kind of religious, so the conversation somehow got coded in Jesus-talk, but it was clear enough what the subject matter was. They must have thought I was out of earshot.

"I heard you and Paolo had a little 'Bible study' last night," said Latona.

"Oh, *yes*," Barbara saucily replied. "We delved *deeply* into Revelation."

"And how hangeth the fruit of his loins?"

"Why, verily his athletic cup runneth over." They both giggled like school girls.

*Out of the mouths of babes*, I thought. And that's how Paolo Escobar became known to us as Paolo Escapade.

My own opportunity at workplace romance came on the first night of our anti-gravity training. We were about to go up in the specially modified Boeing 727-200, *G-Force One*, affectionately nicknamed the "Vomit Comet." In over a century of astronaut training, this old airplane was still the main method used to expose astronauts and tourists alike to weightlessness. Virgin Galactic, Space X, Blue Origin, and other companies had space hotels up in low Earth orbit which catered to ultra-wealthy clientele, but the Vomit Comet was much less expensive and did the job reasonably well – especially for an antique airplane.

We were just starting to find our seats inside the plane when Tawney casually asked me, "So, do any of the girls in this program catch your fancy?"

I was caught off-guard by the question, so as I sat down, I simply blurted out, "They all pass the hot-or-not test, I suppose."

"That's good," she replied. "Because I'm kind of hoping you like older women." Then she gave me a flirtatious wink before taking a seat directly in front of mine.

The pilot was explaining certain procedures to us, like about when the green light told us that it was okay to float out of our seats, when the warning light would come on to warn us to find our seats again, proper safety procedures, stuff like that. But to be honest, I wasn't paying much attention. Tawney had planted a lively little bee in my bonnet, and I was too busy enjoying the buzz.

She was indeed a *well*-salted pistachio, I later discovered.

We took eight trips up on the Vomit Comet, each totaling fourteen parabolic dives. First the plane would climb up at a 45 degree angle and then, at about 34,000 feet, it would dive downward, giving us about 25 seconds worth of weightlessness. I needn't tell you, that part was fun! Then the plane gently pulled up, giving us just enough gravity to get back to our seats. When we were all secured, the plane pulled up sharply, and we all experienced something more than two G's. Poor Satchel Pisser's bladder couldn't take the extra gravity, and he had to wear Depends after that first trip. Kimmie passed out during one of the climbs. But surprisingly, in spite of the well-earned nickname, 'Vomit Comet,' most of us kept our lunches down. Except for Barfy, of course.

We were allowed to indulge for the first few dives, but then Over Behring stepped in, and had us running drills. We were given tools like the ones we would use on our mission and told to do some lame-assed task with them, like tightening and loosening a bolt or some such silly nonsense. Other times we had to float down the length of the fuselage and back again, do tucks and rolls, and otherwise learn how to really navigate without any gravity to guide you. It sounds easy, but it's much harder than it seems.

This was when we began noticing that Barbara had a really bad case of the fumbles. She constantly lost control of her tools in zero-G, and often lost control of them in normal gravity, too. It was only a matter of time before she earned the first and only nickname among the women – Bumble Barbie. If we ever heard something fall or break, we all assumed it was her.

I still wanted out, but I was actually beginning to enjoy space camp a little bit, mostly thanks to the extra-curricular activities I was enjoying with Tawney. So naturally, it was at this point when things took a dramatic turn for the worse. Apparently, someone higher up decided that we all needed an additional "incentive" to assist us in our training, and we were formally addressed by a representative of Branch Charlie, the agency which operated the Scotty under the supervision of various world governments. This representative was some woman named Sarita Shantay, and she claimed to be a "public relations official." She wasn't fooling me with that one, not with the impressive way she power-dressed. She was in a women's business suit which featured shoulder-pads in her sport coat and a skirt which left absolutely nothing to the imagination regarding her posterior. Any woman who dressed like that while visiting a facility where a lot of military personnel were stationed was one who had a lot of power at her disposal. Hell, she probably *ran* Branch Charlie. Either that, or she was sleeping with the person who was.

"I'm here to tell you about the Marlin Kettrell Exobiology Prize," she announced. "We believe very strongly in the possibility of life on Europa, so much so that we are willing to grant a special commendation to the person who is determined to find conclusive evidence of such life, past or present. This person, whomever he or she may be, will already be a hero in the eyes of the general public, and so we are willing to go the extra mile to make that person a public icon. He or she will become the primary spokesperson for ISA, given the choicest assignments in outer space, and will achieve a high degree of fame. As for fortune, a five-million-dollar award will be given to this individual. This might be enough in its own right, but this person will also be forever remembered in the history books as a notable figure. Best of luck to you, and may the best person win!"

Well, that pretty much made me the most unpopular guy in the program. Everybody wanted to win the prize, but since I was the one with the base-jack, I was going to be the person piloting the main exploratory vehicle. That meant the prize would most likely come to me. But I wanted *nothing* to do with it, damn it all! Fame, fortune, public appearances… none of that shit appealed to me! I'd already made all the money I really needed, and such a prize was nothing more to me than a great, big pain in my ass. But my "classmates" wanted it. Badly! I became the guy standing in the way, and everyone resented me for it.

Finally, we were put through the Virtual Reality simulators at the Marshall Space Flight Center in Huntsville, Alabama. For the most part, this was exactly what you might expect, but there were a few highlights. For example, Satchel and I were once doing a docking exercise, simulating what it was like to dock a Soyuz-7 capsule with the New International Space Station. 30 seconds prior to mating, I noticed that we were drifting off to the right. So I said to Satchel, "Lister, we're three degrees right. Correct." But he didn't do anything, and we kept drifting while we approached the station. "Correct! Correct!" I shouted, but we still drifted to the right, and were headed for a collision. Even in a simulator, we'd get shaken up pretty good if we hit anything. So, I did something completely unorthodox and pulled off my helmet. I then uncoupled the safety harnesses and went over to where Satchel was sitting. The distinct sound of *snoring* was coming from inside his helmet. I couldn't believe it! The old fart had fallen *asleep!* I tried shaking him, but it was too late. The capsule hit the station, and I was thrown into the console.

You know, Satchel actually slept right through the crash! His body must have felt the jolt, but he was strapped into his safety harness rather snugly. Only when we pulled his helmet off did he come to and groggily say, "Wh-? Oh! Sorry. Must have dozed off."

Behring decided that Pisser could catch up on his sleep while in solitary.

Towards the end of our training, we were introduced to the Roger Avon Memorial training facility, which housed a full-scale mock-up of what would be our ship during the Europa mission, the *Talos*. The real ship was already out there orbiting Europa, waiting for us, having been previously constructed remotely by robots and micro-robots which had been sent there by Scotty beforehand. Meanwhile, at the training facility, we were trained on the hands-on aspects of working with our equipment and the ship's controls. Oh, all the necessary information was already downloaded to my colleagues' Ex Drives, and I had memorized it out of the manuals, but all that was just book knowledge. For any mission, nothing beats hands-on experience.

The Talos was a pretty cool-looking ship. In Greek mythology, Europa was taken to the island of Crete by Zeus. There, Zeus gave her three gifts, the first of which was a winged guardian named Talos, who would fly around the island three times each day to protect her. Our ship would be circling Europa 3.4 times every 24 hours. Very fitting. Most depictions of Talos make him look like a winged angel, and the ship did resemble an angel somewhat, except that the "wings" were platforms which rotated to simulate one G of gravity. In the mock-up, these platforms were angled downward to make use of the gravity already present on Earth.

Finally, Scotty-Day, the day of our mission, arrived. There was no ignition, no lift-off. Simply one by one, each of us got onto something that looked like a gigantic stove-top heater coil, and vanished in a flash. We then re-appeared on board the Talos. The media was there to broadcast the send-off, with some guy pretending to be a technician spouting off complicated sounding stuff, and then doing a countdown from ten down to one before the switch was thrown. None of that was necessary, of course. It was all theater, as the use of the Scotty had never been broadcast live on the Netstream before.

Latona went first, then Brenda, Bruce, and me. When we materialized, I discovered that we did so right on top of the onboard Scotty pad as though we were still standing. But in the weightlessness of micro-gravity, I didn't quite realize this until I tried to step off the pad and accidentally sent my body careening out of control. My momentum finally stopped when I reached the bulkhead on the opposite side. Fortunately, I landed on my head. So much for my Vomit Comet training.

Jupiter has a powerful magnetic field which bombards everything near it with huge amounts of radiation, including Europa. The Talos, however, was well-shielded against harmful ions. We were literally flying in a lead balloon. Once on board, we went through all our preliminary start-up procedures, ran first safety checks, got things ready, then fired the platform rockets to start them spinning so that we could have gravity. The others arrived shortly afterward.

Once everybody was aboard, we all took stations for launching, monitoring and doing experiments with the L-3, the Laelaps Lunar Lander. Bruce, Tawney and I were its pilots, with the others remaining in orbit up above. The second of the three gifts given to Europa by Zeus, Laelaps was a hunting dog which never failed to catch its prey. Naming the lander after this efficacious canine reflected a kind of wild-eyed optimism on the part of the ISA administrators, but it did at least fit Greek mythology.

What a sight we were treated to as soon as the lander touched down! It was impossible not to take a moment. We were situated on the edge of one of the *linae* – those red lines that streak across Europa's surface – and the view was spectacular! The red line was at the bottom of an impossibly large, ruler-straight ice canyon which stretched out well beyond our field of vision, while the massive planet Jupiter filled the sky overhead in a way that made all our jaws drop. You could see the planet's swirling gasses and be easily mesmerized by them. The white-red-brown hues reflected light off the sun to give the icy landscape a soft, pinkish glow, and the red line we were situated on top of seemed like a long, maroon shadow at the bottom of a ruler-straight canyon. The images we gathered cannot do the experience justice. You just had to be there.

Still, we had work to do. We grudgingly ignored the beauty around us and went to work running tests. Back on board the Talos, our colleagues did the same. ISA was very interested in this part, and so was monitoring us very closely. Because the Scotty doubles as an ansible as well as a transport, we had instantaneous audio/visual communications with Houston. We'd nicknamed this feature of the Scotty the U.K.L. communicator (after Ursula K. LeGuin, the sci-fi author who first wrote about ansibles). Through it, they were watching us like a hawk.

I then played the part they'd specially selected me to perform. The lander had a probe on it known as the *Javelin*. It was a self-heating submersible, designed to melt into Europa's thick ice layer and break through to the watery depths beneath. This was the big test, the one that everyone was so very anxious to see – what wonders could possibly lie beneath a Galilean, lunar ocean? A javelin which never missed its target was the third gift Zeus gave to Europa, hence the name, but I found this somewhat misleading. Penetrating Europa's ice layer was easier than hitting the broad side of a barn. I mean, how could you possibly miss when your target was anywhere and everywhere straight down?

Still, once through the ice, someone had to pilot the probe, which was a real problem. Someone with an ExDrive couldn't do it. Any sort of conventional radio-transmitted signal wouldn't be able to reach the probe, both due to the thickness of the ice and the intense radiation which constantly bombarded Europa. That meant that any radio-based controllers were ruled out. Attaching the probe to a long extension-cord was impossible both because the length of cord needed would be too large to manage, and because the ice would simply re-freeze behind the probe anyway, freezing the cord in place and trapping it. You could heat the cord, but that gets more and more expensive in terms of energy usage the further down one goes. What about an ansible? Well, equipping the Javelin with a U.K.L. would be impossibly bulky. So, what does one do? The solution to this problem was me – someone who could pilot any craft by thought using his base-jack. A base-jack receiver is reasonably small, and the human brain is also great at conserving space. All one had to do was rob me of my civil liberties and – *voila!* Problem solved.

I had the boom with the Javelin lowered and positioned just as the others were getting their tests and experiments underway. Then, with great fanfare, the Javelin was released, and the nuclear-fission-powered heating system of the probe began to melt into the ice. Gravity did the rest. The probe sank down until it was invisible, and new ice almost immediately froze behind it, letting out a huge, but temporary, cloud of steam. I could hear through the U.K.L. that people were cheering back home.

But seriously, that was about it as far as initial excitement was concerned. The Javelin needed to melt through more than sixty miles of solid ice, and was moving downward at a maximum rate of not quite three miles per hour. That meant that once the surface tests were done and over with, it was going to be rather boring for at least an entire day. Sure enough, the others were finished with their duties inside of a few hours. Now all we had to do was sit there and wait for the Javelin to reach the subsurface oceans we were certain had to be there.

You could almost feel people watching the Netstream back home losing interest. I was not pleased at this, but felt utterly helpless to be able to do anything about it. But then, I got a little bit of inspiration by seeing Min through the monitor, and she was apparently trying to alleviate her boredom by typing something into her console.

"Hey, Min, what are you doing?" I asked.

"Writing a letter to my husband," she said.

"Which one?"

We all burst out laughing at this, because Min really did have multiple husbands. She was Korean by heritage, but Indian by nationality, and that meant she lived in one of the few nations which allowed women to marry more than one man at a time. China, on the other hand, was still a nation with a few billion more men than women, which created its own special set of problems. So, to deal with them, China legalized the export of husbands by mail-order. In fact, China became as well known for its mail-order husbands as Ukraine once was for its mail-order brides, and believe me when I say that the Chinese officials had no qualms whatsoever about polyandry. Min collected these Chinese husbands the way some people did Chinese dolls. At that particular time, she had six.

"*Six?*" Barbara had said back when she'd first heard about this. "Wow. Doesn't that, you know, cause problems? You know, in the bedroom?"

Min had given her an odd look. "Are you asking me if I let them take turns?"

"No! Well – yes, maybe. Sort of. I mean, I'm sure you don't take them all at once." She blushed. "*Do* you?"

She'd given Barbie a wry grin. "Only if I'm *really* in the mood." It was impossible to tell if she was serious.

"They're all probably cleaning her house, tending her garden and doing her laundry," joked Latona.

"And drinking up any beer I may have left in the house," Min shot back. We had all had a good laugh over that one.

This gave me a bit of insight as to what we should do with our dead-time while we were orbiting Europa, waiting for the Javelin to hit liquid water. I decided to start telling jokes. I didn't know if this was a wise course of action, but I remembered something Buzz Aldrin said to a reporter years ago: *"You know, up there, it's life or death. But down on Earth, it's just another television show. Everyone's too busy watching reruns of Happy Days to really worry about you."* So, I figured, what the hell? Why not? Maybe I could get a gig as a comic when it was all over.

By the time I got done insulting everyone on the mission, they all ganged up on me. It turned into one, gigantic roast, and whatever it cost us in pride was regained in ratings.

After twenty-five hours and forty-three minutes of oddball anecdotes and world-champion put-downs, the Javelin sounded its alarm.

"We've broken through!" I announced. "We've reached liquid water!" Over the ansible I could hear hundreds of people cheering back home.

"Let's see!" shouted Latona.

And we did see – almost nothing, that is. The illuminating lamps came on, the video feed came in, and all we saw was a kind of chocolate haze.

"It's like we're in some sort of muddy lagoon," said Bjorn.

"Turn upwards," Latona suggested. "Let's see what the ice looks like from underneath."

I followed her suggestion and turned the Javelin upwards. At first, we still saw nothing. Then the submersible came close enough to the ice for us to see it through the muddiness. The ice did not at all look like the pristine, blue-glowing shapes that have been seen in the waters beneath the Arctic. Rather, the ice was completely dark. No sunlight trickled down to these massive depths. The ice also appeared to have a reddish brown substance coating it, as though whatever was muddying the water was also staining the upper surfaces. It looked less like sub-arctic ice and more like the interior of Carlsbad Caverns. The one white spot was the brilliantly white circle marking where the Javelin had broken through.

"Hey, let me see the video feed," begged Satchel.

"Better not," said Kimmie. "He might start urinating in his flight suit."

"Hey!" he protested. "That's not very funny!"

"*I* thought it was funny," said Latona. "Min? Tawney? Did you think that was funny?"

They didn't answer. They were still too busy laughing.

We decided to test the substances in the water as well as the residue on the ice. They contained complex organic compounds along with various minerals, especially iron oxide. This paralleled the kinds of substances we found in the linae – the red color in the lines was caused by rust and organic compounds. So, this was an ocean composed almost entirely of iron-laden primordial soup. But so far, no signs of life were seen. This suited me just fine, since I was the only one who didn't want to win the Kettrell Exobiology Prize, and finding nothing amounted to me getting off that particular hook.

With the upper surface viewed, the only thing left to do was dive down and try to find the sea floor. Of course, this meant another long wait, as the depths of Europa's subsurface ocean were unknown. So again, we resorted to various short insults and tall tales to keep people interested. The Javelin was descending now at a rate of eight miles per hour, but how long would it take before it would hit bottom?

As it turned out, it took about another 12 hours, which meant the watery depths extended another 96 miles below the ice layer. We were using sonar to get a digital readout of the terrain below, and so had a good idea about how far down it was. But even then, the sea floor came up so suddenly that I didn't have time to react when it appeared and ended up accidentally ramming the Javelin right into it.

"Doink!" said Tawney.

"Hey, give me a break! I can't see anything through this pea soup."

"Pull back," ordered Latona. "Make sure you're not stuck."

I wasn't stuck. I was able to pull out of the sedimentary bottom and pivot the Javelin around, taking a look. Visibility was barely a few meters, but all we could see was a flat, brown benthic terrain. Boring. I had the probe collect and analyze a sediment sample, and we discovered that the chemistry was similar to the muddy substance covering the underside of the ice – rusty, mineral-rich organic clay.

"Well?" I asked. "What now?"

"Head south," Latona directed. "Sonar detected an equatorial striation of some sort in that direction."

"Aye, aye, Captain!"

Sometime after that, Min expressed some puzzlement over what we were seeing. "Something's not right about this."

"How do you mean?" asked Paulo.

"I mean, there's muddy water, and a sedimentary bottom, but nothing's alive."

"So what?"

"So, something has to be *churning* the water, that's what," she answered him. "In order to get sediments, something has to be putting particulates into the water. And in order to get such muddy water, something has to be continuously churning the water up."

"In other words," I said, "someone or something is stirring the pot."

"Yeah, pretty much."

"Maybe it's E.T. making crop circles on the ocean floor," suggested Bruce.

"That's lame," Kimmie told him.

We continued on, occasionally cracking the odd joke, but we didn't need to resort to that as much. We knew every eye that could watch was glued to the Netstream as new Europan terrain, boring though it was, was continuously revealed through the Javelin's camera. Finally, as the equatorial striation came near, we saw a shadowy hill directly ahead. It resolved into a complication which looked like a pile of black rocks at first. As the probe got closer, we could see that some of the black rocks spiked upwards, like the jagged towers of a gothic castle.

"Black smokers!" said Barfy.

"No, the remnants of them," Min corrected. "These are dormant. But there must be some live ones somewhere. That must be what's churning up the water."

"Volcanism under the waves of Europa!" cried Latona. "What a moment!"

Through the U.K.L., the cheering we heard indicated that people back on Earth agreed whole-heartedly.

"It's official," said Paolo. "Europa blows."

"Do a radio-isotope analysis," said Latona, ignoring him.

I was already on it, taking a sample with the Javelin to be analyzed using the miniaturized on-board mass spectrometers. In moments, we had results for uranium-lead, rubidium-strontium and potassium-argon dates. In each case, the results were that the sample was too young to date accurately. When the results came in for argon-argon dating, the result was that the sample was too old. That put a date range for the sample between 50,000 and 150,000 years. Fairly recent.

"Try nuclear magnetic resonance dating," ordered Latona.

"We can only get a rough estimate using that technique," I pointed out.

"Yeah, but do it anyway."

I did. We got back an estimate of about 100,000 years.

"Amazing!" cried Min. "When Neanderthals roamed the planet Earth, these smokers were active."

"But where are the *currently* active ones?" asked Satchel. "There must be some. You said so, yourself."

"The leftover structures lie in a straight line equatorially, so there's only two directions to choose from," I said. "So which way, East or West?"

"East," ordered Latona.

So, East it was. We followed the black smoker remnants carefully, making sure to note everything that looked unusual. Always we looked for any signs that life may have been there, but there was none. No moss, no lichens, no endoskeletons, no exoskeletons, no wilted tubors, no alien trilobites, no calcified sponges – nothing.

After a while, we began sleeping in shifts, as we had been awake for well over a day. I was able to set the probe on auto-pilot and catch some z's myself. It was near the end of my six-hour sleep cycle that the sonar alarm went off, and I was jolted awake.

"Whoa! Something up ahead!" I blurted out. In moments, everyone on board was wide awake and alert, too.

The Javelin slowed, and its camera slowly brought ghostly images into view through the grainy water. A hemispherical shape emerged from the gloom to astound us. The downward side was perfectly round, like a crystal ball, but the upper half looked smashed in. The structure measured about four meters across. It looked, for all the world, just like a gigantic, broken goldfish bowl.

"Looks like Bumble Barbie has been down here, already," cracked Bruce.

"Oh, you are *so* hilarious," Barbara shot back.

"Look!" cried Kimmie. "There's another one!"

Sure enough, less than a meter behind the first one, was another broken sphere, about the same size. And then another appeared on the opposite side of the black smoker remnants. Beyond that was another, and another… In all, we found about two dozen of those smashed goldfish bowls, all of them more or less identical.

"What are they?" Barbara asked aloud.

"Take a sample and date them," said Latona.

I tried, but the spheres were largely silicate, and had few radio-isotopes to do a date with.

"Any carbon?" she asked.

"Trace amounts," I replied. "Why?"

"Do a carbon-14 analysis."

"What? You're kidding, right?"

"No, I'm not. And cross-correlate it with a uranium-thorium analysis while you're at it."

I thought she was crazy, but she was the captain, so I did as she asked. I had to use the trace amounts of carbon present in the water-borne particulates as a benchmark, and hope that would be accurate. There was no atmosphere to generate Carbon-14 on Europa, and so I thought it would be a fruitless exercise, but to my surprise, there was actually C-14 present in the water. As for the silicates, there was only barely enough of the trace elements needed to do a rough date at all, but to my surprise again, the estimates of both dates came up with the same result: about 80,000 years old.

"Now date the black smokers," she said. "NMR technique, just like before."

I did. The estimate came back. About 80,000 years.

"The broken spheres are contemporary to the time period the black smokers in this area were active," noted Min.

"My god!" gasped Tawney. "They're *eggs!*"

"What?!" several of us said at once.

"They're eggs, I'm telling you. Not smashed in, broken *out*. Something comes along, lays its eggs next to the black smokers, right where it's warm, and then leaves. Sometime later, they hatch, leaving these broken shells behind."

"Hatch? Hatch and go where?" I asked.

"Maybe they're still here someplace," she said.

"Still here?" cried Escapade. "Do you see the *size* of those things? If those are the babies, how big are the adults? Pretty fucking huge, I'd say!"

"So what are you saying?" asked Bruce. "That some gigantic sea monster is going to come along and swallow our probe?"

"Exactly!" Paulo replied. "And *then* what will we do?"

"Well," I responded coolly, "I suppose I'll pilot the Javelin up its gut, and make sure the camera's rolling when it gets shit out its ass-end."

"Oh, for heaven's sake," scolded Tawney. "Will you be serious for one damned second?"

"I *am* serious!" I told her. "Look, we're up here, and the monsters, if they're even around, are down there. If the probe gets eaten by one of them, big deal! That might be the scientific discovery of the century!"

"Great," said Bruce. "Our first encounter with a space alien gets to be a gastro-colonoscopy."

"I'm more concerned about the *lander* getting eaten," said Tawney.

"Well, if Laelaps gets in trouble, we can do an emergency Scotty transport to get you out of there, so let's stay focused," said Latona. "Have the Javelin continue eastward. Let's see if there are any more of these eggs lying around."

There were. Doing dates on them each time we found a new batch, we found that the black smokers and the eggs dated around the same time. We found hatcheries at about 60,000, 40,000 and 20,000 years in the past. Then, we finally found the black smokers themselves!

The hot spot stretched out for about forty yards. Billowing clouds of black smoke continually and violently darkened the water, and tests revealed that the superheated jets contained copious amounts of sulfur, silica, iron, nickel, copper, sodium, chlorine and even simple hydrocarbons.

But there were no eggs to be found. Nor were there any little organisms living off the heat or feeding off the minerals like the black smokers on Earth.

We stayed in orbit around Europa for some days after that, exploring with the Javelin, trying to find the creatures, but were unsuccessful. We had discovered their eggs, but whatever had hatched from them was gone long ago. Several of the crew eventually came back home via the Scotty, with myself, Latona and Tawney remaining behind a few days longer, but then we were recalled home too. The ISA sent me up several more times to follow up, as the Javelin was left behind in the water to be used on future occasions. Sometimes Tawney and some of the others were there with me, other times not.

Of course, they awarded the Marlin Kettrell Exobiology Prize to me. I protested loudly that Tawney was the one with the insight regarding the eggs and that the prize therefore rightly should have gone to her. But I was the one who had started the jokes during the long descent of the Javelin, and kept them going during the boring periods of the mission. Everyone back home loved *me*, and so that meant the prize had to be given to the popular guy. The fact that it was a punishment for myself and everyone else in the program didn't bother the bureaucrats in the slightest.

Subsequent missions to the Talos sent down even more probes, and it was found that there were at least several other striations, caused by other volcanic hot-spots that continually moved equatorially from West to East. Geologists have been eager to learn why ever since. Some of the smokers dated back millions of years. Some conjectured that there were remnants of some which were billions of years old, long-since buried somewhere deep under the sediments. All the modern striations had broken egg-shells at similar intervals in the past. But there was no trace of the creatures who'd laid them.

Wherever they were, whatever they were, they had left Europa, leaving behind only one other thing: the chocolate haze of the water. Yes, the black smokers churned the water up, which explained the presence of minerals, but there was far too much organic material to account for – unless it came from the creatures. Yes, the brown coloring and ruddiness of the linae were all due to one thing: alien feces. We had discovered a hatchery, *and* a sewer. The public was disgusted. But the scientists were as happy, literally, as Ph.D's in shit.

If the geochronology proves right, these creatures leave, then return every 20,000 years or so. That means we're due for another visit very soon. These giant aquatic aliens, whatever they might be, could return as soon as this century. Only *this* time, they'll find humans waiting for them. I'm not entirely certain how they'll react upon seeing interlopers invading their favorite breeding ground. I mean, if I found some alien lurking in my bedroom just I was about to have sex with a hot woman, I'd be really pissed off. Still, perhaps they'll barely notice. Perhaps these are simple creatures, akin to giant space turtles, coming in to break through the ice of a Jovian moon to spawn and then break out of the ice again to travel through space away out into the stars, maybe carrying their newborn young with them, leaving red-colored linae behind where they'd broken through. Trace amounts of Carbon-14 would then get created as solar and Jovian radiation affected the brief exposure of liquid water through the cracks. Perhaps these creatures have bodies which are akin to giant spaceships. On the other hand, perhaps they are beings of fantastic intelligence who will react to our presence with hostility. Parents tend to defend their young with extreme violence, after all. Or worse still, wherever there are young being hatched, there are often predators. Would such predators find humans a tasty treat? It's possible. After all, this puts a new spin on the panspermia hypothesis, doesn't it? These creatures might be the distant ancestors of life on Earth. Or perhaps it's the other way around. Perhaps it's neither. Who knows?

I certainly don't. All that is above my pay grade. You lot are going to be the ones who will find out. Most of you are having your brains surgically altered, by Scotty, to take away the fear responses from your amygdalae. Well, if you have enough courage to do *that* before your fear is even removed, I suppose you'll make good Scotty astronauts, even if you *are* crazy. A few of you are even getting base-jacks installed. I feel for you. But my worry is that you won't be used to a life without fear. Those of us born with our condition learn over the course of a lifetime how to safeguard ourselves through trial and error, and we have more than our share of close calls along the way. Many of us die young because we climbed out onto a tree branch we shouldn't have, or acted too cool around the wrong thug. I hope you're careful out there.

Anyway, that's all I have to say about what it was like to be an astronaut. Good luck in space camp.

You're gonna need it.

## Chapter 6: Mother

"She'll destroy you if you do this."

Adorjan Jaire Baptise Napolitano, President of the New United Nations, let the words spoken to him by his chief of staff ring in his ears a moment before responding. "Yes, Claude," he said. "I know."

"It's an obvious trap." Claude Remy went on. "You *must* reconsider."

President Napolitano stared at the document in front of him. His signature upon it would seal the fates of two people: himself, and a woman who, technically, he had never met before.

"It may be a trap," the President said, "but we're talking about a living, breathing woman, and she has rights."

"Not according to the law." Claude protested. "She's an illegal. She should have been terminated the moment she came into existence!"

The president gave him a burning stare. "Well, she *wasn't,* was she?" Napolitano said. It wasn't really a question. "This is a moral decision, not a legal one." He took his pen, and resolutely signed the form – a permanent stay of execution.

"*Sir,*" cried Claude. "Please! Allow me to shred that. It's not too late to change your mind. No one need know…"

"It's *decided*, Claude." The president's eyes never left the surface of his desk as he picked up the paper, and handed it to him. "Please submit this to the Council of Ministers. And then contact the Vice President, and tell her that her services will likely be needed soon."

Claude simply stood there, unable for the moment to take the paper, knowing what it meant.

"Take it," the president insisted, still avoiding his gaze. "And send the woman in as you leave."

"Sir…"

"Please," he insisted again. "She has a right to know. Even as she has a right to live."

Reluctantly, Claude took the document, and walked to the door. Before opening it, he turned around. "It's been an honor serving with you, sir."

The president slowly nodded. He wasn't done yet, and neither was Remy, but the end was certainly looming. He understood the gesture. "It's been a pleasure serving with you as well, Claude," he answered. "Now, please…"

Claude opened the door and exited. Outside in the hall, Napolitano heard him say, "He will see you, now." He could tell by the pitch of Claude's voice that his chief of staff was choking back tears.

A young woman then entered, dressed in sweat clothes that were clearly not her size – no doubt gifted to her out of some charitable necessity. Her hair was black, her face was white, and her eyes had the wide look of someone completely frightened of her situation. As those eyes met the president's, they grew even wider.

"Ajay?" she asked.

The president opened his mouth to speak but couldn't find any words. So he simply nodded.

"Oh, my God! *Ajay!*" She flew across the room and threw her arms around him. "Oh, my sweet boy. You're *here!* You're alive! Let me look at you."

She pulled away from him just long enough to look at his face, at his eyes, and then threw herself into him again in a tight embrace.

"Ajay!" she cried, her tears soaking into his designer suit. "Oh, Ajay! They won't tell me what's going on. I beg and plead with them, but they won't answer any of my questions. It's been such a nightmare!" She pulled back from him. "Son, why do you look so much older? Why do I seem so much younger? What's happened to us? What's going on?!"

The president's large hands took her by the shoulders and firmly pushed her back from him. He kept his gaze down, averting her eyes.

"Susan…" he began.

"*Susan?!*" she protested. "What is this 'Susan' nonsense? I'm your *mother*, for heaven's sake!"

"No," he answered resolutely, still holding her back. "You're not."

She blinked several times, trying to process what he said. "Of course, I am! I'm your *mother!* I birthed you, I diapered you – I know everything *about* you."

"Please…" He almost said 'mother,' but caught himself. "Please sit down."

"Sit down?!" she protested. "Why should I have to sit down? I'm fine!"

"Please, just sit," the president said. "It will be easier if you sit."

She backed away a step, unsure of what to make of what was happening. Then saw that Ajay, the president, was gesturing towards an array of sofas in the center of the room.

"Please," he repeated.

She complied, went over and took a seat, unable to relax the worried muscles in her brow, even if she'd wanted to.

The president took a seat directly opposite her. He took a deep breath, and began.

"When I called you 'Susan,' I meant no disrespect, but I was being accurate. You see, you are not actually my mother." He paused for emphasis. "You are a copy of her."

"A *copy?*" she repeated.

The president nodded.

"That's impossible! How could I be a copy? I remember everything! I remember your entire childhood. Those memories are real!"

"The memories are real," he agreed. "But they've been copied, too."

She sat there a long time, apparently trying to process what was being said to her. "I'm – only a *copy?*"

"Not *only* a copy, no," he answered. "No one is 'only' anything. But this is why your body looks so much younger now."

"I don't understand," she said, starting to cry. "How could I be a copy? How could I…" She couldn't continue, as her sobs took over.

"I'm so sorry," said the president. "What happened to you was wrong. This is unprecedented. You have no idea how much."

Susan eventually controlled her sobs long enough to choke out the words, "What happened?"

President Napolitano heaved a deep sigh before answering. "There's this new device. It's called the Scotty. It was meant as a simple transport, but the number of unexpected consequences the technology presented were… well, they were impossible to plan for." He paused, then added, "It's the device that was used to make a copy of my mother. It's – what created you."

A look of horror brought her tears to a sudden stop. "Scotty? You mean, 'Scotty,' as in 'Beam me up, Scotty?'" she asked. "But that was just a gimmick they used on TV. How could that work?"

The president paused, trying to find the words. "I'm having a hard time with this. You see, I need to sum up an awful lot of history and I'm not exactly sure where to begin. What you need to understand is, the Scotty was found to not only be able to transport things across space. It could transport things across *time* as well. Space and time are the same continuum, you see. That meant the past was no longer secluded from us. If someone can go back in the past, scan a brain, and then obtain a DNA sample, that's all they need to copy an entire person, literally resurrecting them from the dead."

"You mean, people can simply be brought back like this?" she asked.

"No," the president answered. "What happened to you is extremely illegal. The dead aren't allowed to be brought back. It only happened a couple of times before, and there was huge public outcry."

Susan's tears abated, but she was still clearly troubled by this. She got up and began pacing. Eventually she turned to President Napolitano – to the son who was not actually her son – and said, "So, we can't bring back Tom?"

The president hung his head. "Dad's gone. I'm sorry."

She hung her head as well, managing to keep from sobbing. "So why me? Why now?"

The president shook his head. "That's complicated."

"How complicated?"

The president didn't answer right away. Eventually, he said, "The law states that the dead cannot be raised. I already told you about that. The part that I hadn't gotten to yet was…" he paused, trying to force out the words, "that any resurrected copies must be dematerialized by the Scotty again." Another pause. "Dematerialized, and *not* rematerialized again."

"*What?!*" Susan yelped.

"Relax, relax! You won't die. I've already signed the order preventing it. You're going to be fine." He paused again. "But in signing that order, that stay of execution, if you will, I've technically violated the law and – it has put me into some political jeopardy."

She stared at him, utterly flabbergasted. "You're sacrificing yourself to save me?"

Sitting there, elbows on his knees, his hands folded, he didn't even bother to look at her. He simply nodded.

"Oh," she said, her voice quavering. "You really *are* my son."

President Napolitano responded too quickly for his answer to be anything other than a political talking point. "Who you are copied from is irrelevant. You are a sentient being with rights, and you didn't ask to be resurrected. The law is an abomination."

"Still…" She smiled sweetly at him.

The president, for his part, smiled back. And though the rational part of him knew that this woman was not really his mother, that there was no way his elderly body could have come from that young, nubile one, he found himself warmed as though his real mother was really there with him at this troubling time.

"What will happen to you?" she asked.

He sighed. "There will be a challenge to my executive order, of course. There will be a hearing. The constitutionality of the law will be questioned…"

"But you'll still be president?"

He shook his head. "I deliberately violated a law which was clearly on the books. Whether I did so for ethical reasons is secondary to that. The World Parliament is probably already debating my impeachment as we speak."

Now, *she* shook her head in disagreement. "But that's crazy!" she blurted out. "You're absolutely right, I didn't ask to be brought back. Why should you be punished just for protecting…"

The proverbial penny dropped.

"Oh my god," she said. "I'm a trap!"

"Susan…" the president tried, consolingly.

"No! This is why they brought me back. To be used as a weapon against you! Your opponents couldn't get at you any other way, could they? No, of course not. They probably don't have anything on you. Or, at least, nothing that would get someone impeached. So, they *force* you to do something illegal; corner you into breaking the law for the sake…" she gasped as it fully hit her, "…for the sake of your long-dead mother!"

"Her copy," he said.

"*Irrelevant*, remember? *You* said so." She came back to the sofa opposite his, and sat down. "They had no good reason to do this to either of us."

"They had plenty of reason to do this to me."

She stared at him, taking in his demeanor. It wasn't so much shame upon his face as remorse; something which caused him a measure of regret. "What did you do?" she asked.

"There was a trial," he said at length. "Several years ago. Some kid named Iousef Irfan sued his parents and – oh, the particulars of the trial don't matter. Bottom line is that it ruled that children had the right not to be indoctrinated into their parents' religion. That offended a *lot* of religious people.[1] They felt that their faiths couldn't survive the court ruling. So much so that they felt they had to leave Earth. It's turned into a mass exodus. They're planning on colonizing everything from Mars to the moons of Saturn. They claim they have no choice. They ultimately blame me."

"You?" she responded. "Why should they blame you over what happened in some silly trial?"

---

[1] To learn exactly what happened at that trial, please read my novelette, *Sariah's Run* (2024).

"Because I could have spoken out against the verdict," he answered. "I could have invoked emergency powers which could have limited or even overruled the World Court's power. Instead, I supported it. I set precedent. I argued that emergency powers were only meant for defending civilians from military threat. They were not meant to overrule a controversial World Court verdict. Because of that, they see my actions as endorsing the World Court's ruling. They blame me for the entire thing."

He got up, and went over to the edge of the room where there was a service table. Upon it was a crystal water pitcher and a few glasses. He poured himself a glass of water from the pitcher and secretly wished it was gin.

"They weren't wrong, you know," he said, taking a drink. "I did agree with the ruling. I never liked fundamentalists and I've never cared for their politics, either. The ironic thing is, the part of the law which states that resurrected people must be permanently re-energized? Effectively executed? That part only got enacted because the religious contingent insisted it be put there. They saw the possibility of the dead returning as an abomination. Some even saw it as cheating God's justice by coming back from the pits of Hell. Execution was the only solution they would consider. 'Put the wayward souls back where they belong!' they cried.

"In the meantime, though, they've stuck me with the dilemma of you. Oh, their timing was perfect! Now, with most of them leaving Earth, it will soon be an easy matter to get that part of the law reversed with almost no opposition. It might even happen in a couple of years. Once that's done, you'll be safe forever. But for now, the law is still on the books – just long enough to nail me."

He downed the rest of the water in his glass. "Oh, it will always be illegal to resurrect the dead, that's for certain," he said. "Most people agree with that part. But at least those who happen to be brought back, for good or ill, won't be forced to pay the ultimate price just for simply living."

"I don't understand," said Susan. "If religious people are the ones who object to resurrecting the dead, what about abortion? Isn't all life sacred?"

"Hah!" he scoffed. "Don't get me started on *that* logical contradiction." He sighed heavily. "But seriously, your stay of execution only buys you a little bit of time, that's all. You'll have to go into hiding until that law is reversed. After that," he paused, "things will be a lot smoother."

"You should let me die," Susan said.

He rounded on her. "What?"

"If I'm a trap, you should let me die," she insisted. "Put me back into that Scotty thing and turn me back into energy. This isn't my time. My time has passed. I don't deserve another lifetime if living it means watching you pick up the pieces of your broken life."

"It's done!" he snapped. "I signed the order before you even came in here."

"But you can reverse it? You can tell them it was all just a mistake…"

"*I won't watch you die!*" he roared. His anger quickly subsided into a look of intense sadness as he added, tearfully, "Not again."

Susan's hands clasped over her mouth as she realized what he meant.

Just then, the door to the office opened, and Claude Remy reentered.

"Mr. President," he said, "I must inform you that the judiciary committee has voted to schedule your impeachment hearing." He paused. "Wednesday morning."

"Very well," the president replied. "Please take Susan to her pre-arranged living arrangements for me?"

"Of course, sir."

"Ajay?" Susan softly cried.

"Go on," said the president. "You'll be fine."

"But your career…"

"Was all but over anyway. Three years into a second four-year term. I never intended to run for a third term. I'm a lame duck."

"What if they put you in jail?"

"Country club for a few months at worst. Don't worry about me. I've been playing this game a long time. Now go. Go with Mr. Remy." He teared up slightly before adding, "I'll see you soon…

"…mother."

## Chapter 7: The Bullet That Shattered Time

He was going to commit the perfect crime. No, not crime. Crime was the wrong word because this was to be a righteous act. It was, however, the perfect assassination, by the perfect assassin. He was about to kill the greatest enemy the world had ever known: Adorjan Jaire Baptise Napolitano, President of the New United Nations.

He assembled his rifle carefully, piece by piece, removing each component from its case with delicate care, knowing he would have plenty of time to focus in on his target. His pulse rate quickened, as it always did when the critical moment was about to arrive, and savored the thrill. He loved this.

The only downside was that it was going to be too damned easy.

Armand Sanfelippo had experienced the thrill of killing like this before. The planning, the anticipation, the preparation, and then, double entendre intended, the execution. As a soldier, he'd done this many times in special forces, fighting the sort of battles that newsfeeds didn't report, but garnered one plenty of medals. Officially, there were no wars to fight. Not anymore. Unofficially, there was always someone the government wanted killed at a distance. Plus, there were always Third World clashes where Western Powers wanted to safeguard their interests. He could go into such situations and accomplish what was needed with a single shot – and did so often.

Sanfelippo was a sniper, one of the best the Navy Seals ever had. Or at least, he was, until he found his military career cut short by an injury to his left leg – the result of a drunken bar fight he should probably have never gotten into. But, some guy was being an absolute dick to a woman at a bar in Annapolis, so he decided to teach him a lesson about which lines ought not to be crossed. Bastard had it coming. He gave more than he got in terms of the actual fistfight, but he hadn't counted on the other guy packing heat. A single shot to his leg, and the fight was over. The gun-toting dumbass ran off. The woman, last he heard, went home alone. He hadn't even fancied her, and she never even thanked him.

He was taken to Bethesda Naval Hospital. The bullet had shattered his femur, nearly costing him his leg entirely. Multiple surgeries saved it, but he would never walk quite the same way again. He remained holed up for weeks in rehab, knowing his time as a soldier was over, and wondering what to do with his life. He lived for the kill. How could he cope without being given another target? Something to hunt?

He seldom talked to people, but he found himself confiding in a fellow soldier who was holed up in rehab, much the same way he was, except that he was a very old war vet recovering from a heart operation, a triple-bypass. When he told him about the sorrow he felt at not being able to legally kill anymore, his triple-bypass friend just laughed.

"You're pining after the wrong thing," he said. "People don't hunt with bullets anymore. Not really. The real hunting these days is done with computers. Hackers go in for the kill, just like snipers. But unlike snipers, they've got a lot more to things to target, and it's a lot easier to stay anonymous."

Armand scoffed at this. "That doesn't sound much like being a soldier."

Triple-bypass laughed again. "Son, the only wars that will be fought anymore are cyber wars. In a cyber war, only hackers are truly soldiers." Then he added with a wink, "And in a cyber *world*, only hackers are citizens."

That resonated with him. So, after getting processed out, he used his G.I. bill benefits to go to college at UVA to study computer engineering. It wasn't long before he picked up the basics of programming, and he was soon prowling the dark web for victims. Ostensibly, all hackers were white-hat hackers, as he soon learned, and everyone talked about doing "pen tests" to help corporations defend themselves from attacks, but Armand loved the kill. He took to black hat hacking, and soon picked up a small circle of friends online who were grey hats who helped him. He quickly developed a reputation as an unstoppable troll, as well as a formidable hacking threat. Few people knew who he really was. And when he found a suitable victim, he felt that same thrill he once felt as a sniper, having a target within his sights.

He never chose his victims at random. They were always people whom he deemed fit for destruction, people who had it coming. Sexual predators, Muslim extremists, communists, neo-Nazis, the sort of people who clearly deserved to have all their secrets exposed and their bank accounts drained. Besides, picking victims at random was child's play. Far too easy. He knew many hackers who played the numbers game – made their attack so multitudinous and wide that a few victims eventually always fell prey. But for him, that sort of thing was too non-specific. He preferred the challenge of finding a *specific* person, and overcoming whatever obstacles lay between it and himself.

The rest of his college life, and indeed the rest of his life in general, might have been a simple one of online predation, had *she* not come along.

She frequented the study lounge in the student union, and whenever she did, he couldn't take his eyes off her. She was perfect, perfect, perfect. Perfect ass, perfect breasts, perfect red hair, and though she dressed tastefully, her outfits left little to the imagination. He tried not to stare, but he couldn't help it. He leered, like she was something he had acquired in his crosshairs. Sometimes she would look his way, catch him staring, and smile. He would smile back. He couldn't help it. It felt strange, since he didn't really smile otherwise.

Day after day, that was their routine. He would take his lunch after morning classes, then spend the early afternoon in the lounge. At ten minutes past one, she would come in. At about 1:19, she would turn, smile, and he smiled back. That was it. That was all he expected it would ever be.

Until one day, she sauntered over and actually spoke to him.

"There's a rally going on tonight," she said. "Want to come?"

He was so utterly dumbfounded that she'd said something that he took a moment to recover. "Uh, *what?*"

"There's a rally tonight," she repeated. "You interested?" She was handing him a flier.

He took a look at it. It was some student Christian group called Chi Alpha. The rally was to feature some sort of Jesus-rock group followed by some message by a preacher he'd never heard of. So that was it. She wasn't truly interested in him. She smiled at him because she was a good little Jesus-freak, and she probably smiled like that at everybody. Well, fuck.

So, no one was more surprised than him when he heard the words come out of his mouth, as if spoken by someone else, "Sure, I'll go."

"Great!" she said. "See you there."

He watched her beautiful, beautiful ass leave the lounge, then looked back at the flier. Why the hell did he say that? He wasn't entirely sure. It wasn't like he disliked religion, but he'd never taken it all that seriously, either. Maybe he was bored. Then again, a girl like that could have asked him to swallow a cyanide pill and he would have momentarily considered it.

The rally, held off-campus at a nearby Lutheran church, was a little bit odd for him. The music was actually not half bad. The preaching was moderately tolerable. But oddest of all, *she* was there, and actually said 'hello,' to him, as though she somehow cared after she'd gotten him through the front door. She introduced herself as "Jessie." Armand nervously shook her hand and gave his own name. Then she stayed by his side during the entire event, as if she were actually glad he was there. It all felt surreal.

Towards the end, when the alter call came, something even stranger happened. He stood up, strode to the front of the church, and dedicated his life to God. Jessie came up behind him, laid her hand on his back, and prayed with him. So did a lot of other people.

She stayed right there with him afterwards through the night. In fact, she stayed with him long after the rally was over.

She stayed. Permanently.

He often wondered what she saw in him. He wondered more frequently why he was so damned lucky. He didn't feel he deserved a girlfriend like her. Maybe, he reasoned, it was just one of those situations where certain types exhibited special magnetism. She was the perfect 'good girl,' and he was her perfect, 'bad boy,' although he had a very difficult time believing himself to be even remotely perfect by any measure. All he really knew was that, when he dedicated his life to God, he knew that he was purposing himself for goodness and righteousness. That's all he really cared about. Let the theologians argue about the rest of it. If there was a God, he was on His side. And if there wasn't, well, he was on His side anyway.

Either way, he was on *her* side, and that's all that really mattered.

They married on June 11$^{th}$, 2068, a year after he graduated college.

His new, Christian lifestyle changed him. But he didn't stop hacking. He did, however, change the types of targets he chose. He started going after atheists, socialists, and liberals. These were the natural enemies of Christianity, and by extension, his wife. He didn't kill anyone, but he was able to destroy many aspects of their lives that existed online. Deep down, he still felt like a killer. Only now, he was a killer for God, taking out the trash wherever it needed removing. His young wife didn't understand his activities and simply took them to be an extension of his chosen career. He was fine keeping that part of his life sequestered from her.

When she told him in their first year of marriage that she was pregnant, he was delighted beyond measure. When she told him in their third year of marriage that she was pregnant again, he was happily overwhelmed. He had some pilfered funds from his earlier days of hacking where he'd preyed upon a deserving victim's bank account, and could move that money around skillfully so that Jessie didn't suspect anything, but even those financial resources would be stretched to the limit with two children.

Then came the day the liberals took things way too far. The New United Nations had been robbing nations of their sovereignty for years, but then some kid named Iousef Irfan actually dared to sue his parents to prevent them from indoctrinating him into the religion of Islam – and won. Armand didn't much care for Islam. In fact, he thought it was one of the worst blights ever vomited upon the human race. But now, thanks to this upstart kid and his victory in the meddlesome World Court, children had the "right" to not be indoctrinated. By *any* religion.

That meant all children, *everywhere*. That meant some bureaucrat having some "representative" in his kids' preschool, telling him that he couldn't raise his own, perfect babies, borne by their unbelievably perfect mother, to be perfect Christians.

It made him so angry at times he could barely breathe. Jessie started talking about selling the house and joining some of their fellow congregation members in leaving Earth to join a colony on Mars – just to escape the U.N.'s damnable jurisdiction. His blood absolutely boiled. If anyone was a deserving target for a hacker attack, it was those numbskulls on the World Court!

Perhaps that's why, on a cold November night, he took things a bit too far.

There were twenty-four justices on the World Court. Armand could have targeted any of them, but he wanted the biggest one. Chief Justice Antonin Kleczka was not only an American, but he wrote the majority opinion. Taking him out would send a clear and unambiguous message about not crossing certain lines.

He went into full stealth mode, bringing all his experience to the fore. Public officials were the toughest to get information on, but he'd hacked the back-channels years ago. The protection services that most people used to black out their Netstream footprints were his to access. So he did. He soon knew where Kleczka lived, the route he took to work, the name of his wife, the names of his relatives, the names of his wife's relatives, his kids names, all of it. But they weren't his targets. He did not hold it against someone to be related to a criminal. A child does not choose his parents, nor a child his siblings. Even choosing a spouse was largely a matter of luck, as he knew all too well. So he held nothing against those other people. They were merely leverage – if he should need it. But with the speed and efficiency of his work, he wouldn't.

Finding the man's bank account numbers was pathetically easy. The man trusted the U.N. to keep his financial information secure, but that firewall was vulnerable. So did the email system that the U.N.N. used. The silly man actually used his work email as his personal email most of the time, so cracking that one gave him access to everything else. Using the personal information he'd garnered, he quickly gained access to Kleczka's bank account. He intercepted the confirmation email from the bank, sent back the confirmation code, and deleted the evidence. He was also able to block and reroute the bank's SMS message to a dummy phone – a hacker trick he'd perfected with a little bit of know-how, some discarded military hardware, and a road trip to Virginia where he attached his homemade device to the cell tower nearest Kleczka's home. The bank account was now, effectively, his.

He watched that account for a few weeks, seeing the ebb and flow of money. He saw the bills, the groceries, the usual transactions – nothing untoward. This guy was pure-bean vanilla. But he also saw the regular deposit of 230,000 Euros, twice each month, every 1st and 15th.

He also saw the regular deposit of €15,000 to a retirement account. And that account was a cool 1.5 million.

On week seven of his stealth operation, he struck. He emptied Kleczka's account of €240,000 right on the morning of payday, and quickly emptied the €1.5 million savings account into several dozen banks worldwide almost simultaneously, never exceeding the 2,000 Euro limit which would trigger investigation. He then moved that money around several more dozen levels, with hundreds of transactions at each level, making it a shell-game of transactions.

He buried his tracks so deep even Interpol wouldn't find them.

Had he been single, he would have left the money alone indefinitely. Not having any pressing need for cash meant that one could simply let hot money cool off until it was safer to launder. And it wasn't about stealing the money – it was about denying the money to the target. But being a father meant meeting certain obligations, and his wife let him manage the money, so he could slide some cash under the rug from time to time, and often had. This money, however, was too recent. Too hot. If he were just a little bit more patient, he could have moved the money into Marsmarks, since Mars was the only entity that still used crypto-currency. Or he could even have gone old school and converted the money into untraceable assets like gold or silver before daring to bring any of it closer to him. But he was just a little too over-confident. And the sure knowledge that he was righteous in his actions before God made him a little too sure that he would not be found.

He was.

He only converted a few hundred Euros into dollars and moved it into the U.S., but that's all it took. They nabbed him when he visited a local café he was fond of. It had Netstream access, and it was one of several locations he chose to bury his access just one more level, keeping it that much farther from home, although his VPN and multiple-port strings made certain that one more level was merely superfluous.

Within ten minutes of accessing one of his accounts in Johannesburg, two men in black business suits entered the Café.

"Armand Sanfelippo?" one of them asked.

He played it cool. "Who wants to know?" he asked.

"You're coming with us," the man replied.

He could have put up a struggle. Made a scene. Fought tooth and toenail. But went with the men willingly. He wasn't quite sure why. He just had a feeling it was the right thing to do. They put him into a black SUV (some cliché's never change) and drove him off, hood-over-head.

After about 45 minutes of driving, they pulled him from the vehicle and escorted him inside a building. He wasn't sure where, but it had a lot of stairs. In his hooded state, he nearly tripped over all of them. He realized he'd been shoved into some sort of room when he heard a door latch click behind him. He was pushed backward into a chair and then someone finally removed his hood.

Armand didn't recognize him. He was short, middle-aged, and unassuming. Yet he held the air of someone who'd held power for a very long time.

"DarkPatriot180," the man said, using his most common hacker name. "Never thought I'd see the day."

"Who's that?" Armand asked.

The man gave a look as though he'd just been handed a three-dollar-bill. "Don't even try. We've been following you for years." He drew close. "And rather *personally* for the better part of a year."

Armand wasn't sure what that meant. He'd never been caught before, so he had no usual response. He decided to stick to his guns and said, "I have no idea what you're talking about."

"Have it your way," said the man. "Your name is Armand Sanfelippo, service number 229-34-6087. Retired Navy, honorable medical discharge at the rank of Petty Officer First Class. Your wife's name is Jessie Crumbacher, your sons are Martin and Greyson, you're a former Navy Seal Team 8 sniper, and you recently defunded Justice Antonin Kleczka of nearly every single penny to his name. How am I doing so far?"

Armand remained silent.

"So let me save you some time. My name is Marlin Kettrel. I'm the director of Homeland Security. I know you're a hacker, and I know you're damned good. I also know you're in a world of trouble. But you're a hacker for God, and that goes a long way towards getting on my good side. You want to get out of this? You'll do what I tell you."

He resisted the urge to swallow hard. "What the hell do you want from me?"

Kettrel, smiled. "I want you to put your skills to work for us. I looked up your service record. You were a damned good soldier. You could be a damned good soldier again. Does that interest you?"

Armand felt a divine presence. This was it. This was what the Lord wanted him to do.

"Yes, sir!"

"Then go home to your wife. We'll be in touch."

He was hooded again and driven home.

For almost two weeks, he didn't hear anything. His wife noticed his change in mood, and commented about it. He told her that it was just problems at work and nothing to really worry about. That explanation seemed to satisfy her.

Finally, an anonymous phone call came at work. He was given an assignment in the form of a target to kill. He didn't know who the target was. He didn't particularly care. Whoever it was, it was a test. They wanted to see if he could follow orders to the letter. He didn't care about that. He only cared that this was a chance to be God's vengeance.

This was a chance to feel the thrill of killing once more.

He'd kept his sniper rifle in storage for years. Getting it out felt like a holy ritual. He cleaned it, checked it, repacked it in its case, and then took it with him to his assignment. He wanted to take it to a remote field and re-calibrate it. Maybe practice a bit to get the feel of it once more. But there wasn't time. He would simply have to rely on whatever training and skills he'd retained after all these years.

His old training did not desert him. He followed the plan to the letter, took out his target flawlessly, and got out of his perch without leaving a trace. One shot, clean through the head. It was beautiful.

Kettrel was impressed. During the debriefing he said, "That was a fine job you did. You've told no one about it? Not even your wife?"

"No, sir," he said. "You were specific about that."

"And it doesn't bother you? The person you killed? Who he was? What he did for a living?"

"Sir, if the Good Lord meant him to live, He would have stopped me," Armand answered. He was surprised at how deeply he believed it when he said it.

Ketrrel smiled. "Very well. You'll get your payment, plus a little bonus. But perhaps you'd like to work for me full-time?"

Armand couldn't imagine anything he wanted more.

He was delighted to share the news of this new "job" with his wife, even though it meant the two of them would have to stay on Earth permanently. He didn't really know what the job would entail, but he'd been given a cover story and he stuck to it. The amount of money he'd just brought home was impressive. She acquiesced, and vowed that she would teach her kids Christianity in secret. A lot of parents were doing that, anyway.

As it turned out, the job basically involved being Kettrel's hatchet-man. Sometimes Armand was asked to hack a particular target. Other times, he was asked to shoot one. It didn't matter. If Kettrel said there was a mess to clean up, he'd go in and do so. Usually with a single shot or final keystroke. And the FBI made sure nothing ever traced back to him.

Then came the day Armand saw it: the most wonderous device he'd ever seen. Kettrel called it a Scotty, apparently because it could turn matter directly into energy, just like Scotty could do on that old television show. Kettrel had stepped down as Homeland Security director to become head of something called the Temporal Bureau – because the Scotty could materialize things across time as well as space. Armand was put under the command of a Colonel named Ajith Acharya, and assigned to be trained by a skeletally thin man named Randall Gosling. Ostensibly, Armand was to serve as Gosling's assistant. In reality, he was there to learn how to use the Scotty for Kettrel's secret missions.

The Scotty could do amazing things. Armand saw how it could scan a computer for dematerialization and, in so doing, learn *exactly* what information the device contained! *No wonder they found me so quickly*, Armand realized. Such information harvesting could even theoretically be done with the human brain, once they perfected it. It seemed like there was nothing this machine couldn't do.

It could even give him the perfect cover to commit an assassination.

When Kettrel informed him it was time to use the Scotty to kill U.N. President Napolitano, Armand felt a surge of righteous fervor. Who needed a colony on Mars when one could simply re-take Earth! He'd learned enough about the Scotty's capabilities to be able to pick a target and take it out, but no one had ever tried to fire a sniper bullet through a Scotty transport aperture before. It could transport objects in motion easily, but a sniper bullet was much faster than anything they'd attempted before.

"Our calculations say it's possible, but we're not exactly sure. Give it a try on a neutral target after hours tomorrow," Kettrel ordered. "Do it after Gosling goes home. See if it works."

Armand did. It was remarkably easy. A simple pumpkin in the middle of a farm he knew of in Pennsylvania provided plenty of targets with no one around to notice. Using the Scotty's Macroscope, he picked out a pumpkin. Then he took aim and shot it. The pumpkin shattered. Then, he closed the aperture. Just like that, the concept was proven sound. The Scotty could enable a mobile sniper bullet to materialize hundreds of miles away! Even with an object travelling in excess of 2,000 miles per hour, the matter-energy conversion was nearly instantaneous, with no loss of velocity!

That brought Armand to the present moment, where he prepared to shoot Napolitano, just as he had that pumpkin. It would be the easiest kill he'd ever made. Too easy, in fact. Furthermore, he would be bending time in order to do it. He was targeting Napolitano's location one hour into the future. In so doing, he would be able to shoot, kill him, and then go to the National Mall in Washington D.C. and see his own shot take the bastard out! It would be spectacular!

The vantagepoint Armand chose was especially cruel. He made the Scotty aperture appear directly above the podium, over where Napolitano's head would be. The shot would come straight down, through the top of his skull and down the center of his torso. His brain would turn to mush at the same time his aorta would be shredded. Nothing would save him.

One of the beautiful aspects of his plan was how the Scotty aperture would be concealed. A Scotty detection field could cause such an aperture to glow with blue light. Having such detection fields were now standard procedure around heads of state. But Napolitano was giving a speech outdoors, and the sky was clear. A blue light against a blue background would be nearly invisible. It was perfect.

Armand adjusted the Scotty's materialization axis so that the bullet would enter the aperture horizontally, but exit vertically. From his vantagepoint, he would see Napolitano as though the entire world were tilted up on its side.

Napolitano took the stage to the screaming cheers of his supporters. Armand grinned at the thought those cheering screams would be transformed into screams of horror. He took aim as he approached the podium. He let him say a few introductory words. Then…

…he took the shot.

Napolitano crumpled like a dropped marionette. The cheers of the spectators indeed turned to screams of horror. People began looking around to see where the shot had come from. In their confusion, not one person, *not one*, ever thought to look straight up.

He closed the aperture, then shut down the Scotty. With practiced efficiency, he packed up his gun, re-cased it, then recovered his shell casing, as he always did. He never left a nest without making sure it was absolutely clean.

He wiped the Scotty's logs. Then he wiped the panel clean of any fingerprints.

In the short time it took to drive to the National Mall, where Napolitano was giving his address, he chuckled to himself about how easy the assassination had been. That made the kill slightly less satisfying. But that was compensated for by *who* had been killed. Heads of state were the most difficult to kill, but this one had been easy. Every future assassination would be equally as easy given Scotty technology. But he'd been the first. His was the initial kill. If he were somehow to be caught, he would be remembered forever.

But catching him was impossible. The Scotty was the ultimate in stealth technology. No one would be able to determine how it was done, much less who had taken the shot. Hell, he was about to attend the event itself and witness the event as a bystander – the ultimate alibi!

He had placed his rifle back in its secret location long before arriving at the National Mall. It was always much easier to find parking by going east of the White House to a structure there, then walking to the National Mall and the Lincoln Memorial. He wove his way through the crowds who had gathered to hear Napolitano speak. He checked the time on his iris-link. He'd arrived ten minutes before his fired shot. Ten excruciating minutes of waiting before he got to see his handiwork. He used the time to look for a suitable place to get the best view. There wasn't an ideal one, but a small knoll Northeast of the Lincoln Memorial sufficed.

Finally, Napolitano took the stage and he felt the thrill of killing he'd felt before – only this time, he was about to feel it *twice!* He felt privileged.

Out of curiosity, he looked up to see if the Scotty aperture were visible. It was – barely. That meant there was a Scotty detection field in place. But the blue light was so faint against the blue sky he could scarcely make it out, and that was with him *knowing* it was there. For everyone else, that aperture was practically invisible.

He heard no shot, but saw Napolitano crumple. He felt the satisfaction of seeing it. He heard the same screams he'd heard an hour earlier, replayed as though it were a recording. People rushed to Napolitano's side, looking to help him.

Then, hands *seized* him from seemingly everywhere!

He wasn't sure what was going on. Everything was a blur. He felt himself being pushed to the ground, rolled over, someone put handcuffs on him, and he heard an unfamiliar voice speaking:

"We got him, sir. He's in custody."

"What?!" he shouted. "What the hell are you talking about?"

Nobody answered him. He was pulled to his feet by strong arms, then pushed along somewhere. He couldn't see on account of all the dark suits which surrounded him. The crush of the crowd was overwhelming. He heard people screaming at him. He felt things being thrown, but he couldn't tell what they were. Finally, the crowd of dark suits parted in front of him wide enough to reveal a black sky pod. He was shoved into the back seat and then began to comprehend his surroundings.

In the front of the vehicle sat two people. He didn't know the driver. But the front passenger he knew! The red hair over an Asian face was unmistakable. It was Sarita Shantay, Deputy Director for Scotty Operations, second behind Marlin Kettrel.

She turned in her seat to face him.

"Thought you could assassinate the President of the New U.N. and get away with it, did you?"

He was gabberflasted. He tried to ask, 'How could you possibly know?' but caught himself. He didn't want to accidentally incriminate himself. After all, they *couldn't* know anything. The Scotty made his activities completely untraceable.

Could they?

Sarita saw the expression on his face. "You're wondering how we could possibly know, aren't you?" she asked. "It's quite simple, really. Historians from the future clued us in to who you were and where we would find you."

His thoughts raced. That simply *wasn't* possible! Numerous attempts to change the past had been attempted and they had all failed. Something about the past prevented anything from interfering with it. It was an immutable law of spacetime mechanics. They had even given it a name: *The Twelve Monkeys Effect*. Named after an old classic of sci fi where someone travelled back in time to alter history and failed.

"You're wondering about the Twelve Monkeys effect, right?" she added. "Funny thing about that. If the attempt to change history is done before the event occurs, it *can* be changed." She turned around to face forward, and the vehicle took off into the air. "A couple of kids on Mars, of all places, stumbled upon that little fact. We took note of it ever since. You see, the moment we saw the president had been shot, we hit a panic button that automatically messaged future Scotty users, inquiring as to the whereabouts of the perpetrator." She turned around again, and smiled. "They dutifully let us know where you would be after the assassination. Oh, we couldn't change the part where Napolitano got shot. That part was history. Unchangeable. But we could at least catch his murderer."

So that was it. That was the loophole that allowed Scotty users to alter a historical event. And they had used it to catch him.

He said nothing. There was nothing to be said.

He would be put on trial. It would be a circus. Provision for the death penalty would almost certainly be made. His fate was pre-ordained.

He thought about Jamie, and their two boys. They'd stayed on Earth for his sake. For the sake of being able to make a difference and take back the planet for God. Well, perhaps he had. Perhaps Napolitano's death had actually made the heathens pause and re-evaluate. At the very least, he'd struck a sizeable blow.

No major head of state had been assassinated since Kennedy, and none had been shot since Reagan. He'd been the first to actually accomplish that feat in well over a century. No matter what else happened, he would be remembered. That seemed small compensation for Jamie and the boys not having a father, but at least he would die a martyr.

They would try to make him talk. But no. He decided he was done talking. He would surrender no information, nor give up any names. He was caught. Keeping quiet was the only thing left he could control.

He began feeling the thrill of death one last time. Only this time, the death was his own.

He decided to welcome it. One more completed mission. So what if the target was himself?

He was a martyr. He was immortal. His reward was with God.

## Chapter 8: Scotty-Free

"But I didn't do it!" cried Randall Gosling as he jumped to his feet. The wide-eyed, frantic look on his face, and the way he held his clenched fists at his temples, caused several people on the jury to recall Edvard Munch's 'The Scream.'

"Order in the court!" Barked the overweight and appropriately named Judge Rover. His sagging cheeks and jowls flopped about like those of a baying St. Bernard as he spoke. "Ms. Rockport, you will restrain your client from any further outbursts, or I will rule him in contempt of court."

"Yes, your honor," the nervous lawyer replied. Turning to her client, she hoarsely whispered "For God's sake, Randall, sit down!"

"But – it's a *lie*, can't you see?" Randall objected, refusing to lower his volume one bit. His trembling finger pointed to the viewscreen at the front of the courtroom – the one that, a moment ago, clearly showed him killing Bernard Lewis, the former head of the Republican National Committee. Two gunshots to the head, one in each eye.

"As a matter of fact, *no*, I can't see," Rockport told him, still trying to keep her voice down. "All I can see is clear footage showing your guilt."

She was annoyed, but tried not to show it. The footage was as much a surprise for her as it was for her client. All they knew beforehand was that Macroscope surveillance footage of the crime would be shown. Nobody knew how damning it would be, except maybe the prosecution. Her client had insisted that any such footage would exonerate him; maybe reveal that the crime was committed by a look-alike.

"But it's not true!" Gosling pleaded, as loud as ever.

"Ms. Rockport!" called the judge.

"One moment, your honor," Jenna called back, then faced her client. "At least *try* to keep your voice down, will you?"

"But don't you see?" Gosling tried again. "It *can't* be true. I mean, it looks convincing, but the footage must be *faked*, somehow."

"Faked?" She contemplated the idea for all of a nanosecond. "Impossible. The Scotty's Macroscope is infallible at revealing the past. You know that better than anyone. You helped develop the technology. You've even testified in other court cases as to how impossible it is to fake such evidence."

"Then I was *wrong*, wasn't I? Someone found a way to hack the system. I don't know how, but they must have. Maybe they replaced the footage with a deepfake or something. But whatever they did, that's *not* me! You've *got* to believe me!"

Jenna looked into the pleading eyes of her thoroughly *fucked* client and saw the sincerity, the panic, and the utter desperation that was apparent there. Gosling was either innocent, or completely stark-raving mad.

Jenna Rockport was newly minted off the bar, looking to make her way in the world any way she could after daring to open her own practice right out of the gate. When an impossibly thin, middle-aged man named Randall Gosling came into her office complaining that nobody else would take his case, Jenna took it. Hell, she needed the money. She'd take anything. But she hadn't expected a shit storm like *this* to be the result.

"Ms. Rockport," the judge interrupted again, "are you able to restrain your client, or not?"

Jenna threw up her hands as if trying to throw the weight of the whole situation onto the floor. "Your Honor, may I have a brief recess to confer with my client?"

The judge considered this for a moment. "Oh, very well," he conceded. "But only because we've mostly put in a full day already. We'll adjourn early today and re-convene at 9:00 A.M. tomorrow morning."

The sound of the pounding gavel made Gosling startle so badly that Jenna thought his nerves would jump out and flee the courtroom, writhing away like living ramen noodles.

Back at Jenna's rather Spartan office, they reviewed the footage that was shown at trial, which she had received from the D.A. that evening.

There were special rules regarding Macroscope footage, thanks largely to international laws imposed by the New United Nations. Macroscope footage was only allowed to be initially shown at trial by an official of DARPA to prevent anyone from tampering with it. Jenna had naturally requested a copy immediately after the court session ended, and the D.A. obliged since it had already been presented at trial. There was nothing to gain by withholding it.

Together, Jenna and her client went over every minute of the startling footage, looking for anything which might provide a clue as to the severe disparity between what the Macroscope showed as historical fact, and what Randall Gosling remembered about that day. The Macroscope had captured several dozen different angles spanning several hours. Repeatedly they viewed the images and saw the same progression of events. Randall could be seen taking his usual route to work at DARPA Headquarters in Arlington County, Virginia. His dark hair, which barely showed any grey, plus his remarkably slim body type, made him easy to follow, even in a crowd. He boarded the Metra, got off at Virginia Square, then walked the remainder of the way down Wilson Boulevard, turning left onto Randolph Street just before entering the DARPA complex.

The only part where Gosling's memory and the footage disagreed was where it showed him veering off course to enter Gold's Gym, pull a .357 Magnum from some random person's gym bag, and then shoot Bernard Lewis twice in the face with it.

"I don't get it," said Jenna. "There you are, clearly shooting the guy."

"And *I'm* telling you, I didn't do it. I have no memory of it," Randall insisted.

The lawyer shook her head. "Do you remember boarding the Metra?" she asked.

"Yes," her client answered.

"And walking down Wilson?"

"Certainly."

"But you don't remember going into Gold's Gym?"

"Hell, as far as I can remember, I've *never* been inside that place!" Randall insisted. "Do I look like I work out? I must have walked past the place hundreds of times, but never once thought to go inside."

Jenna scratched her chin for a moment as though she were a man with a five-o'clock-shadow, and briefly wondered what that would feel like. Randall certainly had a point. His frame had no muscle on it whatsoever. He was middle-aged, and probably hadn't lifted a single weight since high school, and even then only because his gym teacher made him do it. "Well, it sure *looks* like you entered there at least once," she finally said.

"I never did, I'm telling you!"

"Fine. Then how do you explain what the Macroscope is showing?"

Randall threw up his arms in exasperation. "Damned if I know! I have a clear memory up to about Pollard Street. I remember walking by the pet store. After that…"

Jenna knew the rest. After that, nothing. "When do you recall walking again?"

Randall thought for a moment. "Somewhere around the corner of Wilson and Randolph, I guess. I remember distinctly turning the corner."

"So, that means that for a block and a half, you just blacked out?"

Randall shrugged. "I guess I must have."

Jenna's eyebrows crunched together like two trains colliding on the same track. "And it didn't strike you as odd that you were suddenly missing a chunk of time?"

"Not really," he admitted. "To be honest, I just figured I was daydreaming or something."

"Shit," she said. "That's not helpful at all. The defense of 'I just blacked out, Your Honor,' is about as cliché an excuse as you can possibly get, and no jury's going to buy it. Can't you recall anything else? I mean, seriously, if we can't find something more solid than you having a blackout, we're screwed."

Now it was Randall's turn to shake his head. "Right now, the fact that I can't remember anything is the only basis for my defense."

"Well, that's empirical for *you*. For the rest of us, you're asking us to take your word for it." Jenna reversed the footage to the point of the murder and replayed it. She paused when the man who was presumably Gosling reached for the gun. "So odd that you went right to *that* particular bag to get the gun…"

"It wasn't me!"

"Okay, okay, it wasn't *you*," Jenna conceded. "So, for want of an alternate hypothesis, let's call it the demon that temporarily possessed you…"

"Seriously?"

"You have something better?"

He didn't.

"Okay, then," Jenna continued. "The 'demon' goes straight for the gun. See that? No hesitation. It's like he knows the gun is there beforehand. As though it were planned."

Randall watched the footage as though seeing it for the first time. "Yeah," he said. "That's really weird."

"So how did you… I mean, how did *he* know it was there?"

"How the fuck should I know?" Randall answered.

"Don't be like that. I'm trying to help you, here. Do you know whose bag that is?"

"Jesus, Jenna, I don't even know whose *gun* that is!"

Neither did Jenna. The gun, as had been revealed during trial, was unregistered. The gym bag belonged to the murdered man. "So why would you… er, the man in the video, go straight for *that* particular bag?"

The DARPA scientist thought about that a moment, putting his engineering brain cells to work. "It *must* have been planned," he agreed. "There's no other logical explanation."

"That's my impression, too," Jenna agreed.

"So that's evidence of a conspiracy, right?" Randall said, sounding hopeful.

"It's not nearly enough," Jenna said. "It's a clue, from our perspective, but for the prosecution, it's still tantamount to nothing. We're going to need a lot more than that if we're saying the camera… er, the *Scotty Macroscope*, was lying. Or, at least not telling the whole story."

Jenna rewound and played the scene over again a few more times, looking for any particular detail that might stand out. None did. But it was then that she heard a beeping noise. She looked over at her client and noticed that the beeping was coming from a classic-style Smartwatch Randall was wearing.

Randall tapped his Smartwatch to stop the beeping, looking slightly annoyed.

"Nice Scimitar," she said.

"Huh?"

"Your old-fashioned Smartwatch."

"Oh," said Randall. "Yeah, it's a bit old-school, but I like it. Makes me look distinguished."

Jenna didn't think he looked distinguished at all. 'Vintage' was the kindest word she could come up with, although 'dated' was a lot more precise. It basically shouted to the world that he was a man who refused to change with the times and would rather have something old bulging out on his wrist like some 20$^{th}$ century piece of clockwork than have an iris-link contact-lens, or an Ex-Drive wired into his brain, or something else more modern. Sure, Smartwatches were vogue when celebrities wore them while jogging around Hollywood in the twenty-twenties, but those same celebrities ditched them when people started hacking them to track their movements.

That train of thought made Jenna realize something. "Hey, does that wrist-thing of yours have a fitness monitor app?" she asked.

"Well, sure, but I never use it. I told you, I don't work out."

"But it's there? Step monitor, heart rate, all that?"

"I guess so. Why?"

"Think it has your health-related data for the time period on this Macroscope footage?"

Randall let that sink in, then his eyes widened. "*Sure*, it would! Give me a sec…" He fussed with the icons on his wrist phone and found the data inside the app. For once, default settings paid off. Porting the data over to the computer screen, Jenna was able to sync up the time markers and juxtapose it with the Macroscope footage. Sure enough, during the exact moments Randall was having his mysterious 'blackout,' and in the exact same geographic location, the heart rate and respiration recorded by the fitness monitor radically changed. The heart rate was much faster, and the breathing was much shallower.

"That's it!" Randall said. "We've finally got something!"

"Yes," his lawyer agreed. "But I still don't think it will be enough."

"Why not? Such radically different heartbeat and respiration proves it must be someone else inside my body."

"How?" Jenna asked. "I mean, if you can't actually *show* that some sort of demonic possession was taking place, the argument could simply be that your heartbeat spiked because you were nervous right around the time of the crime being committed. It's certainly an argument a jury would understand."

Randall started to object, then gave up. Jenna was right. Unless the mechanism of the 'possession' was shown, there was no point in arguing anything about an increased heartbeat.

Randall's Smartwatch beeped again.

Jenna raised an eyebrow. "Who the hell keeps calling you?"

"Oh, it's just my mother," Randall answered.

Jenna looked at him as though he'd just sprouted rabbit ears. "You're kidding."

"No," he admitted. "What can I say? I'm a mama's boy."

She kept staring at him. She'd had some weird clients during the short time she'd been a lawyer, but this one was full of surprises. Still, her own mother called her all the time. Why should it seem so strange when it happened to a man? "Aren't you a little bit old to be helicopter-parented?" she asked.

"Eh," Randall shrugged. "I put up with it because I don't know how much longer I'll have her around. I mean, it's not like the Scotty is being used to make people young, yet."

Jenna tried to formulate an answer but found herself snagged by her own thoughts. There was certainly no reason why the Scotty couldn't be used to make people young. Why hadn't that happened yet? It was already being used in place of most cosmetic surgeries. She suddenly realized that control of this device, which could potentially be an endless fountain of youth, would be quite a compelling motive for framing one of its developers for murder.

If only she could see a connection.

"I keep putting her off," Randall continued. "I mean, we're kind of in the middle of something important, here."

"Might as well answer it," Jenna told him with a sigh. "We're spinning our wheels at the moment. Take a break. Talk to your mother."

Randall shrugged and answered his watch. "Hi, mom," he said.

"Rand! Dear! Honestly, don't you *ever* answer your phone?"

Jenna grinned. Because it was a wrist-phone, she could hear her voice clearly. And the sound of it covered all the cliches. Elderly mothers were the same everywhere.

"I've been a little busy, mom. Haven't you been watching the newsfeeds?"

"Of course, I have. But that was why I was calling. Haven't you been able to find out who framed you for that awful shooting?"

"No, mom, nothing yet," Randall admitted. "Whoever set me up really has me in a pickle."

"Well, you'll solve the puzzle, dear," his mother said. "You always do. After all, you avoided suspicion when that former assistant of yours shot the U.N. president, right?"

Jenna sat bolt upright at this. She'd read that in the newsfeeds and then completely forgot about it. But that was *big* news at the time. In fact, it was the primary reason no other lawyer wanted to take Gosling's case. *Holy shit!* Could her client's case be mixed up with the assassination of President Napolitano?

"I might not be able to solve *this* puzzle, mom," he told her. "Right now, all we can see is a change in the shooter's heartbeat and respiration during the exact time of the shooting. But if we can't find anything more solid than that, I'm afraid we're sunk."

"Well, why don't you check the baby-tracker?" she asked.

Randall and Jenna looked at each other. "The *what?*" they both asked simultaneously.

"The baby-tracker. Back when you were born, everybody was doing it. We wanted to be able to find you if you ever got lost or kidnapped or something. We implanted the chip as soon as you were old enough to walk."

Randall made the sort of face he might make if a fresh lemon had been squeezed into his right eye. "You put a *chip* in me?!"

"Hey, I wouldn't get pissed off about that if I were you," Jenna interrupted. "Right now, that chip is the only thing giving your case a glimmer of hope."

"Is that your lawyer?" said Mrs. Gosling. "Oh, bless your soul for defending my boy! You know, he was always so smart, but somehow, he always found trouble. But it seemed like there was always a good Samaritan who was there at just the right…"

"Yes, yes," Jenna interrupted. "Could you tell us more about this chip?"

"Oh, sure." The old woman's voice seemed to brighten. "It's located in Randall's calf behind his left knee. Like I said, all the young parents were doing that back then. You know, when you're a new mother you're so terrified that something will happen…"

"And this chip monitors your son's movements?" Jenna interrupted again. "Even today?"

"I think so. It was a lifetime contract, after all. The salesman said…"

"Do you think you could remember the name of the company?"

"Certainly. It was LifeSaver Enterprises."

"And do you still have the tracking number of the chip?"

"Oh, let me see, I'm pretty sure I wrote that down and tucked it somewhere. Now where did I leave it?"

Both Jenna and Randall hung their heads and covered their eyes.

Randall suddenly uncovered his face and sat bolt upright as he realized something. "Wait, mother, you didn't use this tracker on me when I was in high school, did you?"

"I neither confirm nor deny anything, dear," she replied.

After some digging on the part of Mrs. Gosling and some incredibly impatient handwringing by both lawyer and client, they were finally able to sign into the LifeSaver Netstream portal and download Randall's movements for the day in question. Not long after, they superimposed that data with the Macroscope footage and aligned the time signatures just like before.

Sure enough, right about the point where Randall crossed Pollard Street, the chip's signal winked out for a few seconds.

"There!" cried Randall. "That's where I blacked out. And the signal goes dead right at that point."

"But it comes back on again," Jenna pointed out. "What could that mean?"

Randall thought about that for a moment. "I'm not sure. Fast forward to the point when my memory resumes."

Jenna did so. Right before Randall was seen approaching Randolph Street, the signal winked out for a few seconds once more.

"It happened again!" Randall practically jumped in the air as he said it. "Something interfered with the signal right at the beginning and end of my blackout."

"Okay, now we're in business," exclaimed Jenna. "We finally have some solid evidence that someone interfered with your life at exactly that time frame. But how did they interfere? What could cause this sort of 'blip' in the tracking chip?"

Randall pondered this, and then suddenly stood up. "Oh!" he cried. "Oh, no, they wouldn't dare!"

"Who wouldn't dare?" asked Jenna.

"Oh, uh," Randall started, "well, I'm actually not exactly sure who, but whoever it was, if they somehow got their hands on a Scotty…"

"Wait, someone could replace you with a Scotty double?" Jenna asked.

"Sure," Randall replied. "The Scotty could rearrange your molecules to make you look like anybody. As long as the molecular pattern is available, you could get Scottied to look like Taylor Swift, Elvis, or Meryl Streep."

"I'd rather be Marilyn Monroe if it came to it," Jenna replied. "But hang on, they could materialize a double which is superimposed over an existing body? At the same time? In mid-stride, no less?"

"Of course. It's much easier if the person is moving the same way when the transfer takes place, but it's not absolutely necessary. Early versions of the Scotty had to transport things that were perfectly stationary, but not anymore. A person who's standing motionless still has movement; heartbeat, respiration, blood flow... all these are moving parts. It would be no problem to replace someone with a body double, even if that person were running at full speed, never mind walking."

Jenna's mind raced. It made sense, and yet was so incredible! She'd always thought of the Scotty as a simple matter-energy transporter. She hadn't thought of using it to switch out a real person for an imposter – right in the middle of a city street in broad daylight, no less!

"So, if that was someone else who got Scottied into your own body, where did you, that is your original body, go?"

"Probably got held in computer memory somewhe – oh, fuck!"

"What?" Jenna jumped, startled by Randall's outburst. "What is it?"

"That means I'm actually a copy of Randall Gosling! Shit!" He started pacing around the room. "I'm going to need to get treated for omphalos psychosis."

Jenna had heard that term before. Where had she heard it? Then she remembered. "Oh yeah, that existential dread thing. The after-effect of using the Scotty that the newsfeeds keep talking about."

"That's the one," Randall said. "Bastards! They killed me and resurrected me just so that they could frame me!"

Jenna's brow furrowed. She understood the general concept of the Scotty not actually being a transport; that it was really a form of death and rebirth. But when it came right down to it, her brain rebelled against that and wanted to believe the same person had simply been transported. It was easier to pretend the person had simply "moved." But that simply wasn't true. And the knowledge that he had died and been re-made as a copy, that he was not the original Randall Gosling, would eventually drive him mad. That's what omphalos psychosis was.

"They can treat people for that now?" she asked.

"After a fashion," Randall replied. "They use the Scotty to alter your brain. So you don't actually feel fear as sharply." He started pacing again. "It's like unplugging the whole mechanism to prevent the ailment, or deliberately severing a nerve to cure chronic pain. But it's basically a micro-lobotomy." He shook his head as he paced. "Fuck!"

Jenna had nothing to say in response to that. It made sense, but in a confusing sort of way. Her attention drifted back to the Macroscope footage, and the tracking chip signal that winked out right at the end of Randall's "blackout." Then, she noticed something.

"Hey," Jenna said, "look at this."

Randall stopped pacing and came back to look at the computer screen. "That's the second time the tracker blinked out," he observed. "So what? What am I supposed to see?"

"The strength of the signal," Jenna replied. "See that?" She pointed to the period just after the second 'blink.' "The signal's output doubles in magnitude."

Randall looked carefully. There was really no way to know whether the signal's strength had actually "doubled" like Jenna claimed. But the little dot on the map, the one that displayed "his" location, certainly looked a lot larger and brighter after the second 'blip' than before.

"What could cause that?" Jenna wondered aloud.

Randall had no answer for her. He was thinking. If his body's pattern had been stored in a computer during the murder, the tracking chip should have remained unaltered. Yet this one apparently was altered in some way. The signal output had been boosted. But why? Did someone want to make it easier to find him after the incident? That would certainly make it easier for law enforcement. But the law had no difficulty in capturing him at all because he'd had no idea he was even a suspect. All the cops had to do was visit DARPA and slap on the handcuffs. Why would he have even thought of running? And by extension, why would those who set this up even consider the possibility? They might not have even known about the tracking chip. So, if ease of tracking wasn't the point, what was?

Then he figured it. If the chip had something added to it, it would need more power. His tracking chip would only need a few microvolts. But if something else got connected to the circuit, such as a fleck-drive, it might need a dozen microvolts or more. That would mean more energy would be needed than simple subdermal biochemical conversion could provide. A tiny battery would have to be added to the ensemble. And the net result of that…

…would be a much stronger signal from the chip.

"I think we need to remove my tracking chip so that we can have a look at it," Randall eventually said.

Jenna gave Randall a sour look. "It's late," she told him. "And you have to be in court again tomorrow morning. Where on Earth are you going to get someone willing to remove and analyze an outdated, childhood tracking chip at this hour?"

"I work at DARPA, remember?" Randall answered. "Believe me, I know a guy."

The following day in court, Jenna and Randall sat before the jowly judge and prepared to face the music. Only this time, the tune was about to change, because they had a melody of their own to play.

On the strength of the Macroscope footage, the prosecution gave no further arguments. It was then Jenna's moment to shine.

"Your honor," she began, "if it please the court, we have new evidence to present which was discovered last night. It is a recorded testimony from a person who has confessed to the crime, thus exonerating my client."

The entire courtroom went abuzz at this, and the judge had to gavel the proceeding back to order.

"Ms. Rockport," said the judge, "the prosecution has already presented a Macroscope recording as evidence and that evidence is quite compelling. If you have recorded testimony from someone confessing, it will likely simply be argued that the person confessing was either coerced or insane."

"Not when you hear the additional evidence we have to present, your honor," Jenna replied. "And I think you will agree, our evidence is also compelling."

His Honor-of-the-St.-Bernard-jowls looked over towards the prosecution. "Has the D.A.'s office been properly notified of this development?" he asked.

"We have, your honor," said Sam Gillick, the prosecuting attorney, getting to his feet. "But if the defense really has anything she thinks can satisfactorily thwart proof obtained by Macroscope footage, I'd love to see it."

"Very well," said the Judge. "You may proceed."

"Thank you, Your Honor," said Jenna. "The video of the confession is here on this fleck-drive, which I will now play for the benefit of the court."

Jenna inserted the fleck-drive into a console which had been specially built into the defense's table. The large display screen opposite the jury box – the same screen which had shown the seemingly-impossible-to-dispute Scotty Macroscope footage only yesterday – now showed something quite different. It showed a small young woman with hair so dark and a face so white that she looked almost like a porcelain doll. She spoke concisely and with confidence.

> "Hello. My name is Susan Julienne Baptiste Napolitano. I am the copy of the woman of the same name who gave birth to Adorjan Jaire Baptise Napolitano, the former President of the New United Nations. As you know, President Napolitano was assassinated in the year 2081, and the gunman, Armand Sanfelippo, was immediately arrested for the crime. But what isn't known is Sanfelippo's true motives, and who gave him the order to kill the president of the U.N. Most people believe that Sanfelippo took that knowledge with him to the grave. But he did not. I'm about to reveal that knowledge, and it will shock you.
>
> "The bullet that struck down President Napolitano was materialized at great speed remotely using a device popularly known as the Scotty. It's the same technology that created me. Resurrected me, if you will. But there are more terrifying aspects to this device than simply the ability to kill with pinpoint precision over vast distances. The Scotty records the molecular patterns of the human body – all the molecular patterns. Including the ones found in the human brain. Now, this is a truly terrifying fact, and it will most likely still be classified at the time you are watching this recording, but it has now become possible to unlock the contents of the human mind, simply by scanning it using a Scotty device. Our thoughts, our memories, our most intimate desires, and our deepest secrets… these are no longer private anymore. The researchers who developed the Scotty can now use it to spy inside anyone's brain. Anyone.
>
> "But as frightening as that is, that's how I discovered the truth about Armand Sanfelippo. Because his brain contained the memories of RNC Director Bernard Lewis ordering him to assassinate Ajay… I mean, the President of the U.N.

Susan's speech paused slightly, and the courtroom began to murmur. When she continued, the room went quiet.

> "Sanfelippo was given the order via Marlin Kettrel, the Director of Scotty Operations, but Kettrel received it from Bernard Lewis first. Lewis and Kettrel were both members of the terrorist group known as the Sons of God's Justice, and Kettrel was Lewis' right-hand man.
>
> "This information came to me by way of Mr. Claude Remy, Ajay's former Chief of Staff. It was he who helped me cope with my 'resurrection.' He set me up with housing, food, money, and he taught me how to manage the technological shock of being re-created 30 years after one's own death. Perhaps he only did so because Ajay ordered him to, but I believe he came to genuinely care about me. Maybe that's why, after Ajay was killed, he decided to make me part of his inner circle.
>
> "Claude worked with Sarita Shantay, the deputy head of Scotty Operations for the U.N., to secretly scan Sanfelippo and extract the information from his brain. We did this because all other avenues at achieving justice seemed to fail, and we couldn't let that happen. Our love for Ajay wouldn't allow it.
>
> "In doing this, we learned not only that Sanfelippo was ordered to kill Ajay through Marlin Kettrel, who received the order from Bernard Lewis, but also that it was Sanfelippo who resurrected me in the year 2079 in an attempt to trap the president into disobeying an established law – however unjust that law might be. The plan nearly worked, except that the vote to impeach President Napolitano failed. Popular support for me and my plight was one of the main reasons why, and for that, I'm extremely grateful.
>
> "We learned that Lewis is much more than a right-wing extremist. He has worked behind the scenes with religious fundamentalists to commit terrorist acts throughout the world, hoping to 'force the planet back to God.' Before he died, Sanfelippo held the knowledge that Lewis had orchestrated the assassinations of at least five members of the World Court who ruled in favor of the now-infamous Iousef Irfan Case, and may have assassinated many other government officials who oppose their particular brand of zealousness. The world sees Bernard Lewis as a firebrand. We discovered that he was an outright murderer.
>
> "For these and many other reasons, we realized that Bernard Lewis had to die. And here is where I give you the most shocking statement in this recording: I was the one who killed him!"

At this, the courtroom murmured loudly, and several gasps were heard. The judge nearly gaveled the room back into order, but did not need to, because Susan continued, causing the room to again fall silent.

"I did so because he ordered Ajay killed, and then got away with it. Let me be clear, I killed him, but it was not murder. I committed an act of maverick justice, but only when the system failed. I took the law into my own hands, after it fell off Lady Justice's scales.

"I may merely be Susan Napolitano's Scotty-made copy, but I still have the heart of Ajay Napolitano's mother. And nobody fucks with my boy and gets away with it! For me, saving civilization from a madman was just a bonus.

"With the help of Claude Remy, I used a Scotty device to put myself in perfect position to kill Bernard Lewis. We framed Randall Gosling for the crime by having me be Scottied into his exact location at the same time we Scottied him out, while simultaneously using his bodily pattern to make me look exactly like him. Then, perfectly disguised as Gosling, I simply walked into his fitness center and killed Lewis during his regular morning workout. Claude arranged for Lewis' gym bag to be left behind in a particular location, and provided the unregistered gun. Then, when the deed was done, I was Scottied back out again with Gosling simultaneously replaced. Anyone examining the Macroscope footage afterward would simply assume Gosling had killed him in cold blood. There would be no motive, but who would need one? Seeing is believing.

"Why frame Gosling? Because Sanfelippo had once been his assistant. It seemed fitting, since he was the one who trained my son's assassin, whether knowingly or not. Serves him right for playing God, and the same goes for the rest of those iconoclasts at DARPA. The Scotty probably should never have been invented – humans are just too irresponsible to use it properly. Then again, I'm one of the ones who abused the device, so who am I to really judge?

"But Gosling is only tangentially guilty, and being framed for murder is probably overkill. Also, the world deserves to know the truth, one way or another. They should learn, even by an accidental discovery later on, why Bernard Lewis was shot and killed. So, I decided to give Gosling a sporting chance. Since he has no motive to kill Lewis, or at least, none that I know of, his defense will likely exhaust every resource trying to exonerate him. With that in mind, I recorded this confession and implanted it inside his body – attached to a tracking chip that his parents put inside him when he was a kid. Anyway, on the off chance he finds it, he'll be able to clear his name. If historians find it years or even centuries later, that's fine, too. If the authorities come for me after the truth is known – well, I have a contingency plan for that.

"That's all I have to say. Good luck finding this recording. Fuck Bernard Lewis, fuck the Scotty, and fuck our flawed justice system for failing.

"And thank you Claude. For everything. I love you."

The recording ended, and for a moment, the courtroom was as silent as a dropped pin's grave.

Jenna broke the silence like She-Hulk breaking a glass ceiling. "I present as further evidence, the fitness data from Mr. Gosling's wrist-phone, and the tracking data from a child-finder chip which was present inside his body. As you can see," she posted the overlayed data to the screen, "the child-tracker signal is interrupted at time-stamp 07:23:22 and 07:26:14. Between those exact intervals, the fitness tracker shows a marked change in terms of heartbeat and respiration. Both are much faster. Now, this may have been due to nerves on the part of someone about to commit murder, but I submit that there is another explanation that is far more plausible. The body that resembled Randall Gosling was being occupied by the mind of a person with a different metabolism. A person much smaller, whose heartbeat and respiration were not used to being inside a male body. The heartbeat and respiration were those of a shorter, smaller person. In this case, a short, slender woman."

She turned to address the judge. "Your honor, if it please the court, I would like at this time to skip ahead and give my closing statement."

"Mr. Gillick," the judge asked, "You would ordinarily give your closing statement first. Do you have any objections?"

"Honestly, I don't think I'll have much to say, Your Honor," the prosecutor replied.

"Very well, Ms. Rockport, you may proceed."

Jenna walked out from behind the defense's desk and strode to the center of the courtroom, holding its attention as firmly as Rosie holding her riveter. "People of the jury, my client is innocent! We have the recorded confession of the true assailant, and her explanation as to how she did it makes perfect sense. Susan Napolitano had a strong motive. My client does not. She provided a reasonable explanation as to how she knew precisely where and when to find the murder weapon and use it. My client did not. The recording I provided explains the facts perfectly, and the prosecution's does not. The Macroscope did not lie. But neither did it tell the whole truth. And the whole truth is that the Scotty was used to deceive us all."

She walked back to her place behind the defense's desk, fearless as Mother Jones.

The judge took a moment to re-collect his jowls before speaking. "Mr. Gillick, do you have anything to say in response?"

Sam Gillick slowly stood as though he were a marionette being pulled up by its strings. "Your Honor, in light of this development, the State of

Virginia concedes to the defense and withdraws its case against Mr. Randall Gosling."

"Very well," said His Honor. "The jury is relieved. The case against you is dismissed, Mr. Gosling, with the sincerest apologies from the Commonwealth of Virginia."

At Sly's Bar & Grill later that night, four people celebrated their notable courtroom victory. Randall Gosling and Jenna Rockport were joined by Randall's boss, Dr. Gregory Lampert, director of DARPA, and Emma Gosling, Randall's mother.

"Here's to a non-miscarriage of justice for once," said Lampert, raising his glass.

"Hear, hear," agreed Randall. "And to the start of a brilliant legal career," he added, nodding towards Jenna.

"Oh, nonsense," she said. "You're not my first client. And we were adrift until your mother threw us a lifeline."

"I did no such thing," said Emma, the only person holding a non-alcoholic beverage. "I'm simply an old, wise mother who benefitted from once having been a young, paranoid one."

"Nevertheless," said Jenna, "it was you who remembered the chip. I don't think our case would have stood a chance if you hadn't done that."

"I was a nag," said Emma. "I couldn't have told anyone about the chip if I hadn't phoned repeatedly."

"On any other day, mother, I would resent you nagging," said Randall. "But not today."

The four clinked their glasses and enjoyed the toast. It would not be their last that night.

"Now," continued Emma, "all we need to do is get Tessa over here so that you can celebrate properly, Randall."

Randall winced as though he'd been handed a dirty diaper. "I know you liked her, mom, but we're divorced. That's that."

"Well, I have hopes, that's all," answered Emma. "You're not too old to give me grandkids, you know. Maybe Jenna here would…"

"Mother!"

"It's all right, Randall," said Jenna. "But seriously, Mrs. Gosling, I don't date clients."

"What a pity," the old woman sighed.

"I, for one, am anxious for you to finally get back to work, Randall," said Lampert. "I keep losing man hours from you because of these legal scrapes."

"Hey, neither this nor the assassin thing was my fault," complained Randall.

"I know. Still, these sorts of things do tend to crop up around you," Lampert pressed.

"Around the Scotty," said Jenna. "I'm sorry, but that device is a lightning rod of trouble."

"I don't think I can argue with that," Lampert conceded.

Just then, a man entered the bar, spotted them, and approached.. The business suit he wore would have made it obvious to them that he was a lawyer, even if they hadn't seen him in court earlier that day.

"Sam Gillick," said Randall, seeing who it was. "Well, look what the cat dragged in."

"The cat," said the D.A., looking smug, "digested me long ago. What's left of me is being fought over by the dogs, who keep burying me in various gardens."

"Well, I must say," said Jenna, "I've never had a post-trial drink with the opposition, before. Come to toast the District Attorney's record-beating loss record?"

Gillick smiled, still smug. "Nothing so casual. I come bearing news. Though, if you're offering alcohol, I won't say no."

"The answer to the alcohol question is yes," said Randall. "But news first."

"Very well," said Gillick. "I thought you should know that Susan Napolitano has been arrested."

"That qualifies!" said Lampert. "Bartender? Another round, plus one!"

"What will you have, Sam?" asked Randall.

"Scotch and soda will be fine," answered Gillick.

Jenna saw the reservation on the D.A.'s face. "You could have told us this by text. Or we could have learned it from the newsfeeds. You're bothering to tell us in person. There's more to it, isn't there?" she said.

"There is," he replied.

It was then that Randall looked over, read Gillick's face, and surmised what was going on. "Let me guess," he said. "She claims she has no knowledge of any of it?"

Gillick was taken aback. "How did you know?"

Randall nodded and smiled. "Intuition," he said. "It was an idea long kicked around at DARPA, ever since we first started mucking about with the Scotty. If one uses the Scotty to dematerialize, then re-materialize again, the newly materialized person is really only a copy. So, by extension, if one commits a post-meditated crime after that point, one could simply de-materialize in the Scotty and re-materialize again using the old molecular pattern. The newly materialized person is the former version of themselves, thus wiping out any memory of having done the misdeed. We used to talk about various scenarios where one might be willing to do that."

"He's not kidding," Lampert confirmed. "I was there."

Gillick's jaw dropped almost down to his oversized necktie. "Holy shit," he exclaimed. "We're still trying to confirm the details, but that's pretty much exactly what we think happened!"

"Wait a minute," said Jenna. "You're telling me that someone could use the Scotty, commit a crime, and then regress to their previously Scottied form in order to escape justice?"

"It's technically not escaping justice," said Randall. "The person who committed the crime will have committed suicide by Scotty. The person whom the Scotty re-materialized is a different person, completely ignorant of the deed in question."

"My God," exclaimed Gillick. "As if the consequences of the Scotty weren't bad enough. Now it's become the perfect alibi!"

"No," said Lampert. "Not the perfect alibi. People have committed suicide to escape justice before. This is just another form of it."

"Maybe," admitted Gillick, "but it seems like a horrifying loophole to me. Based on what we've been able to piece together, Claude Remy pulled exactly the same stunt Susan did."

Randall raised his eyebrows at him. "You mean, he's now claiming complete ignorance?"

"Yes," said Gillick. "Exactly."

"Oh!" gasped Jenna. "I think I understand, now. Remember in the video when Susan said, 'I have a contingency plan for that?'"

"Sort of," said Randall. "What are you suggesting?"

"She knew," Jenna exclaimed. "She'd planned on regressing using the Scotty this entire time."

"You mean," asked Lampert, "she used the Scotty knowing that she would plot something afterward?"

"No," Jenna clarified. "Nothing that fancy. I think it far more likely that she was told to use the Scotty beforehand by someone who knew how to use it that way. Someone professional. Someone experienced."

"Like Claude Remy?" asked Gillick.

"Exactly like Claude Remy," Jenna answered. "Remember at the end, she said, 'Thank you Claude, for everything. I love you?'"

"Yeah," said Randall. "That much I remember."

"Think they had a relationship?" asked Lampert.

"I know it," she answered. "You don't need my womanly intuition to figure that one out. Claude Remy fed her, housed her, clothed her, and after her president-slash-son was killed, she must have begged to help capture his killer."

"Not her son," said Randall. "She was a copy of Napolitano's mother, remember?"

"You know what I mean," she chided. "She still had a mother's emotions. It was only natural that she should want to protect the man who, in a different version of herself, was her son. It was also natural to feel some affinity towards Remy. He likely felt something towards her, too. Especially after his favorite boss got killed. She became his only connection to the former president. And Claude became her only connection to her lost son. It was almost inevitable that something romantic would have developed between them."

"But when she regressed, she would have lost all that romantic knowledge," said Lampert. "Remy would have lost that knowledge, too."

"Exactly!" said Jenna. "Her message of, 'I love you,' was a deliberate reminder, both to him, and to herself. She didn't want either of them to forget their love for each other."

That thought sunk in with everybody. Risking it all was one thing. Knowing beforehand that it would cost everything was quite another. Claude Remy and Susan Napolitano didn't just put it all on the line, they put it all on the line and then some. Both their lives, and their love.

"Think she'll ever see the message?" asked Randall. "You know, and see how the other version of herself felt about Claude?"

"I'm sure she will," said Jenna. "By now, that video will have been leaked by someone and have already been halfway around the Netstream by now."

"How romantic," said Emma. "Too bad Susan had to kill someone over it."

The next round of drinks arrived, and everyone raised their glasses. Gillick nearly drained his drink in one gulp.

"So who's going to be prosecuting the cases against Napolitano and Remy?" Jenna asked Gillick. "Will it be you?"

"Hell, no," Gillick answered. "I wouldn't touch it. Besides, this is a federal case, not a state one. But I'm fairly certain there won't be a trial. I mean, how could there be? The identities of the perpetrators can't even be verified."

"Fair point," Jenna conceded. "Stay for another round?"

"No thank you," said Gillick. "I'm going home and going to bed. I've had quite enough of Scotty-related shenanigans for one day. Good night." He spun around and walked off.

They watched him go, then returned to their celebration. All except Randall, who found himself feeling somewhat jealous. Gillick could simply walk away from the Scotty after losing one court case. Hell, everyone involved in this caper could simply walk away. Everyone but him. Even Lampert was close to retiring. He, on the other hand, was stuck working with the Scotty at DARPA, pretty much forever. If he even considered leaving for some other job, various government interests would claim eminent domain and force him back again. There was no escape for him.

No escape for the copy, the facsimile, the xerox of Randall Gosling. Omphalos psychosis was setting in. He could feel the existential dread of it closing in on him like twilight darkness. He knew he was going to use much more than alcohol to deal with it, but that wouldn't keep him from getting blind, stinking drunk anyway. He decided to seek treatment for his O.P. in the morning – along with his hangover.

He thought back on his earliest days with the Scotty. He'd once gotten caught abusing the device to sneak peeks at young women in showers. President Cullen, the U.S. president at the time, nearly had his ass fired for that one. Or worse, if the rumors were true. Looking back on it, he almost wished she had fired him. He would have gotten away from this line of work scot-free.

No, not scot-free, *Scotty*-free. Like the sort of Scotty-free Susan Napolitano was able to obtain. Like the one Claude Remy was likewise able to. They'd used the Scotty to get away from the device's influence forever.

He could not. He'd been falsely accused, then exonerated, but he still had a lifetime sentence to serve.

One without parole.

## Chapter 9: Scotty, The Destroyer of Worlds

The bomb was set to go off on August 27th, 117 A.T. (the year 2085, Gregorian) 7:30 a.m., Mountain Standard Time.

In a remote region of the New Mexico desert, stood a tower. It was fittingly only a dozen or so miles away from the Trinity site, where a similar test regarding nuclear fission had occurred nearly a century and a half earlier. At the tower's pinnacle, a small amount of material was about to be converted instantly into energy, which would result in a spectacular explosion. But this was no nuclear bomb, nor was there any massive contraption at the tower's apex which was to be dropped. Fission would not be involved this time. This test involved the Scotty – the now-infamous device which science fiction writers long thought of as a convenient method of transportation in cinema. But when it finally became reality, it carried far darker consequences than merely transit.

This test involved the darkest of those consequences, the instant release of energy. Under normal operation, the Scotty converted matter into energy slowly – usually into electrons, positrons, and gamma rays – with a small amount of energy lost in the form of heat and light. That energy was then captured, stored, and used later, such as in the re-materialization of whatever got converted. But if the Scotty could convert matter into energy slowly, what would happen if it did so rapidly, and that energy were simply released?

The calculations predicted an explosion more powerful than anything unleashed before.

The researchers of Scotty Operations, a division of DARPA, and operating under the prevue of the United Nations, were about to test this hypothesis. A small piece of matter, a mere one quarter of a gram of graphite, would be instantaneously energized by Scotty, with zero energy capture. The process was called RAMEC, for rapid mass-energy conversion, and if successful, it would redefine the word, 'power.'

Standing outside the entrance to the lead-lined concrete bunker, located several miles from the detonation site, Randall Gosling viewed the tower through polaroid-tinted binoculars.

Kenneth Graves, a young college intern, and only recently lured out of Cal Tech to serve as the test site's lead assistant, rushed out of the bunker door to Gosling's side. "Sir," he said nervously. "It's less than a minute, now. Director Shantay says you should come in."

Gosling didn't move, causing the intern to wonder if he'd been heard.

"Sir," Kenneth tried again. "Please come in. You really don't want to get hit with all those gamma rays." He paused. "Unless you *want* to turn into the Hulk?"

Gosling finally lowered his binoculars to give the youth a side-eye. "Tell Director Shantay I'll be in in a minute."

"But you don't *have* a minute! That's what I've been trying to tell you." He checked his iris-link. "It's down to forty-three…"

"I said I'll be right in," Gosling deadpanned, going back to his binoculars.

The kid looked inside the doorway, where he saw Director Sarita Shantay standing inside, alongside several heads of state. He shrugged at her.

She motioned him inside, and he dashed over.

"Ma'am?" he started. "He won't come in. I told him…"

"Don't worry about him, Kenny" said Director Shantay. "He's fear-deficient. Has been ever since getting treatment for omphalos psychosis a few years ago. He'll come in at the last second. He'll be fine. Just take your position."

"Yes, ma'am!"

The intern dashed off, leaving the director to share anxious looks with the others in her immediate vicinity. To her left stood President Rachel Ambrose of the New U.N. and her vice president, an android named Stalwart. To her right, U.S. President Mario Shalambay stood, with his vice president, Marigold, also an android, right behind him. Surrounding those five, within the expansive bunker, was a large assemblage of scientists, engineers, researchers, military personnel, and journalists – all of them waiting to see the dawning of a new age, or else working busily to make it happen.

"Twenty seconds," came the announcement over the P.A.

"Nervous, Director?" President Ambrose asked Sarita.

"Nah," she answered. "Not really." And in truth, she wasn't. She'd endured numerous trials, political winds of change, and even office relationships in order to claw her way up to being Director. To her, this seemed just one more challenge.

"Well, *I'm* terrified," President Shalambay admitted. "My great grandfather was there at the Trinity detonation. He voluntarily stood outside the bunker when the blast wave hit and got knocked off his feet. He laughed it off at the time, but he died of cancer several years later."

"There won't be as much radiation this time," Shantay told him. "Only a small percentage of matter will be converted into gamma rays, and we're well protected against that."

The voice over the P.A. issued the final countdown. "Energy conversion in ten, nine, eight, seven, six…"

"Okay," Shantay breathed, "*now* I'm nervous."

"…three, two…"

Gosling finally stepped inside.

"…one."

The windows were darkly tinted, but the flash was so bright no one, not even Stalwart and Marigold, could look directly at it. Even some of those who were watching the event on video screens covered their eyes. For a moment, it was eerily silent, as the brightness beyond the light of a second sun dimmed, and the all-too-familiar image of a giant, mushroom cloud appeared and began rising into the clear skies over New Mexico.

The shockwave hit. A thunderous, ground-based, "Boom!" was *felt*, not heard, throughout the entire bunker, causing nearly everyone not sitting down to reach out to something, or someone, to steady themselves. When the secondary airborne shockwave was heard a few seconds later, the sudden blast and roar made it impossible to hear anyone speaking for several seconds, even when those talking were in close proximity.

After the roar subsided, it gave way to shouting. Numerous cries of "Whoop!" and "Yeah!" to say nothing of any number of exuberant expletives were heard throughout the bunker everywhere. People broke out into applause. They exchanged high-fives with perfect strangers. Some of the scientists even overcame their shyness to give each other hugs.

Numerous people came up to Director Shantay and congratulated her. It went on for a few minutes. Some of them even dared to shake her hand. No one dared hug her, though. Oddly, the well-wishers pushed their way right past both presidents, *and* their security detail, as though they weren't even there, much to their shagrin.

In the cacophony, one of the scientists began shouting, "Thirty-four-point-three kilotons!" He repeated it over and over, "Thirty-four-point-three kilotons!"

The figure was soon repeated by others and evolved into a chant: *"Thir-ty-four, point-three, kil-o-tons! *Clap! Clap!* Thir-ty-four, point-three, kil-o-tons! *Clap! Clap!*"*

"I don't understand," President Ambrose shouted to Director Shantay over the din. "Is that figure significant?"

"It's as I calculated," answered Gosling, who'd overheard. "The Trinity detonation was an eighteen-point-six kiloton blast with barely a gram of matter being converted into energy. But some of that energy was kinetic, released in the form of alpha and beta particles. *This* time, the conversion into heat and light was nearly 100%. No atomic debris, other than a few beta particles, got propelled out. All electrons and quarks were converted into energy. That resulted in a blast nearly twice as powerful."

Director Shantay held up her hand, signaling for Gosling to stop talking. Turning back to Ambrose, she said, "You'll have to forgive him, Madam President. He was the lead researcher on this development project, and he's a little proud."

"Pride has nothing to do with it," Gosling countered, ignoring the director. "It's a predictive calculation, that's all."

But President Ambrose had already turned her back to them, retreating towards the rear of the bunker – away from the cheering scientists and researchers. She was joined by President Shalambay, who looked equally melancholy, along with their less emotional mechanical colleagues.

Director Shantay followed them. "You're not happy at this development?" she asked Ambrose. "How could you not be? It's the single most significant development in Scotty technology since time travel."

She slowly shook her head. "We're all bastards, now."

Shantay was taken aback. It was a quote similar to the one Kenneth Bainbridge had given after the Trinity detonation, only he'd said, 'Now we're all sons of bitches.' "You can't possibly be squeamish about the Scotty's power *now*, can you?" she asked. "Not after everything else it's demonstrated?"

"Of course I can," President Ambrose said. "When the Scotty ruined the minds of those who used it, we ignored the consequences. When we used it to spy on people, we came up with justifications for that, too. When it was used to send information across the eons through time, we overreacted, then pretended it wasn't a big deal afterward. At no point have we ever taken responsibility for the massive powers of this device. And now it has the power to destroy everything, everywhere, without even the courtesy of a goddamned *missile?*" She shook her head. "No. This whole thing has finally gone too far."

"Madam President," said Gosling, "I've felt the consequences of the Scotty first-hand. I can absolutely relate to your worries. Yes, there is a certain danger. But think of all we could do with this capability that doesn't involve destruction. Can you imagine what this could do for space travel? Imagine if a RAMEC process were used on an Orion-style starship. Instead of a series of nuclear bombs propelling the ship, a steady stream of matter could be fed through a filament and turned into energy within the drive-cone, propelling the ship. We've never been able to design a ship that would be so incredibly fast, until now. Humans could begin exploring the cosmos, visiting other solar systems, and actually doing so within their own lifetimes!"

"We're perfectly aware of the potential benefits, Assistant Director," said President Shalambay. "But as you already know, the cosmos is already being explored by astronauts who are willing to die and be re-made elsewhere using the Scotty. The Europa Project was a prime example. You are correct that sending people out to explore without having to give them a Scotty-death first is quite desirable. But as amazing as the Scotty's benefits are, what about the dangers? If some lunatic was to convert, say, a baseball-sized amount of matter into energy inside the Earth's core and blow the entire *planet* to smithereens, is there anything about your device that would prevent it?"

Director Shantay was incensed, yet remained cool before answering. "We do have *safeguards* in place to prevent that."

"Safeguards?!" President Ambrose whirled on her. "What good have your safeguards ever done? So far, the Scotty has been abused at *every* turn! People have illicitly spied on others using it. People have raised the *dead* with it. People have even committed *murder* using it. Hell, my predecessor was *assassinated* by someone using this device! And now you dare argue that your 'safeguards' are going to keep our entire *planet* safe? What a load of bullshit! Rogue agents have gone so far as to try to alter *history* with it, you know."

"They failed," said Gosling. "Twelve Monkeys effect."

Ambrose glared at him. "Yes, Gosling, they failed. But the *attempt* was still made. And *you're* a fine one to talk! You once abused the Scotty *yourself* to spy on naked women. Oh, yes, don't think President Cullen didn't tell me about that! And when it was used to commit murder, *you* were the one framed for it. *Again*, thanks to this device. I'd keep my mouth shut, if I were you!"

"I don't think you're being fair," Director Shantay said. "Judicial systems now have a near-perfect record of actual justice, thanks to the Scotty being able to re-play past events using its Macroscope. Crime has all but disappeared. And the medical benefits are incalculable. Maladies that used to be death sentences are now things of the past. Cancer has been cured. People can look young virtually forever. Hell, they can *be* young! Lifespans have been lengthened to such an extent that people might actually be immortal. Surely you can't be upset at the near Utopia the Scotty has been able to provide?"

"Utopia?" said Stalwart. As the first N.B.I. (non-biological intelligence) among the group to speak, he grabbed everyone's attention instantly. "I hardly think the examples you cite are a Utopia. Yes, lifespans have lengthened, but the population crisis has never been worse. And yes, medicine and jurisprudence have improved, but these advancements are still largely dominated by those with wealth. The poor have yet to benefit from the Scotty, and that's inequality in its purest form."

"Those benefits will work their way down," Director Shantay insisted. "Poverty was not solved before the Scotty was invented, and it's not been solved afterward. But with lengthened lifespans and the collective wisdom of elders retained, it soon will be."

President Ambrose scoffed. "You're a woman of *faith*, if you think that. Because the 'wisdom of the elders,' as you call it will include their biases and prejudices as well. Need I remind you that just such a biased elder attempted to subvert history by implanting a *baby Jesus* into the past? And that *you*, yourself were married to this very man?"

Sarita Shantay could muster only one response to that. "My *ex*-husband, Marlin Kettrel, the former Director of Scotty Operations, was brought to justice – by *me!*"

Ambrose looked at her for a moment. "Yes," she conceded. "That's true. I haven't forgotten. It's the primary reason you still have a job. Nevertheless, Kettrel was a member of the Sons of God's Justice and managed to keep said membership a secret for years, despite your close proximity to him. If even *you* are vulnerable to such a Manchurian candidate as he, then it's time for a surer hand to govern the Scotty – especially since the fate of the entire planet is now constantly at stake."

Shantay's jaw dropped. "What are you suggesting? That you're taking the Scotty away from me?" She sounded almost like a woman who'd been told her pet dog was about to be executed.

Ambrose smiled, though not sweetly. "Too many people, myself included, recognize that your expertise, and that of Randall Gosling, are too valuable to dispose of. No, I won't take the Scotty away from you." She paused, then added, "But you will not be calling the final shots anymore."

Shantay looked as though the U.N. president had just slapped her. *"What?!"*

"The U.N. assumed jurisdiction over the Scotty after the Temporal Bureau failed," Ambrose continued. "But it largely let Scotty Operations operate autonomously. From now on, that will change. Safety protocols and final say of usage will now be entirely controlled by the New United Nations."

This time, Shantay looked as though, if the president *had* in fact slapped her, that slap would have sent her spinning. She did a double take, then a triple take, and finally a *quadruple* take before answering. "Let me get this straight," she started. "You're letting me keep my job, yet taking final say *away* from me?"

Ambrose nodded. "That is correct. And don't act so shocked. This move has been a long time coming, and Scotty Operations has been practically begging for it."

Shantay not only snapped, but *cracked* – on the level of a seismic fault. "You unbelievable bitch!" She spat the words like a pit viper. "And after the demonstration of our greatest achievement, no less! After everything I've done. After *all* I've suffered through! You're going to rip control away from me before I've even barely settled into my office? How *dare* you! This is nothing short of a power grab, pure and simple!"

"A power grab?" Ambrose answered. "Oh, no. I'm stepping down as president."

The words thudded into Director Shantay's consciousness like dropped cinderblocks. Even the fear-deficient Randall Gosling looked startled.

"Android Stalwart will take over for me," Ambrose continued. "And you needn't act so dramatic about losing the authority of your office. You've held your position for nearly three years."

If Shantay had been crushed before, now she was outright pulverized. The bottom dropped out from under her world, and everything seemed to go into free fall. She even swooned slightly, prompting Gosling to make a move to catch her. But she didn't fall. When she recovered, she closed her eyes a moment to compose herself, then spoke. "Three years? You mean three years of fighting to retain my interim position. Three years of legal battles with my predecessor's lawyers who tried to dislodge me. I've only been officially confirmed as director for a month. And *now*," her eyes locked onto Android Stalwart. "you're going to rip control away from me and hand it over to this – this *thing?!*"

Neither Android Stalwart nor Android Marigold gave the slightest reaction to Shantay's obvious prejudice. Rather, it was President Shalambay who answered. "This is something we've been discussing for quite some time," he said. "I intend to step down as president of the United States as well. Humanity has progressed well beyond the point where our inherent flaws could merely destroy us all. Now we're poised to destroy everything on every world. One emotional misstep could end it all, everywhere. It's time for incorruptible, un-emotional hands to take the wheel."

Shantay looked from Shalambay, to Ambrose, and back to Shalambay again. "I don't believe what I'm hearing," she said. "You're both such cowards that you would hand complete control over to *machines?*"

"Is that really so shocking?" Shalambay answered. "President Ambrose and I both have Ex-Drives implanted in our brains. Our memories are augmented. Our faculties, computer-enhanced. Let's face it, most people today are practically half-robot, themselves."

"Half robot is one thing," Shantay shot back. "Complete robot is something else. Sure, N.B.I.'s have been holding public office here and there over the last several years, but has anyone really *proven* that their integrity is infallible? That they won't misuse their power?"

"You're asking us to prove a negative, and that's impossible," said Android Stalwart, finally speaking in his own defense. "One might as well ask to prove that the sunrise will never cease happening. Can you prove that the integrity of *humans* is infallible? I cannot say whether no android, anywhere, will ever malfunction or make a mistake. I can merely point out that, so far, no android ever has."

"That you *know* of," Shantay countered. "This is insane."

"Insane?" asked President Ambrose. "Look at what's left of that mushroom cloud rising out there. *That's* insane! We now have the capability to make any city, any *planet*, become that. Not just at the touch of a button. We had that power before. But at the touch of a button *instantly*. No waiting. No, this is just too big. We're only human, after all. And only human just isn't enough. Not anymore."

The director crossed her arms and looked at both presidents with utter disdain. "I had it all wrong," she told them. "You're not simply cowards. You're *automacrats!*"

The word seemed to make President Ambrose recoil slightly. "Automacrats?" she repeated. "Yes, I suppose circumstances have forced me to adopt that philosophy. Fair enough. But if so, it's quite clear that you are also an automaphobe. All of that is quite moot, however. This has been decided, and that's that."

"Now I am become Death, the destroyer of worlds," said Randall Gosling.

His interruption was unexpected, and such a drastic change of topic that no one could quite fathom why he had chosen that particular moment to say it. For a long time, no one said anything.

“Are you quoting Robert Oppenheimer?” asked President Shalambay, finally.

“Yes, and no,” Gosling answered. “Yes, it was what Oppenheimer said after the Trinity detonation in 1945, but he was quoting the Bhagavad Gita.”

“That was a mistranslation,” Vice President Marigold told him. “It should be read, ‘Now I am become the time of destruction, the *consumer* of worlds.’”

“That doesn’t matter,” Gosling responded, “it is a true sentiment. We have become like Shiva the Destroyer, and we don’t like it.”

“No,” said Ambrose. “It is not we who are the destroyers. The Scotty has become the Destroyer of Worlds. That’s why we’re handing that tool off to someone else.”

Director Shantay looked as though she were about to reply, then stopped. She spun about on her heel, and stormed off. She had nothing more to say to them, and even if she did, she knew damned well it would do little good.

They thought they could take control of the Scotty *away* from her? Hell, she was the one who had *procured* the Scotty. She had shaped its capabilities. *She* had defended it against those who tried to abuse it. If it weren’t for her, it would still belong to Gormann Industries, serving corporate interests. Or worse, in the hands of her insane ex-husband, Kettrell! And now *they* thought they should have ultimate say?

Oh, no. Automophobe or not, no machine was ever going to wrest control away from her. She had fought too long and too hard.

This wasn’t over.

## Chapter 10: The Phoenix

"She's launching!" shouted Randall Gosling.

"But that's impossible!" Administrator Blasingame shouted back. "She hasn't been enabled to launch!"

"But she has," Gosling said. "Look!"

Gosling was pointing at the cockpit monitor whose camera was aimed at the filament feed for the Avon drive. The filament spool, which provided the fuel for the drive, fed a carbonized thread into the drive cone where the tip of the filament was transformed into energy via a Scotty process, providing a continual blast powerful enough to propel any starship to nearly the speed of light. As such, the spool had been removed to ensure that something exactly like the current situation could not happen. Yet somehow, the spool was there. Someone must have used another Scotty device to materialize it back into place.

And it had just ignited. With eight passengers on board, including Gosling and Blasingame.

The acceleration threw the other six of them into the aft bulkhead of the main cabin. Gosling was close enough to the pilot's chair that he was able to grab it and pull himself in, but Blasingame was not so lucky. He only had time to grip the auxiliary console, and there wasn't a grav-support chair close enough for him to reach.

Blasingame knew the ship's capabilities better than anyone, so he knew how dire their situation was. As administrator for ISA, the International Space Agency, he had overseen the successful test mission of this very same ship as it took a four-man crew on a round-trip to Jupiter and back – the first non-Scotty manned mission to Jupiter, and the first Jupiter-related mission since the Talos missions to Europa.

"Phoenix!" Blasingame shouted to the ship's computer, "Emergency shutdown! Code alpha four Charlie!"

Nothing happened. The ship continued to accelerate.

"Damn it!"

Having a successful Earth-to-Jupiter trip was no small accomplishment. But the real history was made due to the ship's transit time. Only 12.71 days. Accelerating at a constant 1-G, the ship achieved a speed record of 0.009c, nearly 1% the speed of light, two million, six hundred and ninety-eight miles per second.

All that was barely two weeks ago. And Blasingame knew that 1-G was only a *fraction* of what the vessel was capable of.

"Hit the emergency shutdown button!" he shrieked to Gosling. "If the G-forces get too strong we'll never be able to reach it!"

Gosling knew this. He had helped perfect the Scotty device that made the Avon drive possible, so his knowledge of what the ship was capable of was almost as great as Blasingame's. But he was too preoccupied at that moment to complain about the condescension.

The Scotty worked by converting matter into energy slowly, then converting energy back into matter again. But a slow conversion process implied that a fast one was also possible. With Gosling's help, a rapid matter-energy conversion process was eventually tested with the energy being released instead of captured. The results were explosive, on a nuclear blast level! Almost immediately afterward, an old idea called Project Orion was retrieved from NASA's archives, dusted off, and put into production. Project Orion explored the feasibility of using nuclear bombs to propel a starship. But if one could produce a continuous blast akin to that of a series of nuclear detonations, without the actual bombs themselves, why not try it?

The result, after three years of research and development by ISA, DARPA (the Defense Advanced Research Projects Agency), and Scotty Operations (of which Gosling was the lead researcher and Assistant Director), was the very ship Blasingame, Gosling, and the others were now trapped on. It was the first ever starship engine powered by Rapid Mass-Energy Conversion, or RAMEC. Since it was the Scotty that ultimately made the spacecraft possible, the vessel received a name from the Star Trek franchise as well. It was dubbed the *Phoenix*, which was, in Star Trek canon, the name of Zefram Cochrane's warp-drive ship.

The burn cycle was growing exponentially larger and Gosling could feel the pull of acceleration increasing, as could the other seven people on board. Three G's, then four, then five… Gosling managed to reach the control panel. With tremendous effort, he punched the red button for the emergency shutdown sequence – hard.

Nothing happened. He pushed it three more times just to be sure.

"We've been sabotaged!" yelled Gosling. He was stating the obvious, yet some part of him appreciated returning the condescension back towards Blasingame, in spite of their peril.

"Kick… out… the… panel!" Blasingame grunted out. And that was the last thing he ever said, because at six G's, he lost his grip. He fell three and a half feet – to his death. The fall onto the control cabin's rear bulkhead may have been short, but the impact was deadly. The six other passengers aft were treated to a very unwelcome shower of gory, red rain.

Gosling tried moving his leg into position to kick out the panel in a last-ditch effort to sever the circuits and disable the craft. If he could do that, they would be adrift, but no longer accelerating. But it was far too late. The ship had nearly reached eight G's and he couldn't lift either leg, much less kick anything. Even trained fighter pilots couldn't withstand that much gravitational force for more than a few seconds. He could feel himself beginning to black out.

Then he lost consciousness, never to regain it.

The ship went past ten G's, then twelve…

On the aft bulkhead of the main cabin, two women and four men lay pinned, barely able to move, and spattered with Administrator Blasingame's blood. Four of them were secret service agents, charged with protecting the other two, President Stalwart of the New United Nations (still referred to simply as the U.N.), and President Marigold of the United States. But there was nothing the agents could do to protect them, now. They couldn't even protect themselves.

It was odd to have two heads of state on board a single craft. Such a concentration of high-profile targets posed an unnecessarily high security risk. It was odder still to have two of them on board a vessel as highly scrutinized as the Phoenix. But political schedules, often subject to change, and launch schedules, often subject to budget limitations, dictated the best opportunity for both presidents to visit the vessel was simultaneously. They reasoned that the risks could be mitigated by keeping their travel plans absolutely secret. They were wrong.

When the Phoenix completed its Jupiter mission, it became the most famous starship in the world. For heads of state not to pay it a visit for the obligatory photo-op was unthinkable. So, the plans were made, the flights were booked (unlisted), and Presidents Stalwart and Marigold remained concealed until their surprise arrival at ISS-2, where the Phoenix was docked. Because space is unforgiving about resources, each president brought only a two-person security detail. It was thought that this, plus the absolute secrecy, would be enough to protect them.

That was, until the airlock doors had slammed shut, and the launch sequence began. When the Phoenix blasted away, silently in the vacuum of space, the entire crew of ISS-2 were left utterly baffled as to what the hell had just happened.

On board the Phoenix, two of the four secret service agents silently passed away. One of them died of a burst aorta. The other had landed face-first onto the bulkhead and slowly suffocated under the strain of nearly 15-Gs. One of the two that remained active was a secret service agent named Brenda Phillips, who had the strongest cardiovascular system out of all of them. But even she couldn't last. She managed to gasp out the words, "I'm sorry, Mr. President, and Madam President. I… I don't think I can save you this time." Then she stroked out and died.

But she was the last to do so. The other three could withstand 15-G. They could withstand 100-G, if they really had to.

Because they weren't human.

They were N.B.I.'s, non-biological intelligences. Androids, in plain parlance. Such androids had been serving as politicians for over a decade, but Marigold and Stalwart were the first to assume preeminent roles of leadership in major Western democracies. Both had become presidents when their predecessors stepped down. Both were figures of controversy, as some regarded androids as not being fit to hold office, much less be heads of state. Despite this, Marigold had been confirmed in her role by election one year prior and had won easily. Stalwart's election was pending.

Agent Bastion was also controversial. He was the only android in the International Intelligence Agency. Other androids had tried to complete the rigorous training at the academy, but failed. They were earlier models with minds that were too literal. But Bastion's brain was as advanced as that of Marigold and Stalwart – perhaps more so. Some felt that having N.B.I. secret service agents was one step closer to a complete android takeover of all government. But Bastion had earned his place, shrugging off the prejudice of his human colleagues while performing his duties flawlessly, as well as demonstrating unique judgment in difficult circumstances. When he was finally named to Stalwart's detail, the president made sure he stayed there, and not just because androids liked to stick together.

Now the three of them were literally in a boat without a helm. Agent Bastion looked around. There was no telling how high the G-forces could get. The filament spool had enough length to burn continuously for years, relative to ship-time. If the ship hit even a tiny micrometeorite, it could tear the hull to shreds. He had to think of something.

If he could climb to the forward compartment, he could disable the ship's control panel and stop the engines. But how could he do that? There didn't seem to be any obvious way to climb up there, or he would have done so before, when the G-forces were lower. Now, at 17-G and still climbing, he could barely move. His mechanical muscles were ten times stronger than those of a human, but they weighed so much more, even at normal gravity.

Then he saw it: A line of ribbed edges along the starboard bulkhead. It was probably meant as an emergency ladder. But could he climb it?

If he redirected all his battery energy towards movement, he might be able to overcome the massive G's holding him down. But spending that energy would use up all his power in one go. He would have to shut down to recharge, and that meant he would fall right back into the aft bulkhead again. He might be able to lock his limbs before shutting down, but even if he had twice as much battery power, he wouldn't make much progress.

But if he had *three* times the battery power…

"Sir," he croaked out to President Stalwart, "I have… a plan."

"Love to hear it," Stalwart replied.

"I might be able… to climb."

"Climb?" said Stalwart.

"But I'll need your… batteries."

Stalwart didn't hesitate. They were doomed otherwise. "Take them," he said. His chest cavity opened, revealing the power cells. Then Stalwart shut down.

Bastion looked over to President Marigold. "You too, ma'am."

"Don't… waste it," she managed to say. Then she too opened her chest cavity and went into shutdown mode.

It took a long time for Bastion to crawl over to them and collect the batteries. There was only one place he could carry them – in his stomach. He opened his torso panel and jettisoned the stomach pouch. Androids didn't really eat, and the only reason for having one was to look polite at formal dinners. He placed the four batteries, two from each, inside his stomach cavity. His internal systems hooked up the power to augment his own. Then he was ready.

He crawled to the ladder. He could feel the extra energy available to him, but the ship was up to nearly 20-G, now. Pulling upward on the lowest rungs, he managed to get himself on his feet. That was all he could manage before having to lock his limbs and shut down.

When his systems rebooted, his internal clock told him it had been over twelve hours. He moved a finger, sampling the gravity. The ship had topped out at 20-G. If that's what it was after twelve hours, then that was undoubtedly the Phoenix's maximum acceleration. He gathered all available power and put it to the micro-hydraulic systems in his arms and legs. He hoisted himself up, then locked his limbs and was forced to shut down again.

Over and over, the cycle repeated. Rung by rung, cubit by cubit, he slowly made his way towards the pilot's console, taking 12.35 hours to shut down and recharge after every step. Eventually, after dozens of rungs, he got nearly to the top. But there was a problem. The passage into the pilot's cabin was a hatch central to the fuselage, which meant there was a considerable amount of bulkhead blocking Bastion's path. To get through there, he would have to jump, grab the hatch's edge, then pull himself in. But against 20 G's, that was impossible, even for an android. Fortunately, whoever designed the starboard-side ladder had considered this, because there was a small access hatch right above where the ladder ended.

The problem now was getting the damned thing open.

Bastion reached up with his left hand, directing all his energy into that arm, and grasped the release latch. It was a dummy-lever which released the hatch with a downward, counter-clockwise motion. But when he attempted this, it wouldn't budge. A latch that would probably have opened under normal stresses was immobile under the strain of 20-G.

Bastion tried a different approach. Risking the strain of reaching higher, he braced his hand under the latch and prepared to use the edge of his forearm as a lever. It was something no human could attempt on account of the pain it would produce, but Bastion had the luxury of disabling his nerve endings.

After a tremendous strain, the latch finally moved. The latch groaned as it slid until the hatch opened. But at 20 G's, it fell open with such violence that it ripped right off its hinges, taking Bastion's android hand off with it. The force nearly pulled Bastion off the ladder, but somehow, he held on. The hatch door fell aft and landed edgewise on President Stalwart's left leg, severing it, and creating a sizeable dent in the bulkhead.

Bastion had no time to worry about that. He'd spent all his energy getting the door open. He locked his limbs and shut down to recharge.

He needed another hoist and recharge cycle to lift himself high enough to reach the control console, which was even more challenging than before with only one hand. That same handicap meant he couldn't pull the console out with a free hand. He had to punch it out with his stump and punching against 20 G's was extremely difficult. He went through another shutdown and recharge cycle before he finally broke the console free, and the internal circuits were severed. The console flew backward with incredible violence just as the hatch door had. Fortunately, this time it missed everyone – or rather, everyone remaining. The console itself, shattered.

Immediately, the acceleration ceased and the strain of gravity disappeared. Bastion's muscles, which had been tensed against the high G's, suddenly had nothing to push against anymore and threw him forward over what was left of the control console. His body bounced off the view port, but sustained no damage; neither did the high-temperature quartz glass.

He floated backward, completely drained, and shut down again.

This time when he came to, his internal clock showed that he had only been out a few hours. Not having to lock his limbs before shutdown saved on energy and reduced recharge time. He looked around him, and worked out that he was upside-down and facing the port side. He tried righting himself by swimming through the air and found it far more difficult than he expected. He did eventually position himself upright in relation to the ship, and looked forward into the pilot's cabin, through the viewport.

The sight he saw was amazing! Stars that were directly in their path appeared as a brilliant blue, overwhelmingly bright, and clustered densely together. This light-show, caused by the blue-shift of relativity, was as amazing as any pyrotechnics, and more spellbinding than the Aurora Borealis.

He pulled his attention away from the fantastic sight. He needed to revive his remaining shipmates. Swimming through the air again, he eventually reached the starboard bulkhead. He gently pushed off. Then, when he reached the port bulkhead, pushed off again laterally to get over to the presidents. They were drenched in the sticky gore left over from their three human colleagues, as well as that which had rained down from the remains of Blasingame and Gosling. He removed the power cells from his stomach compartment and re-installed them into each of the presidents. He did Marigold first, then Stalwart.

"Aaaaah!" Stalwart yelled when his systems came back online. "What the *hell* did you do to my leg?!" Androids did not feel pain as such, but the loss of a limb gave him an overload of sensory information as his systems came online.

"Sorry, sir," Bastion replied. "Collateral damage from trying to stop the ship."

"*Collateral* damage?" he started to protest. Then he saw the bent and twisted access hatch, and what it had done to the bulkhead beneath him. "Ah," he simply said. Then he saw the stump where Bastion's left hand used to be. "You have some collateral damage of your own, I see."

"I'll be fine, sir."

"Ugh," complained Marigold. "I'm covered in – is this even blood?"

"It's what blood separates into under high gravity, ma'am," Bastion said, "It came from what's left of our human colleagues, I'm sorry to say."

"Shit!" said Stalwart, realizing that he was covered with a fair amount of platelet and plasma himself. "How many G's did we endure?"

"The ship topped out at 20 G's," Bastion told him.

"20 G's?" Stalwart repeated. He lacked the emotional range of humans, but he could still appreciate the acceleration record. Androids weren't completely devoid of emotion; they just didn't feel it as intensely. "Impressive."

Marigold was looking around the inside of the fuselage. Something didn't make sense to her. "Does this ship seem different?" she asked.

"Relativistic effect," said Bastion. "The forward bulkheads look bluer and the aft ones look redder."

"Relativistic effect?" echoed Marigold. "How fast could we be going?"

"Last time I saw the console," said Bastion, "we were a little over half the speed of light."

"Really?" she said. "Only half?"

"51.1865 percent, ma'am," Bastion replied.

On hearing this, Stalwart collected himself, literally, since he had to retrieve his severed leg, and pushed off the aft bulkhead to drift up to the command cabin. There, he saw the blue stars effect which had so mesmerized Bastion a moment earlier.

"Fascinating," he said.

Marigold wasn't far behind him, and also marveled at the sight.

Eventually, Bastion drifted over and interrupted the moment. "I hate to disturb your reverie, but we really should figure out what happened. *And* how to get back."

"What happened?" said Stalwart. "We *know* what happened. Someone wanted us out of the way. They can't kill us, so they blasted us off into deep space."

Bastion knew what he meant. NBI's were extremely difficult to kill. An android state senator from Illinois once took a shotgun blast in the stomach from an assassin and showed up for work in the legislature the following day. She didn't even bother going in for maintenance, wearing the same blouse, and displaying her torso damage for all to see.

Even if an NBI could be killed, another could simply be downloaded into a new body from a back-up. But with android politicians that presented a complication, because technically the backup was a copy, and the copy was not the actual candidate who was elected. It was a sound legality, because if a back-up predated a time when certain political promises were made, that could lead to serious problems. The back-ups for Marigold and Stalwart might be activated if they were presumed dead, but they would not be presidents.

It was a perfectly executed coup.

"I think what Bastion means is," said Marigold, "how was someone able to pull this off? The drive spool was removed from the ship. We all saw it."

"And yet it was right there in plain sight on the monitor when we blasted off," Stalwart added. "Dr. Gosling pointed it out." He drifted aft, finding a portal which allowed him to see the engine room. "It's still there, in fact."

"That means somebody used a Scotty," said Bastion.

"I don't understand," said Marigold. "The secret service knows how to detect a Scotty-lock. If one took place, we would have picked it up and the tour would have been cancelled."

"But we *didn't* detect a Scotty-lock," said Bastion. "And the Phoenix was under constant surveillance, even before it went to Jupiter."

Stalwart thought about this and quickly found the answer. "There is only one logical explanation," he said. "Someone locked onto the Phoenix well before launch date, before the security protocols were in place."

"But that's nearly impossible," countered Marigold. "If they did that, they would need…"

"To have a Scotty permanently locked on to a particular target for months at a time," Stalwart completed her thought. "Yes, I know. That can only mean…"

It was Marigold's turn to interrupt. "Someone has a rogue Scotty!"

Bastion shook his head. "That's also nearly impossible. Someone would need the highest clearances to even have access to the *schematics* required to build a clandestine Scotty device, let alone have the resources to build one."

Marigold and Stalwart exchanged looks as they reached the same conclusion. "Shantay!" they said simultaneously.

No one else could have pulled it off. Also, no one else would have dared. Sarita Shantay, Director of Scotty Operations, had a grudge against the U.N. ever since President Ambrose, Stalwart's predecessor, took control away from her. She must have salivated at the opportunity to take out both Stalwart and Marigold at the same time.

But to what end?

"We need to get back!" said Stalwart.

"Agreed," said Marigold. "Can we just signal for help? Someone at ISA can get a Scotty lock on us and do a locational remake."

'Locational remake,' was the euphemism usually used for a Scotty transport. Since it wasn't really transport at all, it made sense to label it what it was – the death of a person at Point A and a "remake" of a new person at Point B. It was still tempting to think of this as a form of "transport," but everyone knew it wasn't.

"It's logical to assume that whoever sabotaged the ship disabled the ansible as well," said Stalwart. "We'll have to turn around on our own."

Marigold sighed. "But that means it will take the same amount of time to slow to a stop as it took to speed up. And *then* we'll finally be able to get headed back." She paused for a thought. "How long have we been traveling, by the way?"

"My internal clock was pushed slightly off due to the speeds we were traveling," began Bastion, "but when I last looked at the console, the ship time read as twenty days, nine hours, and thirty-six minutes."

"Twenty *days?*"

"Yes, ma'am," he replied. "I'm sorry, but each rung I climbed to get to the control cabin took a little over twelve hours."

Stalwart looked at the starboard bulkhead where the emergency ladder was located. "There are only 30 rungs," he said.

"I had some difficulty when I reached the top, sir," Bastion said, holding up the stump where his left hand used to be.

"Ah. Yes." Stalwart understood. "Well, we'd better hope we don't hit a patch of space dust, or we'll get ripped apart."

"As I recall," said Bastion, "this ship uses a Scotty field to energize space dust before it hits us."

"Nevertheless," Stalwart continued, "we'll need to do a flip and burn right away. Bastion, what did you do with the console after you removed it?"

Bastion pointed to the aft bulkhead where bits and pieces of what used to be the control console were mingled with the plasmatic blood and gore of what remained of the five humans who died.

"Well, shit, *that's* a problem," Stalwart huffed.

"Any other obstacles we should know about?" asked Marigold.

Bastion took a few nanoseconds to think about that. "Before he died, Doctor Gosling complained that he'd been locked out of the control console. That means we won't be able to use it either, because once it's re-connected, it will simply resume the same course it had been previously set to. We'll need to find and circumvent the sabotage before we can fix the ship and turn around."

"Great," said Stalwart.

"There must be a manual override somewhere," said Marigold.

"Yes, ma'am," said Bastion. "But even with our NBI reflexes, are you confident that you can do a perfect one-hundred-and-eighty-degree flip and burn accurately enough to hit Earth again? Because if we're even the tiniest bit off, we'll miss our target and never reach home. If my internal math is right, we're .015 light years away from home. That's a really distant target. It's far better to let the shipboard computer handle it."

It isn't easy to stump an android, even for another android, but Bastion managed to do it.

"What do you suggest?" Stalwart eventually asked.

"There are only two possibilities," said Bastion. "Hardware or software. If the sabotage is caused by hardware, then Shantay Scottied it there, and we can find and remove it. If it's software, well, I'm a secret service android. I've had the latest counter-hack software uploaded into my neural net. Once I'm plugged in, I can root the problem out."

Stalwart nodded. "I'm glad I kept you around. You're kind of handy."

"Yes, sir."

"Let's get to work," said Marigold.

They began to hunt through the electrical systems looking for any sort of hijacking device. It took Bastion only a few seconds to find it. Plugged into the diagnostic systems interface was a device large enough to be a Scotty-based ansible, also called a UKL. Through that device, whoever was running the rogue Scotty could feed overriding commands directly into the ship's mainframe.

"Ah!" Stalwart exclaimed. "Perhaps we can use this device to repair the ship's ansible and signal home."

"Not possible, sir," said Bastion. "This device has an ansible connection, but no audio or visual capabilities. If we want to signal home, we're going to have to jerry-rig something else." He reached in with his one remaining hand and started to yank it out.

"No, wait!" President Stalwart said. "If we yank it out, then Shantay will know we've detected her."

"So what?" asked Marigold. "What could she do?"

"Energize us and the entire ship *with* us, for starters," Stalwart replied. "And *not* materialize us back."

"She could have done that at any time," Bastion pointed out. "So why didn't she?"

"Probably because she didn't need to," Stalwart replied. "As soon as the ship took off, the secret services of both the U.S. and U.N. would have engaged emergency measures to pinpoint us by Scotty, possibly even doing a locational remake back to Earth, if it really came to that. But that didn't happen. By the time they attempted a new Scotty-lock, we must have already been travelling too fast for them to pinpoint us."

"Great," said Marigold. "So the only person with a Scotty-lock on us…"

"Is Sarita Shantay, yes," Stalwart completed her thought. "But we all heard Dr. Blasingame mention that this ship always has a Macroscope detection field. We haven't seen any blue halos, so she's not spying on us visually. She's only keeping tabs on us by the Scotty-lock. If we shut down the ship's power, and simultaneously yank the hijack device out, it should appear as though we blew up."

Neither Bastion nor President Marigold responded immediately. Finally, Bastion said, "None of us is an engineering android. Are you sure this will make the ship look as though it got destroyed?"

"No," Stalwart admitted. "But what other option is there?"

There wasn't one. So they got to work. As it turned out, shutting down the ship's power was not as simple as throwing a switch. There were multiple redundancies and backups designed to make sure the ship did *not* lose power. They had to disable those systems first before they could shut down, which was no easy task. After numerous consultations with the ship's onboard manuals, emergency procedures, and more than a few expletives, they finally got the systems ready to be shut down. It involved throwing two switches simultaneously. Bastion stood by on one of them with his remaining right hand, Stalwart waited by the other, and Marigold readied herself at the UKL. When Stalwart finished counting to three, they all yanked simultaneously.

Inside the now pitch-black ship, the eerie blue stars glowing through the ship's forward viewport had an even more spellbinding effect than before. But they had no time to enjoy it, because with the power shut down, there was nothing to prevent space dust from colliding with the ship and ripping it apart. So after a few seconds, they turned the power back on again.

They waited, knowing that if Shantay suspected anything funny, they would likely be energized before long. But eventually, it became clear that their stunt had worked. They were free!

"This is the Phoenix calling any and all ISA personnel. We have returned and are in dire need of assistance, please come in."

The androids had spent nearly 81 days in space. But that was ship-time. Decelerating at 20-G, it had taken them 20 days to slow down, another 20 days to accelerate the opposite direction, do a flip and burn half-way, and decelerate for 20 days during the return home. They could have endured higher G's to get home faster, but 20 G's was strain enough on their systems, so they decided not to risk it. They went into sleep mode for most of the trip.

There was little need for consciousness in the long, dark boredom of space. They didn't arrive exactly back at Earth. But they knew they were somewhere inside the orbital sphere of Mars. Beyond that, they weren't experienced enough navigators to know their position with certainty.

They jerry-rigged a radio and tried signaling. For a long time, they heard nothing in response.

President Stalwart was taking the lead. "To any ISA bases or vessels who may be listening, this is the Phoenix. Please acknowledge."

"Think anyone's listening?" asked Marigold.

"I'm not sure," Stalwart answered. "I've only been at this for twenty minutes."

"I can take over signaling, if you like," offered Bastion.

"Thank you," Stalwart replied, "but I'd prefer to continue trying myself for now."

He made slight adjustments to the radio they'd constructed from various bits of electronics they'd cobbled together.

"I say again, this is the Phoenix, somewhere within the vicinity of planet Earth. We need assistance. Please respond."

Finally, a crackle and a reply came.

"To the vessel claiming to be the Phoenix, this is 9G WFO of the National Oceanographic and Atmospheric Administration. This is a private channel used for scientific research purposes and your broadcasts are disrupting our research station. Please desist these prank broadcasts. It's been a long day, and we're very tired."

Marigold quickly grabbed the makeshift microphone. "9G WFO this is President Andi Marigold. As head of the U.S. government, and by extension the agency you work for, I'm giving you a direct order to put me through to your superiors."

"President Marigold?" came the tired-sounding voice. "Great. Sure. I'm President Richard Millhaus Nixon. I'm right here with my vice-president Elanor Roosevelt. We're having a party here in Camp David, and we're glad you could call in. Now would you please knock it the fuck off? I'm trying to get some sleep."

"My good man," said Marigold, "what's your name?"

An audible sigh came through. "Not that it's any of your fucking business, but I'm Keith Zelinski. And I'm turning the radio off, now."

"No, wait!" Marigold cried. "Give your superiors the following identification code: Bravo 1479 Alpha Mike 1. If that doesn't pan out you can turn the radio off and get all the sleep you want. Just give them that code. Please?"

There was a long silence, and they all feared that Keith Zelinski had indeed turned his radio receiver off. Then the reply came. "You're *serious*, aren't you?"

"Yes!" gasped Marigold, relieved. "Give them that code. See if it pans out. I'm not jerking your chain, I promise you."

Another worrisome pause followed. "Well, okay," Keith finally replied. "I guess I'm curious enough to make a phone call. Hell, I don't like my boss that much, anyway. I don't mind waking his ass up. Hang on…" There was a rustling sound. "Okay, I found a pencil. What was that ID code again?"

"President Marigold! Thank goodness you're all right. It's been three *months!* It's so good to hear your voice again." Brenda Scarsbury, the woman who had been Marigold's Secretary of State, genuinely sounded relieved. "Is President Stalwart there with you?"

"Yes, I'm here," Stalwart replied.

"Thank heaven! We thought you were gone for good. By the time we realized what had happened, it was too late to do anything about it."

"You'll be able to retrieve us?" Stalwart asked.

"You're actually not too far out," said Scarsbury. "JAXA informs us that the Hope-6 is on her way out to retrieve you. She should be there in several hours."

"Great. Thank you." Stalwart answered.

"Can you tell us what happened?" asked Marigold. "We have a pretty good idea who did this to us, but we don't know the details."

A pause came at the other end. "We know who did this as well, ma'am," Scarbury said. "There was a coup, you see."

"We know," said Marigold. "We worked that part out for ourselves."

"Yes. It was done by a group of anti-android radicals called Humans First. They killed Vice Presidents Long and Ivanova right about the time you disappeared. They were successful at seizing power for a little while, but it didn't last more than a couple of days. We won it back."

"What happened to Sarita Shantay?" asked Stalwart. "We're certain she was involved."

Another pause. "She's dead, sir."

Stalwart and Marigold exchanged looks. Behind them, Bastion raised a skeptical eyebrow.

"She seized control of Scotty Operations during the coup and managed to retain control of it in the fallout that came afterward. The World

Court had a strong case against her. They were about to arrest and indict her for her role in the coup, but when they raided her office, she'd already energized herself."

Bastion finally spoke first. "Incredible. Suicide by Scotty! It almost seems fitting."

"We think it was all about the control of Scotty Operations," said Scarbury. "Shantay didn't seem to care about the politics. All she wanted was to regain control over the technology."

"That sounds like her," said Stalwart. "It worked, too! For a little while, anyway."

"Good Lord!" Marigold exclaimed. "She sided with a global coup! And all just for three more months of control? What on earth could she have been thinking?"

"Who knows?" said Stalwart. "But I don't think we're done with Sarita Shantay just yet. A woman like that having complete control over Scotty technology? Even for three months? Who knows what she could have done with all that power. And we'd be fools to think she hasn't remade herself in another timeline or hidden her molecular pattern in some tertiary computer system."

"Many of us feel the same way, sir," said Scarbury. "In the meantime, it will be nice to have you back. Androids are openly accepted in society now. That happened with the backlash after the coup attempt. Oh, I'm sure there are still some hold-outs around. People take a long time to change their minds about things. But polite society doesn't speak ill of NBI's anymore. You'll be welcomed home as heroes!"

"Good to know," said Stalwart. "But I sure hope the crew of the Hope-6 has an android tech on board. This little excursion literally cost us an arm and a leg."

## Chapter 11: Hall of Fame

Robert Anson Heinlein's eyelids flicked open like a zippo lighter. It wasn't waking up; it was a sudden snapping into awareness, without any of the grogginess or slow emergence from mental fog that waking from sleep has.

He immediately realized he was lying down, and sat up. Odd. That was easy. Not the slow, almost evolutionary process of becoming upright he was used to. What was going on? He looked around. It seemed to be his room. It certainly *looked* just like his room. But something felt different – like himself, for starters.

He tried to remember the last thing that happened before he'd laid down for his nap. He'd given Ginny instructions on his cremation, scattering his ashes at sea, full military honors, the whole nine yards. Yet now, it seemed those nine yards would have to be walked back a few paces, because he felt *wonderful.* Like the proverbial new man, or at least a refurbished one. He stood up out of bed with all the labored difficulty of a child on Christmas morning. Did the nurses give him some new kind of medication during his nap?

He took a deep breath, then let it out, expecting to cough out whatever cruel and malicious lifeforms had been breeding inside his chest during the night, as he'd always done every morning for the last 50-odd years. Instead, his exhale was as silent as the sigh of a librarian at Sunday Mass. No wheezing, no coughing. If the nurses had given him anything, it was amazing.

Then he looked at his hands.

They were youthful. They were strong. No liver spots, no swollen, arthritic knuckles. No nurse's medication could have done that!

*What the living hell was going on?*

Whatever it was, Ginny had to know.

"Ginny?" he called but received no answer.

There was no sign of his wheelchair, or cane. No matter, it wasn't as if he needed them anymore. He ventured out into the hallway. "Ginny?" Going past the kitchen, he came to the door to his garage, opened it, and turned on the light. The Cadillac was there. If Ginny left, one of the nurses must have given her a ride.

So, where the blazes *were* they?

He went into the bathroom, where Ginny usually went in the morning, but it was as vacant as his lungs. The railings were in place along the walls, but the toilet seat booster with the handles was gone. Apparently, *all* his mobility aids were off at the church ladies' quilting club.

He glanced at himself in the mirror, not expecting to see anything shocking – and then – saw something completely shocking.

"What the *fuck?!*"

He slowly approached the mirror – and stopped. How many times had he coached his fellow writers not to depict *exactly* this scenario! Yet here he was, living the cliché! Apparently, life sometimes imitated bad art.

In the mirror, he saw that he was – *young!* Almost exactly the way he looked when he was 30! Right down to the carefully trimmed Disney mustache. There were no noticeable lines on his face, his teeth were no longer yellow, and his moustache hadn't been this dark since his 40's. But he was *eighty* years old! Or was he?

Was Ginny?

He bolted out of the bathroom fast enough to take all the bats out of hell with him, determined to look in every room of the house for his wife.

"Ginny!" he shouted, as he checked everywhere including the basement and the attic. But Ginny was gone and oddly, so were many things he had remembered storing. Where were his secondary trophy pile? Navy pins? The old photo books? That was a problem for later, right now he had to contact someone—*anyone.*

He ran to the telephone and snatched the receiver off its cradle as though grasping a literal life-line. No dial-tone.

"*Goddamn* it!" he roared, slamming it down. He would have to find out what was going on some other way. If the phone didn't work, he would have to get the hell out of the house.

That meant getting dressed. For the first time, he took note of what he was wearing. A plain, white, pocketed V-neck t-shirt, grey sweatpants, and compression socks – just what he'd been wearing before he'd lain down for his nap. Everything should have fit more loosely on him now, since he was apparently his more youthful, slender self. But they didn't. *Add that to the list of questions.*

He went to his bedroom to change clothes before going out. But the clothes in his dresser were not the same ones he remembered. They were his style, but not quite the same. And they weren't stowed properly, either. He always put items away military style, but in these drawers, socks were rolled into balls instead of folded. And the shirts were folded as though they were on display in a store.

No matter. He quickly changed into some khaki slacks, a button-front shirt, and argyle socks. Then he took out a belt, and noticed it was brand new.

"Seriously? What the fuck?"

He looked at the other belts. They were *all* brand new!

He brushed it aside, put on the unfamiliar belt, and reached under the bed where he knew he would find his navy-style black dress shoes. *They*, at least, were there, and shined to a mirror polish, just as he'd left them. But when he tried them on, he could easily tell they weren't broken in. Those weren't really his shoes.

"Fuck it."

Now dressed, more or less, he went to the front door and tried to open it.

It wouldn't budge.

He cursed and cursed as he grasped and pulled on the doorknob, unable to make it turn or even rattle the door frame. He then kicked it—an idiotic response as it opened inwards – then he repeated the whole routine. No change.

"FUCK!" He gave up on the door and headed to the garage. Throwing open the side door, he slammed his fist into the button that should have triggered the garage opener.

Nothing.

"*Fuck* you, too!" Robert roared as he banged on the button like a conga drum. Tired of that futility, he went in and pulled on the lanyard to release the garage door opening mechanism and tried pulling the door open by hand. Nothing moved.

"Oh, *hell*, no!"

Utterly enraged, he went to get his rusty, old sledgehammer. Except, again, this one was brand new. *And* kept in the wrong place.

He picked up the unfamiliar sledgehammer anyway. New or old, a heavy block of steel was still a heavy block of steel. He went straight to the garage door and took a large swing at the exact center of it.

*BONG!*

The sledgehammer bounced off, leaving roughly the same amount of damage a June beetle might have left after colliding with the hull of an aircraft carrier. Clearly, this door was *not* made of sheet-metal.

He pounded wildly on the garage door, uttering an expletive with each swing of the sledgehammer. Still nothing, not even a scratch in the paint.

He bellowed a loud, vocal-cord-tearing roar as he brought the sledgehammer down one last time onto the garage floor. *That*, at least, had some effect, as a small chunk of concrete broke and popped into the air. He wondered if he could pound out a tunnel through the concrete. Probably not, he decided. But if there were some other way…

"The *windows!*" he realized.

He ran out into the living room, sledgehammer in hand, and decided that the large, front window was his best bet. He pulled open the curtain.

And froze.

Where his front lawn *should* have been was an iron, grid-floored corridor which ran parallel to the front of the house. On the other side of that, facing his own window, was *another* window, and on the other side of *that*, was a man. He looked very familiar. He smiled and waved.

"Hello, Bob."

"Jesus H. Christ!" Heinlein said, dropping his hammer.

"Nope," the man answered. "Not him. Not *this* time, anyway."

"*Ike?*"

"Yeah," said Isaac Asimov. "It's me."

"Holy shit!" Robert gasped. "You look…*young.* I mean, I almost didn't recognize you."

"You too," his old friend replied. "In fact, you look about the same as you did when we were at the Naval Development Corp during the war."

"Same to you," Robert said, still unsure of his words. "Well, except you have those goofy sideburns you grew later on."

"Yeah. Um, not really sure about that. That was my signature look later on, but not until I was middle-aged."

"How the hell did you get over there?"

Isaac raised his eyebrows and heaved a sigh before answering in his thick, Bronx accent. "Well, that's the real damned question, isn't it? I mean, how in the hell did *you* get over *there?*"

"I have no goddamned idea!" Robert replied. "I'm pretty sure I was dying. I had just told Ginny what to do with my ashes…"

"Good god! Ginny! Is she with you?"

"No. Is Janet with you?"

"No."

Robert sighed, crestfallen. What else could he have expected? "Well," he continued, "after I'd argued with the nurses, I laid down to take a nap, and the next thing I know, I'm *here.* In this newfangled copy of my own house."

"You mean it looks like Bonnie Doon?" asked Isaac.

"No, we sold Bonnie Doon a year ago, remember? This looks like our house in L.A."

"Oh, right. Sorry, I forgot."

"You *forgot?* How could you forget? It was just last year!"

"Last year for *you,*" said Isaac. "That was *five* years ago for me."

"*Five* years ago?" A sudden thought dawned upon Robert. "Let me guess: Your last memories before you came here were on your death-bed?"

"Damn right!" Isaac replied. "I was in the hospital, the doctors were telling me I wasn't going to make it, and then I woke up here."

"And you couldn't get out?"

"Nope. And here's another bit of news: We're not the *only* ones."

Robert stared at him. "What do you mean?"

"Hi, Bob," came another voice he remembered.

Robert couldn't tell where the other voice came from at first. Then he noticed another window off to his right, next to Isaac's. It looked somewhat like a patio door, except that it probably didn't open. Inside was a short man with coke-bottle glasses and the innocent expression of a little boy. The young man had a knob-like nose and an ordinary face, and Robert recognized him instantly. "Well, I'll be damned." he said. "Ray!"

The smiling Ray Bradbury gave him an imaginary tip of the cap. "Yep. In the flesh."

"Holy fucking shit!" Robert took a moment to let it all sink in. Then it hit him. "Wait, *both* of you?"

"Near as we can tell," said Isaac, "all four of us woke up here at the same time."

"All *four* of us?"

Another voice came to his ears. "Robert? Oh, dear me! Robert, is that you?"

The sound of that voice was one he would know anywhere. But no, it *couldn't* be! "Arthur?"

"Ah! My good man," came the voice of Arthur C. Clarke. "It's so good to hear your voice."

"Uh," Robert started, looking around, puzzled. "Likewise. But… where *are* you?"

"I'm in the paddock off to your right, based on what Raymond tells me."

"*Paddock?*" It made sense, really. The term seemed to fit as well as any other.

"We figure that we're prisoners of some sort," said Ray. "But whoever jailed us went to a lot of trouble to put us in cells that look just like our own homes."

"Yeah, I noticed," Robert answered him. "So, your place looks just like your house in L.A.?"

"Right down to my typewriter," Ray replied. "Except that I can't find my girls, and the phones don't work."

Robert knew what he meant by 'his girls.' Ray had four daughters and at least one of them was always looking in on him or calling him every day. But not in this place.

"I'm in a similar predicament," said Arthur. "I can't find Hector *or* Tamara."

Robert again knew. Hector Ekanayake was the brother of Arthur's best friend (and probable lover) Leslie Ekanayake, who died young. Hector and his daughter Tamara became his adopted family.

"And my place looks like my apartment in New York," said Isaac. "Except my window faces you instead of Central Park."

Robert let out a whistle. "So, does that mean your paddock looks like your beach house, Arthur?" Robert asked.

"Pretty much," he answered. "Except there's no access to the water. There's sand and rocks, but instead of any water, there's only this damned window."

"I wish I could see it. You had a lovely house."

Almost like magic, a new window appeared in the bulkhead separating Robert's house from Arthur's, and Robert found that he could see right into Arthur's dwelling perfectly. Arthur's beaming face peered through the new window right at him.'

"Fuck me!" cried Robert.

"Well! Bless my soul!" said Arthur. "Look at this! And look at *you!*"

Robert came over to the mysterious new window. Arthur did the same on his side. Arthur certainly looked younger. He had wispy blond hair, big window-like glasses, and a round, boyish face – so round and egg-like, in fact, that Robert thought his head and shoulders looked like Humpty Dumpty sitting on a wall. He was slimmer, with a hint of a potbelly, and over his thin frame he wore a simple t-shirt, swim trunks, and sandals. A robe barely hung off one shoulder, and he had a goofy smile on his bewildered face. "Well! Mr. Arthur C. Clarke!" he eventually said.

"Mr. Robert A. Heinlein!" Arthur answered. "What a *wonder.* How youthful you look!"

"Wait, what's going on?" asked Isaac.

"A new window just magically appeared right fucking here!" Robert answered.

"Oh yeah," he answered. "That same thing happened over here between my place and Ray's not too long ago."

"I can't tell if I'm hallucinating." said Robert, examining the window. "Is this *real?*"

"I'm not sure," answered Arthur. "I *think* I'm real…"

"No! I meant the *window!*" Robert was feeling along the edges of it. "Perfectly seamless! It's like part of the wall! But I can see right *through* it!"

"Oh, ho, ho, Robert." chuckled Clarke. "How distractible you are, you delicious man."

Here, Robert pulled his attention away from the edges of the window and looked at his old friend straight in the eyes – eyes which seemed to be *undressing* him. "Now, Art, I've told you a hundred times that I don't swing that way."

"A man can *dream*, can't he?"

Robert shook his head. Art had always called himself, 'not gay, just mildly cheerful,' but he knew his old friend better than that. He looked past Arthur towards the beach house. "*Goddamn!* Art, I wish I'd been able to see from this angle before. I'd have recognized your house immediately!"

"That's right," Isaac recalled. "You visited there, didn't you?"

"Yeah. You remember that time, Art, when I dropped by, and the Sri Lankan Army lent us that helicopter?"

Arthur laughed. "Yes, we got to fly all over the entire island, didn't we?"

"I'm surprised they didn't make you *king* of that island!" said Robert.

"They tried making me president," remarked Arthur, "but I wasn't interested."

"It's a shame I never got to see your place in Sri Lanka," said Isaac.

"Well, you were always welcome to come visit, Ike."

"Come on, Arthur," he answered. "You know how much I hate airplanes."

"Yeah," Arthur laughed, turning to Robert. "The man wrote about starships, yet is afraid of flying."

"I'm not afraid of flying!" Isaac protested. "*Crashing*, on the other hand, that's another matter."

"Robert," Arthur asked, "we didn't see you at first, but we heard shouting and something that sounded like pounding. Was that you?"

"Yeah," he answered. "I couldn't find Ginny, then I couldn't get out my own front door. So, I tried the garage door, but when that didn't work, I tried pounding through it with a sledgehammer."

"Didn't work, huh?"

"Not a dent."

"Wait," said Isaac, "you have a *garage?*"

"Yeah. The Cadillac's in there, too," Robert answered. "Too bad I can't drive anywhere."

"My garage is here, too," said Ray, "but no car."

"Okay," said Isaac, "I'm even more confused than I was before. Why would someone build a prison cell with a *car* in it?"

"When I find out, I'll let you know," Robert answered. "I can only assume that whoever copied our homes copied them faithfully, without giving any rational thought as to whether the copy made any sense."

"That would explain why all the books on my shelf are brand new," said Isaac.

"Everything's brand new over here, too," said Arthur. "Even my fishing tackle."

"Okay, said Ray. "We know everything is brand new in here, we can all see into each other's fake homes, and we know we can't get out. Now what?"

Robert thought a moment. "I don't know, kid," he said. "I suppose we try to figure out what this strange place even is."

"Do you figure we're in some sort of zoo?" asked Ray.

"Or *jail*," added Isaac. "Although I'd like to know just what it is that I'm being accused of."

"Are we even sure there's no way out?" asked Robert. "I don't know about any of you, but I'm not willing to abandon that possibility just yet."

"There's always suicide," said Arthur. "Technically we're dead already."

Robert thought about that. "Let's keep that as a last option."

"Maybe the four of us can figure a way out," said Isaac.

"No shit," said Robert, a little annoyed at the condescension. "Like *what?*"

"Well, weren't you about to take that sledgehammer to your window when you first saw me?"

Robert looked and saw that the sledgehammer was right where he'd dropped it. "Yeah. Okay. Worth a shot, I suppose." He picked up the hammer, took a deep breath and swung a mighty blow at the center of the glass. It had as much effect as he'd had with his garage door. Just for good measure, he took several more swings at the window before giving up.

"Okay," Isaac said. "Whatever that is, it's not glass."

"Yeah," agreed Robert. "And the fact that we have tools which aren't effective means this is definitely more of a jail than a zoo."

"Add to that the fact that it's us four," said Arthur, "and it begins to be apparent what this place really is."

"What do you mean?" asked Robert.

"Isn't it obvious?" asked Ray. "We all have only one thing in common."

"Yes! Well done!" said a *fifth* voice, which continued, "You are all universally remembered as the greatest writers of the golden age of science fiction!"

Strolling down the corridor bisecting the four paddocks, was a tall, muscular man dressed in a dark-colored suit that could pass for a uniform. His pale face looked as clean-shaven as baby skin, and his light brown hair so perfectly styled it might as well have been a polystyrene helmet.

"Who the fuck are *you*?" bellowed Robert.

"Tam," he replied. "Tam Valkoviak. And before you ask, you are on board the space station, Lira, in the Eta Carinae star system."

All four men were struck speechless behind the glass of their cages. The sudden appearance of a new stranger, coupled with the revelation that they were apparently in outer space somewhere, combined to temporarily rob them of any ability to retort. Heinlein was about to finally yell something crass at the strange man, but he was beaten to the punch.

"Don't bother insulting me. I've heard it all before. And don't bother dreaming of escaping to Earth. You're so far from Planet Earth that you'll never be able to reach it. You might also want to be aware of *when* we are. Suffice it to say you're in the 27th century by your outdated Gregorian calendar. Only a few historians and one or two collectors, like myself, remember you."

Finally, Asimov found his voice. "*Collectors?*"

"Yes," Tam replied. "Which leads me to tell you *why* you are here. And that, I must tell you, is very relevant." He paused, stopping in the centermost area between all four main windows of their paddocks. "You are all part of *my* collection. The greatest writers in the universe."

"Why you son of a bitch!" yelled Robert. "You kidnap us and hold us prisoner just so we can be in your *trophy* case?!"

For the first time, Tam looked at Robert straight in the eye. "I've kidnapped no one. I merely plucked you out of time and re-created you here. You aren't the original Robert Heinlein, you see. You're a copy. But what's in your *mind,* oh, yes, *that's* very much original! Only your bodies are new. Or haven't you noticed that you're all *young* again?"

"Oh, we noticed," said Isaac. "Young enough to pummel your stupid ass to a pulp as soon as we get out of here!"

“My dear man,” Tam answered, sounding utterly unconcerned, “if there were any chance of your escape, I never would have gathered you here in the first place.” When he said it, his air of confidence was so great that Robert half believed it.

“This is an outrage!” yelled Ray, pounding the glass of his window. “You *can’t* hold us prisoner like this!”

“I’ve imprisoned *millions*, Mr. Bradbury,” Tam answered, dismissively. “I’ve enslaved billions, and murdered *tens* of billions. I assure you; I can absolutely hold you prisoner like this.”

“And what do you expect us to do?” barked Arthur. “*Write* for you?”

“You may write if you wish,” answered Tam. “But I don’t require it.”

“What *do* you require of us?” asked Isaac.

Tam looked at him with an air of surprise. “Not a thing! I already have everything I want from you. You’re in my collection. That’s that.”

A moment went by before Robert pounded on the impenetrable glass of his bay window with his fist. “That’s *that?!*”

Tam looked over at him. “Yes.”

“Why you…!” Robert uttered a string of profanity that would have done the U.S. Navy proud. “When I get out of here…!” he started to say after his expletive invective, but Tam cut him off.

“You *won’t!*” he simply stated. And in so doing, stopped Robert’s tongue-lashing in mid-lash.

“*What?*” asked Arthur.

“You don’t imagine that in the hundreds of years I’ve been in existence that you are the *first* I’ve imprisoned, do you?” Tam asked.

Nobody answered. Perhaps it was because of his casual mentioning that he was a centenarian, or perhaps because they couldn’t think of a way to answer such hubris.

“You are only the latest additions to my overwhelmingly *large* collection,” he added, even as he began strolling off down the corridor. “So, you’d better get used to being a trophy. It’s not a bad existence, really.”

“How would *you* know?” asked Isaac.

Tam stopped in mid-stride for a moment. “You know, I suppose I don’t. You may have a point, there. Not that it matters.” He began walking down the corridor again, then added over his shoulder, “Besides, you’d all still be *dead* if I hadn’t done it.”

“Wait!” yelled Ray. “How are we supposed to live like this? With nothing to do and nowhere to go?”

To everyone’s surprise, Tam stopped again, turned around, and called back, “Any blank wall can become a telescreen. They’re voice-activated.

You can use them to watch or listen to any media items you wish. Keep up on current events. Educate yourselves on the long history you've missed. Keep yourself occupied however you like. But make no mistake, you're *stuck* here."

And with that, he was gone.

Arthur breathed out, "Son of a bitch!"

"Fuck!" shouted Ray, stomping his foot. "*Fuck!*"

"I don't believe this!" said Isaac. "We're just supposed to be this idiot's *action figures?* Stuck here on a *shelf* for all time?!"

"Action figures at least get taken off the shelf once in a while," Arthur replied. "We won't even have that."

"This is stupid!" shouted Robert. "This is so motherfucking *stupid!*"

"Sooner or later, we have to be able to find a way out," said Isaac.

"Why wait?!" bellowed Robert. "I can think of *one* way out right now! And I'm going to take it!"

"Bob! Don't!" said Issac.

"Why the hell not?!" Robert barked back. "I was dead before, and honestly, it wasn't half bad!"

Robert stormed into the bathroom, opened the cabinet behind his mirror and found his straight razor. Brand new, of course, but that didn't matter. He immediately slashed large cuts in his left and right wrists, length-wise to maximize the blood. But he knew that would only end in him passing out if the blood didn't flow even faster. He sat down on the bathroom floor and, taking several breaths to steel himself, he opened a deep cut into his left thigh, right through the fabric of his trousers. It hurt like hell, but he managed to cut deep enough to nick his femoral artery. The blood flowed more rapidly now.

He bit hard down on his lower lip, placed the blade inside of his right thigh, and jerked in and upward. The pain was *excruciating!* But he succeeded. His blood was flowing like a river now, pulsing out with each heartbeat, which was now growing fainter and weaker. Fatigue overwhelmed him and he fell backward, lying in a sticky pool of his own crimson essence. Then, darkness overtook him.

Robert Anson Heinlein's eyelids flicked open like a zippo lighter. No grogginess, no mental fog. Then, remembering, he jerked up.

"Oh, *hell* no!"

He shot out of bed and into the living room. Looking out his bay window, and the strange side-window, he could still see Isaac, Ray, and Arthur.

*It hadn't worked!*

He had only a second to hear Ray's voice cry out, "Bob! Wait!" as he ran into the bathroom. He opened the mirror cabinet and the straight razor was gone. He cursed, ran into the kitchen, turned on the gas on the stove, mildly surprised the gas even worked, and stuck his head in the oven door. He breathed in the gas deeply, actually enjoying the odor of it, waiting for himself to lose consciousness again. Eventually, he did…

And woke up in his own bed again.

"Fuck!"

Returning to the kitchen, he was not in the least bit surprised to find that the stove no longer worked. He went to the bathroom, stoppered the tub, filled it, then submerged himself face up in the water, clothes and all. He consciously exhaled bubbles before deliberately breathing in a deep lungful of water. He gasped, choked, thrashed involuntarily, took in several more breaths of water, and eventually died again.

And once more woke up with bone-dry clothes. This time, the stopper for the bathtub was gone.

He tried a few more versions of this before he gave up. He hanged himself from a rope in the garage. After he awoke, the rope was gone. He found the keys to his car, turned over the engine (which he was surprised actually *worked*), and let the exhaust fumes consume him. Again, he woke up in bed. Neither the keys nor the car disappeared, but the engine wouldn't turn over. He overdosed on aspirin and after awakening all his pharmaceuticals were gone. He was about to set up a trebuchet using coat-hanger wire and his sledgehammer to bash his own head in, when he stopped. Something told him he might *really* want that sledgehammer later on.

Reluctantly, he sulked back into the living room.

"Hey, Ike! Ray! He's back!" called out Arthur.

Isaac soon appeared at his window, and Ray appeared at his. "So? How many times did you die?" asked Isaac.

"Six – I think," Robert replied. "Honestly, I wasn't keeping count."

"That makes sense," said Arthur. "It's been seven days."

Robert was startled. "Seven *days?*"

"Yes," Ray answered. "Apparently, you don't reawaken until the following day."

Robert massaged the back of his neck, as though dealing with one of those pinched nerves he used to get. "How did you guys figure that out?"

"Oh. That was me." Arthur answered. "Hanged myself. Unfortunately, my spearfishing rope disappeared after that, so I couldn't try it again that way. Oh, I could have tried again some *other* way, I suppose, but I'd gotten the point."

"Yeah, several implements of suicide are gone from my paddock now, too," Robert replied. "Did either of *you* two try suicide?" he asked Isaac and Ray.

"Came to the brink with a kitchen knife," answered Isaac. "Then chickened out. I'm quite a coward, when it comes to it."

"I've been on a hunger strike," said Ray. "But it doesn't seem to be working. My body simply resets itself the following morning."

"It's true," Isaac added. "I shaved off my sideburns, just to spite that Tam guy. But the following morning, they were back, just like before."

"Damn!" said Robert. "There's *got* to be a way out! Maybe if we all died at the same time?"

"Robert, if our jailer has as many captives as he's bragging about, then four simultaneous deaths aren't going to overload whatever system he's using," said Arthur.

"Fuck!" hissed Robert.

"But," added Isaac, "in your absence, we've been talking, and we have some ideas."

"Oh, *great*," Robert muttered. "Well, I could use some of *those*, right now."

"All right," Isaac obliged. "It's like this: Remember Forry?"

"Forry? You mean *Ackerman*? Ha!" Robert scoffed at the memory. "That rat bastard still owes me several hundred bucks!"

"That doesn't *matter* anymore, Bob!" said Ray. "Just *listen* to him!"

Robert looked over at Bradbury, and sighed. Forrest J. Ackerman *did* steal one of Robert's stories for his magazine years ago, but Ray was right. That was literally ancient history. "Yeah, all right," he conceded. "What *about* Forry?"

Isaac smiled. "What's the number one thing he was known for?"

Robert thought for a moment. "Getting punched in the stomach by Cyril Kornbluth?"

"Besides that."

"Fangoria magazine? Those ridiculous costumes he wore at Worldcons?"

"No, no, no!" Isaac chided. "His *collection!* The Ackermansion! The biggest assembly of science fiction and horror collectibles in the world at the time!"

Robert's eyes widened. "Ah! So you're saying this guy, Tam, is like Forry?"

"Exactly!"

"Great. How the hell does *that* help us?"

"What do collectors like him always do with their collections?" Isaac asked. "They *show them off.*"

Of course. Nobody loved showing off his collection more than Forry.

"You're saying," said Robert, "that sooner or later, Tam is going to bring guests around so he can brag?"

"Yes," said Isaac. "And when he does, we'll try to appeal to one of them for help."

"Jesus, Ike! That's a long shot! Those guests are probably going to be every bit as sociopathic as *he* is!"

"I know. But it might be our *only* shot. We're outclassed, here, Bob. Probably facing technology even *we* can't imagine. And even if we manage to escape, how far could we get without help? We have no idea what's out there. If we're not careful, we could escape only to find ourselves captured all over again, and whatever means we used for escape taken away from us permanently. We need to get this right the *first* time!"

Robert pursed his lips and stroked his chin. Asimov had a point. "Okay, fine. We'll try it your way. What do we do in the meantime?"

"Use those telescreens," said Arthur. "Get as educated as you possibly can about where we are and what's out there."

"Explore our surroundings," suggested Ray. "Find every access panel. Open every vent. Explore every plumbing pipe. Look for any opening, no matter how small."

Robert brightened. "You know, there's a remote chance that just might *work*," he said. "One of my suicides was to start up my car's engine and let the carbon monoxide kill me…"

"Wait!" said Arthur, "your paddock had a *working car* inside a garage that couldn't *open?*"

"I know!" Robert agreed. "It's *crazy*, right? Now, the engine wouldn't run after that, but it made me realize something. 'Tam,' or whatever he calls himself, gets certain details about the world we came from *dead wrong*. He sets out clothes, and they're our style, but not *exactly* our clothes. Everything he replicates is brand new. Nothing old. It's as if he can't conceive of what something old looks like. And he replicates a vehicle with such detail that it actually *runs*, but can't actually *go* anywhere. That means that he doesn't know everything. He's not omniscient. This asshole, our jailer, *makes mistakes*. We just have to find what they are, and make them work for us."

"I like your sudden optimism," said Arthur. "Even if it took you several deaths to get there. Maybe we can beat the odds and hammer out something out."

"*Hammer* something out?" Robert repeated. "Hang on, that gives me an idea."

Robert looked for his sledgehammer. He was surprised not to find it on the living room floor. Then he realized, it had probably gone back to the garage after everything reset. Sure enough, it was in the garage, exactly in the "wrong" spot he'd found it before. For the next several hours, Robert used the sledgehammer to explore every surface, every wall, ceiling, or floor, with the pounding of his sledgehammer. He drove his fellow "inmates" crazy, especially Arthur, who endured it patiently before finally telling Robert to finally, "Knock off that infernal racket!" But he did not. He kept right on pounding. He did damage to all sorts of superficial ornamentation inside the house, but couldn't budge anything in the walls, windows, or floor. He tried pounding through the concrete floor of the garage. The chip he'd made in it from his previous percussive angst was gone, but he bashed through anyway. When he discovered a solid steel deck beneath the concrete, he finally gave up. He was just as trapped as before, only now his hands were raw with blisters. He collapsed on the bed, exhausted, and fell asleep.

And the following morning, all the damage he'd inflicted, along with the blisters on his hands, were gone.

Robert got up, and realized he felt hungry. All this time, he'd never really eaten, and was scarcely aware of it. Something reset him every time he'd killed himself, and when he was swinging his sledgehammer the previous day, he noticed some hunger and fatigue on occasion, but he was too preoccupied to do anything about it. Now, this morning, he felt ravenous. In the kitchen, he took stock of his supplies. There was a loaf of bread in the breadbox – Roman Meal, his usual brand – and the refrigerator was fully stocked with items like milk, eggs, butter, sandwich meat and bacon. He didn't bother to check the freezer. He fixed himself a bologna and mayonnaise sandwich, wolfed it down, then went back into the bedroom to retrieve his sledgehammer.

It was gone.

Momentarily, he panicked. Like Linus with his security blanket, he relied on the sledgehammer in this strange place. Almost without thinking, he ran to the garage and found the sledgehammer in the 'wrong' spot where he found it before.

Scratching his head, and heaving a sigh of relief, he turned around and went into the living room. The others, Isaac, Ray and Arthur, were all seen present through their respective windows.

"All done smashing things?" asked Isaac.

"Not remotely," Robert replied. "But I think I've learned something. *Everything* resets in this place. Not just us."

"That's true," said Ray. "I went off my hunger strike yesterday while you were off treating all your problems like nails. I ate everything in the refrigerator I could find. But this morning, it was all re-stocked again, just like before."

"Strange," said Robert. "You could probably eat to your heart's content and never get fat because your body resets itself. Anybody here have any booze?"

"Nah, we thought of that," said Isaac. "I gave up on alcohol years before I died. Drinking is more for the young."

"Anybody else?"

"Hector kept some whiskey at his place, but I can't access that, of course," said Arthur.

"Gave up drinking when I turned diabetic," said Ray. "Sorry."

"That's a shame," said Robert. "One of us could have gotten blind, stinking drunk and had no hangover the next morning."

"I'd try to build a still, except that everything would reset the next day," said Isaac. "And I wouldn't be able to share the bounty, regardless."

"Great. Have the rest of you learned anything?"

"Well," began Arthur, "there are news feeds, of a sort, just like Tam said. Voice-activated. The annoying thing is that all the news is hosted by Tam himself."

"What?" Robert answered, somewhat shocked. "Tam does his own *news?*"

"Or a copy of him does," suggested Isaac. "Tam is a replicant, according to what I've read about him."

"Replicant?" asked Robert.

"Yeah," said Ray. "He uploaded his brain into a computer, then downloaded into another body, one which is semi-robotic, and doesn't age. In theory, he could download himself into any *number* of bodies, if he so desired."

"I see," said Robert, who wasn't at all sure he did. "So, there might be *several* of him, is what you're saying."

"Or several hundred."

"Super. Anything else?"

"A war occurred some centuries ago, and, to make a long story short, Tam won," said Arthur. "He's dominated this star system ever since, utilizing every resource it has to offer. Every scrap of metal on every planet, every mineral on every asteroid, every chemical compound he could find. He's even built a Dyson sphere around the star to utilize every photon of light. Other star systems invaded Tam, but he defeated them and seized their raw materials, ships, and weapons." He paused. "I hate to say it, Robert, but Tam isn't just a Type-1 civilization, he's a *one-man*, Type-1 civilization."

Robert let that sink in for a minute. "Holy shit."

"There's more," said Isaac. "I took a couple of coat hangers and used the wire to try and probe the pipes of my toilet. Just to see how far it goes. And, Bob, you're never going to believe this…"

"I dunno, I already don't believe most of it."

"The pipe goes only so far as the bulkhead, and then *stops*."

Robert considered that. "Maybe there's a flange."

"I thought about that. But no. Just as an experiment, I flushed the toilet just to feel if something would open. *Nothing* did!"

Robert considered Isaac's words, but nothing registered with him. "Huh?!"

"Bob, I tried the same thing with the air vents in my apartment, here," said Isaac. "They only go as far as the bulkheads before they just plain stop. I reached my hand in, just to make absolutely sure! There was no opening whatsoever! But in spite of that, air continues to flow *in*."

Robert blinked several times. "Meaning…"

"Isn't it obvious?" Arthur asked. "*Matter-energy* conversion. It's the only logical explanation."

Heinlein's jaw dropped. "Fucking *what?!*"

"Something converts the waste water into energy on the way out, and converts energy into fresh water on the way in!" said Isaac. "Same thing with the air!"

Robert started to feel sick as the full realization hit him. "That would mean…"

"Exactly," said Arthur. "Nothing bigger than an electron gets in or out of this place. Matter-energy conversion is how we got in, and matter-energy conversion is the only way *out*."

Robert's head started swimming. He somehow found his lounge chair and sat down. "Good God!"

"No," answered Isaac. "No god, good or otherwise would have anything to do with this place."

It was several moments before Robert came out of it. He could only rock back and forth in his chair, fists held at his temples. He clenched his teeth and let out a low growl of frustration which grew in duration and volume until he shot up out of his chair and started pounding the floor with his foot. "Fuck! Fuck! Fuck!" he shouted. "This is *bullshit!* We can't escape, we can't kill ourselves… Hell, we can't even grow *old* and die! How the fuck can we live like this?! Fucking *how?!* Damn it, there *must* be a way out of here!"

"Robert, I hate to say it, but Isaac's long-shot plan might be all we've got," said Arthur.

"What, wait for some spectator to come along and signal that person for *help?*" spat Robert.

"Yeah," said Ray. "Exactly."

"And just what sort of people do you think a totalitarian dictator like him will bring *around*, huh?" Robert hissed. "Do you think *any* of the officers brought around by Hitler on his tours through the gas chambers felt any sympathy whatsoever for the Jews they were executing?"

"Probably not," Isaac agreed. "But I have to believe at least a *few* secretly did."

"Oh, come on!" Robert paced back and forth several times, trying to sort things out in his head. Eventually, he said, "Look, the Nazis *hanged* Dietrich Bonhoeffer, and they only had a few years to find him. This guy, Tam, has probably had *centuries* to weed out any dissidents. What makes you think there could possibly be any left?"

"Not a thing," Isaac admitted.

"And here's *another* cheerful thought," Robert continued, "isn't it reasonable to assume that every word we've been uttering is being *monitored?*"

"Probably," said Ray.

Hell, isn't it reasonable to think that every *molecule* in our bodies is under close surveillance?"

"I'm forced to agree with you," said Arthur.

"Well then!" Robert practically shrieked. "What the *shitfuck* are we doing even *considering* this mad plan?!"

"One reason, and one reason, only," answered Isaac. "No other choice."

Robert stared at him. He found he'd gotten so agitated that he had to catch his breath, slightly. "You know what?" he bellowed. "The three of you seem awfully calm considering the predicament we're in!"

"Robert, we've had *days* to deal with the psychological trauma while you were off killing yourself over and over," Arthur pointed out.

Robert didn't know what to reply. Arthur had him there.

Over the next several days, they had no visitors. Each occupied himself in productive ways. Arthur absorbed as much news and information as he could. Isaac familiarized himself with the quantum computer systems which ran the station but found the 11-dimensional physics behind it rather daunting, even for him. Robert delved into the history which took place from the time he died until recently. And Ray? He sulked before finally writing a short story out of sheer boredom. Much to his surprise, the following day, everything he wrote was still there. It hadn't disappeared.

When the others learned about this, they began keeping daily logs and wrote copious notes. Nothing written on paper disappeared the next day unless it was crumpled up or placed in the wastepaper basket. If a ream of paper was used, a fresh one appeared the following day. Stacks of notes and writings soon grew to ridiculous heights. Robert started to paper over his bay window with sheets of paper with 'Fuck you!' scrawled on them, but Isaac talked him out of that. "You need to be able to see out as much as we do!" he said. "Besides, I'm not losing my paper-privileges over your bullshit."

Finally, the day came when Tam brought visitors. There were four men – *all* copies of Tam. There was little point in trying to appeal to any of them.

The following week, the same thing happened. Seven other Tams accompanied the "original" Tam – if it even was the original. They had no way to know. How many of them *were* there?

Months went by, with Tam bringing other Tams to visit his collection. The number of Tams seemed infinite! But really, there was no way to know for certain how many of them were initial visitors or repeat visitors. The Tams might number in the dozens, or the thousands for all they knew.

Until, one fine day, that pattern changed.

Tam brought three Tams with him, along with a *young woman.*

She looked to be about 23, dishwater blonde, long wavy hair, and barely dressed in a midriff-showing spandex outfit that was clearly designed to showcase – well, *everything* about her. Obviously, she was the trophy of one or all of the Tams.

Isaac saw her first. He knocked three times on Ray's window with their secret knock they'd worked out in advance, and Ray immediately dropped what he was typing. He pinged a crystal vase on his bookshelf to alert Arthur, and Arthur used his code knock on Robert's window. Robert ordered his telescreen off and came to the window.

The four of them gawking all at once didn't seem to bother the Tams. They must have realized that the first woman they'd ever brought along might cause a bit of a stir. The "lead" Tam was droning on at length about the historical significance of "the Big Three plus Bradbury, or else, as some historians designate Bradbury above Heinlein, the 'A B C's' of science fiction, for Asimov, Bradbury and Clarke…"

None of the Tams looked at the woman. But the four men behind glass couldn't take their eyes off her, captivated in more ways than one.

When the lead Tam began talking about Robert Heinlein at length, all eyes were on his paddock. It was then that Isaac saw the woman steal a glance his way, and he seized his chance.

He held his left hand out flat, palm up, placed his right fist with hitchhiker-thumb outstretched upward on top of it, and raised them both upwards together. The whole motion took only a split second, and it formed the universal sign-language gesture for "Help."

She saw it. Her eyes quickly darted away, pretending to look at Robert Heinlein.

Robert saw it too. He tried to keep all attention focused on him by flipping the Tams the bird.

Isaac didn't give up after one try. When her glance happened his way again, he repeated the gesture. "Help."

By now, the tourists had moved on to lead-Tam's discussion of Arthur C. Clarke, and all eyes were on that paddock, even the woman's. But then, she reached up with her left hand and seemed to fix something with her hair. While her fingers were nestled within the strands of her semi-blond locks, they formed out two letters in American sign-language:

"O," followed by, "K."

Isaac couldn't believe it! He was elated! He kept his poker face on and conducted zen-breathing exercises to slow his heart rate. No point in giving surveillance any clues that something funny might be happening.

The tour went on to Ray, and then finally to Isaac. Then the tour ended, and the entourage moved on.

When it was clear that they were all out of earshot, Robert exploded. "Well! *That* was fucking useless!"

"Bob," Isaac called.

"What?"

In response, Isaac merely winked.

Robert was about to say something in response, but caught himself. He instead merely gave a facial expression that seemed to say, 'Well?'

Isaac closed his eyes and tilted his head slightly, seeming to say, 'We'll see.'

"Robert?" asked Arthur, who was looking in. When Robert responded by looking his way, Arthur pleaded with his face to know what was going on. In response, Robert rolled his eyes off in the direction the tour had just walked off in, telling him, in effect, that contact had been made.

Almost at the same time, Ray knocked weakly on Isaac's window, and asked if it had worked by giving a 'thumbs up' and giving a hopeful facial expression.

Isaac merely shrugged in reply.

Two days went by before they knew anything, and they didn't dare speak of it among themselves for fear that any monitoring might alert someone. For all they knew, it already had. But there was no point in inviting trouble. Then, on the third night, something strange happened.

Robert thought he woke to see the woman sitting at the foot of his bed.

When Robert finally found his voice, he said, "I must be dreaming."

"You are," she said.

He sat up. "*Really?*"

"Yes. It's the only form of communication we have that isn't detectable by Valkoviak's defenses." She was much more modestly dressed this time, but that didn't prevent Robert from feeling slightly nervous that there was a pretty woman in his bedroom.

He stood up out of bed, silently being grateful he didn't have a morning erection, even while in a dreamscape. "Isaac got through to you?" he asked. "You'll help us?"

"Yes. Come on. We don't have a lot of time," she said, standing up herself. "All four of you have to be in R.E.M. sleep state in order for this meeting to work.

"Meeting?"

"Yes. Hurry!" She went over to the front door of his living room and reached for the handle.

"You can't open that," he started to say. "It's…"

She opened it. Then stepped outside.

Stunned, he reminded himself that he was dreaming. He put on his slippers out of habit, then stepped out of his front door.

Outside was not the front lawn of his California home, nor the dark steel corridor of his captivity. Instead, there was a sunny meadow with tall grass and daisies. The woman moved to the center of the meadow in the blink of an eye. Isaac, Ray, and Arthur converged on her from three different directions. He joined them and ran out.

When they'd all converged on the woman, she began speaking right away.

"First things first," she said. "*Nobody* speaks of this in the real world. The only place you can speak freely is here in the dreamscape. You cannot mention anything while you are awake, not even casually. The central computer already suspects something."

"Wait just a damned minute!" said Isaac. "We're grateful for any help, but who the hell are you?"

She nodded. "Oh. Right. Introductions. Sorry, I get ahead of myself sometimes, and it's been a long while since I had anyone to really talk to. My name is Suzanne Collins. I'm a sci fi writer myself, but I think most of you wouldn't recognize the name. I'm a little after your time."

"The name does sound familiar…" said Ray.

"You mean you were a prisoner as well?" interrupted Robert. "How did you get out?"

"I didn't," she said. "Not really. Female captives get certain privileges in exchange for..." she paused. "certain concessions."

Four male jaws dropped all at once. "My god, child," said Arthur. "I'm so sorry."

"Never mind that, now," she continued. "I was recruited by the Locality. That's what the free systems call themselves. They contacted me by dreamscape, just like we're doing now. It's *their* connection which allows me to reach out to you like this. I spy on Tam, and I give that information to the Locality. The hope is that we'll find a way to defeat him."

"You're a spy!" exclaimed Ray.

"Yes. But also, a prisoner like you."

"*Free* systems?" asked Arthur.

"Yes. Sol, Centauri, Wolf 359, and a few others. But Tam has control of just as many systems as they do."

"Wait, wait…" said Arthur, "Tam controls *more* than just Eta Carinae?"

"*Much* more!" Suzanne replied. "Look, I hate to tell you all this, but you are far more screwed than you realize. Tam Valkoviak is much more than a dictator. Much more than a sociopath. He has the potential to overrun the free systems if he gets enough energy and raw materials together. He could actually conquer the galaxy by sheer strength of numbers."

"Hang on!" barked Robert. "Back up! Can we first start with how the hell we got here?"

Suzanne gave him a brief look of surprise, then relaxed. "Right, of course. Um, how much history have you been able to brush up on?"

Robert scratched his chin. "I was just beginning to catch up with some of the 21st century before I stopped and started focusing on more recent events," he said. "The Internet, Nine-Eleven, the Obama years and the rise and fall of the right-wing media nightmare-cult surrounding Donald Trump."

Suzanne nodded. "About three decades after that, the people of Earth invented the device which brought you all here. It was called 'The Scotty.'"

"The *Scotty?*" asked Ray. "As in, 'Beam me up, Scotty?'"

"Yes. It's the matter-energy converter which imprisoned you. Indeed, it imprisoned all of us."

"But how could Tam get our patterns?" asked Arthur. "He would have to travel back in *time* to do that!"

"The Scotty *does* go back in time, after a fashion," Suzanne said. "If you can materialize something in a distant point in space, you can also do so at a distant point in time because space and time are the same continuum." She paused. "It can transmit and gather information at the quantum level faster than the speed of light."

All four men were dumbstruck. "Are you seriously saying," asked Robert, "that this thing can spy on anything, anywhere, any *when?*"

"Oh, yes," said Suzanne. "The United States kept the device a closely guarded secret until counter-measures could be deployed to prevent abuses such as voyeurism or insider stock trading."

"Amazing!" said Arthur. "So, you could send someone back in time with this thing? Or into the future?"

"Technically, no," Suzanne told him. "Not really. What actually gets sent back in time is only a *copy* of the individual. You see, people are not *transported* through matter-energy conversion so much as they are deconstructed at one end, and re-constructed at the other using indigenous energy. It's actually a death, followed by the rebirth of a copy. Most people who initially tried it found that the knowledge that they had been killed and copied drove them mad. That is, until they found a means of tamping down the brain's fear-response during so-called transit. Only a few time-excursions to the past were made before they gave up on the idea. And as for the future, well, the future *moves* depending upon certain fluctuations. Many future-travelers were lost to some alternate reality, never to return. Since then, the Scotty has only used its Macroscope feature to do surveillance on the past or future."

"Good God!" exclaimed Isaac. "So, this scoundrel, Tam, used the device to steal our minds from the past just prior to death, used our DNA to copy our bodies, and then brought us here?!"

"Unfortunately, yes," Suzanne replied. "Please understand, what he did is *extremely* illegal in the Free Systems. People have been prosecuted and even *executed* for the crime of resurrecting the dead using a Scotty device. It's difficult to get around the safeguards, but an unscrupulous tyrant like Tam has no compunction about reaching across a few star systems and stealing that which isn't his. Once he finds a loophole or a weakness in the systems, he exploits it for his own purposes."

"Holy shit!" breathed Ray.

"Okay," said Robert. "Now we know how we got into this. How the hell do we get *out* of it?"

Suzanne frowned. "Well, that's the real question. I've spent the last twelve years looking for some kind of weakness we could exploit…"

"Twelve *years?!*" shouted Isaac. "You've let this bastard rape you for twelve *years?!*"

"I said don't *worry* about that now!" she spat. "It'll all be for *nothing* if we don't focus!"

Isaac cowed. "Sorry," he said, meekly.

"You've found no weaknesses in all that time?" asked Arthur. "None at all?"

"No," she said. "Any attempt to use an outside Scotty gets detected. Tam reacts immediately."

"So what?" asked Robert. "Strike with overwhelming force. Use the element of surprise."

"Not possible," said Suzanne. "With Tam's countermeasures, the Locality might only get one Scotty transmission in before it got shut down."

"Okay, we can't use an *outside* Scotty," said Ray. "What if we used the *inside* Scotty?"

"No way to get to it," Suzanne answered. "And besides, it's controlled by the main computer."

"Okay," said Isaac, "so what if we took over the main computer?"

At that, she laughed. "No way! Do you even know what the main computer is? It's another copy of Tam's own mind! He even nicknamed it 'Tamerlane,' like the ancient conqueror! It's *impossible* to subvert it!"

"Any computer can be rebooted," Isaac pointed out. "*And* given a new operating system."

"Even if it's rebooted, it will still be Tam," Suzanne pointed out. And rebooting doesn't take long with a quantum computer system. It would only be down for a nanosecond."

All five of them paused for a moment. Then Arthur spoke.

"Maybe we're focusing on the wrong piece of technology," he said. "This guy, Tam, is a replicant, right? That must mean copies of his consciousness get uploaded and downloaded? Maybe from an old body into a new body?"

"Constantly," answered Suzanne.

"So, can't we download one of those copies for ourselves? Know what he knows?"

"No," she replied. "Downloading a consciousness takes time. Tam would shut it down before it barely began."

There was a pause before Robert spoke. "You said the Locality is only able to get a single Scotty signal through?"

"If that," Suzanne answered. "More likely only part of one."

"And you are able to confer with your superiors in the Locality via the dreamscape, just like we're doing?"

"That's right."

Robert smiled. "Guys, I think I'm developing the beginnings of a *plan*."

On the Ops deck of the space station Lira, Tam Valkoviak monitored his empire. He had been siphoning metals and materials from the Procyon system for some time now. In a few weeks, he would be able to launch his fleet of ships into Sol, and in so doing, take out the very heart of the Locality. It would be a critical military and psychological blow, and would ensure his ultimate victory.

Suddenly, an alarm on the tactical panel went off. Tam examined it, then opened a channel to one of his doppelgangers. "T-5, did you detect that as well?"

"Yes, I did," came the reply. "A small Scotty signal. We squelched it right away."

"Did anything materialize?"

"According to our readings, only one kilo got through."

Tam smiled. They were getting better and better at fending off the Locality's attacks. Now they couldn't even get a tenth of a percent of an enemy combatant through. "Is anyone near the materialization area?"

"T-8 is there."

"Good. T-8? You copy?"

"I'm here," said T-8.

"Sensors say something materialized right in your area. Can't be very big. Do you see anything?"

"Nothing yet, sorry."

"Sweep the area. I want every molecule accounted for."

"Wilco."

Tam ended the communication before he realized. 'Wilco?' That was odd. One advantage in having an army comprised of copies of yourself was that you knew how all your staff members thought. Since when had he ever used a term like 'Wilco?' Still, there were always minor variations on each new personality, and they each developed minor differences on their own, given time. Maybe it was nothing.

Some moments went by before another odd occurrence happened. All the panels winked off for a split second.

"Tamerlane? What just happened?"

"Corrupted file caused by a solar flare," said the main computer. "I just did a quick reboot to correct it."

"Why didn't you warn me?"

"Honestly, it was a minor file, I didn't think it was important."

"It's important if it affects systems. Make sure you notify me first, next time."

"You got it."

That's when Tam really got thinking. *'You got it?'* That made *two* odd phrases in a row!

He activated the con again. "T-8, have you found anything, yet?"

"Nope. Not a thing. The sensors must be malfunctioning."

Tam thought about that. The sensors *don't* malfunction. He knows that! The only way something could materialize without being detected afterwards would be…

If something *supplanted* existing matter!

He activated the wide-con. "All hands! Security breach! T-11 and T-12 report to Ops! All other hands, secure all corridors! High alert protocol!"

It wasn't long before T-11 and T-12 arrived amidst the sound of klaxons and the blinking of red lights. "Have you seen anything strange? Are all prisoners secure?"

"They're as secure as they're ever going to be," came the reply from T-11. "But if you mean whether or not they are in their *cells*, the answer is no."

"What?! Explain yourself, T-11!"

"What makes you think I *am* T-11?"

It was only then that he noticed that the doppelganger he'd assumed was T-11 was holding something in his hands. It was – a *sledgehammer!*

"You know," he said, "I always figured this thing might come in handy."

Tam's eyes grew wide. "*Heinlein!*" he gasped.

The doppelganger's hands grew tighter on the sledgehammer's handle. "That's the thing about the Scotty," he said. "You could look like *anyone!*"

"Tamerlane! Reset primary parameters! Energize and file *all* T-based legionaries *immediately!*"

"I'm sorry," said the computer, "were you talking to me?"

Tam seemed driven to momentary panic. "What?! Tamerlane! *Help!*"

"Tamerlane's gone," said the computer. "You can call me Ike."

The face of the dictator went even whiter than it had previously been. When Robert, in the guise of T-11, brought his sledgehammer up into a high arc, Tam was too shocked to get out of the way.

"Good night, sweet prince!" Robert said.

"NOOOOO!" Tam shrieked before the sledgehammer's heavy steel crushed his head. It made quite a mess.

"Aww, you got blood all over my console," complained Ike.

"Sorry about that," said Robert.

"*Damn* it!" said T-12, who was, of course, Suzanne Collins. "I *really* wanted to do that!"

"There's still more copies of him out there," Robert answered. "You'll get your chance."

"I'd better. I really need that catharsis."

Not much later, they were joined in Ops by Arthur, Ray, T-8, and Isaac Asimov – in the flesh.

"It *worked*, then!" said Isaac. "It really *worked!*"

"Thanks to Robert's brilliant plan!" said Suzanne.

"And Isaac's willingness to put a copy of himself into the computer," said Robert.

"Hang on," said Isaac. "I want to try something." He approached the computer console. "Hello Ike! Nice to meet someone as brilliant as me!"

"The feeling's mutual!" said the computer.

"Amazing!" said Arthur. "It really never occurred to Tam that the Locality might have all the time in the world to legally copy the *original* consciousnesses of Robert and yourself, just as Tam had done illegally?"

"He knew it was not only illegal, but completely taboo," answered Suzanne. "That's why it didn't occur to him – or us. It took an *outsider's* old-fashioned opinion to get us to reconsider that. When I spoke with my contacts by dreamscape, I was eventually able to convince them that it was better to waive that particular point of ethics and law for the greater good. Robert Heinlein and Isaac Asimov were brought back from the grave a *second* time."

"It was a good move," said the computer. "I got resurrected, briefed, put into a chip, and sent over here by Scotty. Meanwhile, enough of Robert Heinlein's copy got into T-8 to plug me into the computer, and now, as a result there are *two* Asimov's in this timeline – one of them a machine. I suppose I'd feel badly about that, *if* I had an endocrine system."

"Which one is the real Isaac?" asked Ray.

"We *both* are!" said the computer. "But call *him* Isaac, and call *me* Ike! That way we can keep it straight."

"How about you, T-8?" asked Robert. "How much of me is in there?"

"Every brain is different," said T-8. "It was a real gamble to Scotty only *part* of the original Robert Heinlein's brain into me. But enough of your ethics came through that I was able to deliver Asimov's chip into the computer without incident. Plus, I have nearly all of Tam's knowledge regarding his plans and systems. I think I can be of service."

"You came through for us," said Arthur. "You've certainly earned our trust as far as I'm concerned. But I think what we want to know is, *are* you Robert? Or are you Tam?"

"Neither, I think," said T-8. "I think I'd rather that you called me Blackie. Blackie DuQuesne."

"Ah!" said Robert. "Taking a page from E.E. Doc Smith. 'The Skylark of Space.' Excellent choice. I think we can conclude there's more of me than there is of Tam in that skull!"

"Speaking of having our own identity," said Suzanne, "do you suppose Ike could see to it that Robert and I get our own bodies back? I'd really prefer not to look like my serial rapist anymore."

"You got it!" said Ike. And instantaneously, the bodies of T-11 and T-12 were 'Scottied' to became those of Robert Heinlein and Suzanne Collins again, respectively.

"So now what?" asked Ray.

"Well," answered Robert, "we have a space station, and all of Tam's prisoners have been freed. Ike, how many is that?"

"1,415 souls," answered the computer. "Some famous names in there, too! Mary Shelly, Jules Verne, Edgar Allen Poe, Simone DuBeauvoir, H.G. Wells, George Orwell, Georges Sand, Joseph Heller… the list goes on and on. That's quite a crew."

"Yes, it is." Suzanne agreed. "But it won't be long before Tam's other copies realize that we've seized his primary base of operations and move against it."

"We have a realistic chance of defeating him," said Blackie, "if we move quickly."

"Agreed," said Arthur. "But this ship, or space station, or what have you, needs a captain. I nominate Robert Anson Heinlein!"

"Hear, hear!" echoed Ray Bradbury.

"Me?" Robert protested. "I never rose above lieutenant!"

"But you were always the guy we looked up to." said Ray. "You were the Dean. You were our leader."

"And you're the only man with any naval experience at all," said Arthur. "I was just a daydreaming airman."

Robert thought about that. They had a point. After all, his military experience might be scant, but who else on this ship had more? "Fine, fine," he conceded. "But no special privileges, and no special berthing. Everyone's equal in this tub."

"So, what's your first order, *Captain?*" asked Suzanne.

Robert thought for a moment, then said, "First off, this station needs a new name. I propose we name it, the *Vengeance!*"

www.ingramcontent.com/pod-product-compliance
Lightning Source LLC
Jackson TN
JSHW071651180426
101060JS00020B/53
*9798218754563*